WHAT OTHERS ARE
S...... .....UT ARSON

It's a testament to his talent that Estevan Vega can turn a dark, disturbing story into an intriguing page-turner. Quirky, complex characters and Vega's story-telling skills make *Arson* a must-read ... and Vega an author to watch.

> —Robert Liparulo, bestselling author of
> *Deadlock* and the *Dreamhouse Kings*

Estevan is a gifted young writer, and I expect to see great works from him in the near future.

> —Bryan Davis, bestselling author of the
> *Echoes from the Edge* and *Dragons in our Midst* series

Vega writes well beyond his years, keeping the reader's eye glued to the page with vivid, eloquently penned lines that paint a picture of the tortured young mind that is the main character. With his third literary

attempt, Vega has hit his stride—one that can only pick up speed.

—The Record-Journal

In *Arson*, Estevan Vega has created a character as unique and captivating as Dean Koontz's Odd Thomas. With a fresh voice and an engaging style, Vega's storytelling is something to pay attention to. I expect to see more from this author.

—Mike Dellosso, author of *The Hunted* and *Scream*

Wonderfully envisioned and readable. The story of a young man with a secret talent he doesn't want to be forced to use keeps readers edgy and waiting, and hoping he'll let it all out.

—John Neufeld, author of *Edgar Allan* and *April Fool*

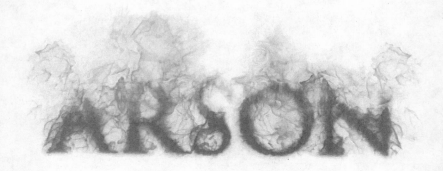

ESTEVAN VEGA

ARSON

"Vega's storytelling skills make *Arson* a must-read...and Vega an author to watch."
—Robert Liparulo, best-selling author of *Deadlock* and *The Dreamhouse Kings*

TATE PUBLISHING *& Enterprises*

Published by Tate Publishing & Enterprises, LLC
127 E. Trade Center Terrace | Mustang, Oklahoma 73064 USA
1.888.361.9473 | www.tatepublishing.com

Tate Publishing is committed to excellence in the publishing industry. The company reflects the philosophy established by the founders, based on Psalm 68:11,
"The Lord gave the word and great was the company of those who published it."

Book design copyright © 2009 by Tate Publishing, LLC. All rights reserved.
Cover design by Tyler Evans
Interior design by Lindsay B. Behrens
Backcover photograph by Steve Teo

Published in the United States of America

ISBN: 978-1-61566-603-4
1. Fiction / Coming Of Age   2. Fiction / Thrillers
09.12.18

For my father, a small spark that lit the great fire.

ACKNOWLEDGMENTS

It's so hard to believe that a few months ago I was lamenting the fact that this book might never actually be published, a simple tragedy that nearly broke me in two. Now, I am overjoyed with its release. The nearly four-year road to publishing this book has been paved with sweat, frustration, tears, and hopes. Yet without the help, encouragement, and support of those around me, I wouldn't have had a shot.

My father is perhaps the biggest supporter of my writing and has been since I was eleven, when he sat me down to write my first short story. I'm so thankful for those nights. He's been there with me every step, every fall, and every doubt.

To Nikki, the calm ripple in a stream of wandering thoughts.

Being one of four brothers makes this next part fun. I'd like to thank each and every one of my bros: Alex, Emilio, and Samuel for their love, fights, and encouragement. We hate each other the most and love each other the most.

I remind myself on occasion that without the love and support of my aunt Carmen, who has been like a mother to me these last three years, I would not have known what true insanity is. Here's to having a million dogs.

My other aunt, Jean, cannot go unrecognized either, for she was the first one to read this manuscript and give me feedback. I am forever thankful.

To the many teachers and professors I have been blessed with over the years, the ones who have shown me a new perspective on the world and helped guide me along the way, God bless you.

I would be a terrible person if I didn't also thank Jo Ann Hernandez, a new friend and author, who has dived into the sea of compassion and found a treasure. Her help and warm compliments have truly given me new hope for my writing career.

Thank you, Stephen Christian, author and lead singer for the band Anberlin, whose great lyrics helped inspire this character.

To all of the other bands whose music has not only been an inspiration to me but has also acted as a catalyst for my view on life, circumstance, and beauty. Art is cool!

Next, to the endorsers, thank you for your support. Your kind and rich words have not only given *Arson* credibility but also have allowed me to think I can actually write a decent book. Thank you! Thank you! Thank you!

For all those bloggers and book reviewers who have helped me along the way, I remain indebted to you.

To every writer who has come before me, whose blood, sweat, and tears have been poured into your works, you have inspired me to capture the essence of a new generation.

To my editor, Audra Marvin, thank you so much for your dedication, encouragement, and faith in this book, even if we didn't always agree.

Lastly, I must extend my gratitude to the editors and agents and publishers who rejected this manuscript over the last year because it allowed room for Tate Publishing to make this dream a reality. For everything there is a season, right? I'm still learning that you never know where this life might take you.

While this is my third book, I feel like a new spark has been lit, and this is a start of something new. Glad you're along for the ride!

Estevan Vega, 2010

ONE

The lake was quiet.

A lazy fog hovered over the surface of the gray water, whispering in the wake of currents and steady ripples. The world seemed dead to Arson Gable, silent anyway. Like the calm before a storm.

It waited.

Arson stepped off the porch onto the lawn; his mind was swimming. This was where he came most mornings while Grandma slept. He cut his gaze toward the lake, that black womb which rested beyond and beneath the rickety dock. It was as if the lake knew his name and his heartbeats, much like the streets and corners of this town knew his name, cold and faceless as they were. Whether he wanted to admit it or not, this place was home, and there was no going back.

A bright light burned in the sky, somewhere far enough for him to notice but close enough to nearly blind him. He breathed deeply and blinked, welcoming the dark rush of black behind his eyelids. From where he stood, he could see the towering oaks rooted deep in the ground. Their thick branches stretched upward into the clouds, some parts draping over the shady spots of the worn-out cabin. One final glance and he was reminded that these tortuous, beaten things seemed to swallow the world. Just thinking about them—how he'd watched them ruin—made him seem small, so worthless.

Arson made a fist and felt the heat swell in his grip. He wanted to run into the brush, to get lost deep in the small section of backwoods Grandma had forced him to avoid ever since they'd moved here. But he didn't move.

This town seemed so close-knit and yet so separated. Less than a mile up the road were a country market, restaurants, and a bowling alley. There was even a liquor store, a cheap pharmacy, and some fast-food chains, and a few miles past that, a movie theater and a nightclub. But at the heart of this place was disunity, a fierce and futile fight to be known and accepted. Arson never understood why Grandpa had picked here to have the cabin built, right beside the lake.

As Arson slowly approached the dock, his mind returned to thoughts of Danny, the only childhood friend he'd ever had. Dim mornings somehow made each memory more real, hard to let go and even harder to erase. Was he always here, always watching? Odd how seven years could come and go without warning, as if the world blinked and somehow forgot to open its eyes again.

In all fairness, it had never been his grandparents' intention to stay anywhere for too long, but it seemed East Hampton, Connecticut, had become a part of them now, a part of him. "One day we'll be like the rest of them," he recalled Grandpa saying—a man of ideals, empty dreams, and hopes Arson could never freely call his own.

Eventually, they had grown tired of running. This dull corner of the world seemed ordinary enough for them to believe starting over again as normal folks would be possible. "Forget what happened all those years ago in Cambridge," Grandma said so many times that Arson imagined her screaming it to him while he slept. But it was always there—the memory—a splinter in the back of his mind. No going back. Ever.

Arson staggered across the dock, images of child play and stupid laughter pouring in all at once. Danny's face stuck out the most, and behind that he glimpsed their old home in Cambridge and flashes of his first birthday. His mother wasn't there, though, nor dear old Dad, but that day had been recounted to him only once by his grandfather, and it stuck.

Nevertheless, with every joyous memory, distilled regret was close behind. He sometimes imagined what it might be like to get thrown in jail by some nameless special agent and be forgotten, or to wake up and find strong hands squeezing the life out of him.

Arson was an unusual boy. A freak. He knew it. And he hated it. Whatever lingered inside his bones always left as quickly as it came, breathing out in short moments of fear or rage. Over the years, he'd asked to be examined to locate the source of his imperfection and if possible terminate it. After all, why did he sometimes wake up in the middle of the night with a fever? How come his sweat sizzled when it hit the ground? What was he?

Grandma always argued there wasn't much point in talking to no-good doctors or even finding out answers to questions he was better off not asking in the first place. Some people were just born with demons, she'd say.

Arson swallowed hard and threw a stone into the water. The splash shattered his reflection, and ripples spread across the dark surface. He wondered why he was the way he was, wondered why those little girl's parents quit looking all of a sudden, why the investigation against two stupid boys evaporated. Perhaps they didn't care about retribution, or maybe they were just sick of chasing shadows.

I want to be free, Arson thought, nausea creeping up into his gut. While boats raced along the surface of the lake, Arson stared in awe. They vanished so easily, like mist gliding across the water and dissolving into nothingness. What if men could do the same? There was a man once, he'd heard, who walked upon water and didn't sink. Maybe he could too. Maybe one day there would be those who believed in him.

Arson's gaze moved over the lake, across to the other side, where Mandy Kimball lived, and her neighbor, his science teacher from the ninth grade. Then his eyes drew back to the ripples spread out before him, to the dying cabin behind him, as he spit. Beads of sweat streamed down his bony frame, his ash-brown hair trapped inside the gritty creases of his forehead. Arson listened for the lake's soothing melody but couldn't hear it. He focused instead on the sound his feet made atop the splintering dock, kind of like the way swings sounded in cheap horror flicks—empty, rocking back and forth to no melody at all. Closer to the edge he came, lingering.

With shut eyes, he stepped out onto the water and began to sink. Peace soon abandoned him to the lake's shallow world. In a blink, he was looking through the eyes of a ten-year-old boy.

"I don't like fire," he heard the boy say, so frightened, so naïve. "It's dangerous."

"Don't be such a wimp," came his older friend's taunts. "Just light it already."

With each shove and curse, the memory turned alive; it was as if it knew he was watching and didn't like it. The pain still stung, images wilting and dying, only to come alive again and again.

I. Hate. Fire.

Arson could feel the cold, could even remember the way everything sounded or how there was no sound at all. Until the night shattered. The weight of remembering dragged him down while he sucked in a filthy drag of water, his coffined body jerking. The veins on his head began to swell. He was choking.

Time to return to the real world, to release the nightmare once more into the dark of the lake. The struggle eventually pulled him to the surface. Slinging his head back and forth, Arson fought to bring himself out of the bitter current, eventually falling upon dead grass. He tasted the grit of sandy dirt in his teeth. Panting, Arson stood up slowly and staggered toward the cabin, where Grandma Kay's shadow guided him in.

There was something strange that came over Grandma when she exacted punishment, like a part of her enjoyed it too much. She said fixing their leaky roof was a good and righteous way of killing the demons inside him. Nothing like hard work. She said there was no way a lake could cleanse a boy's troubled mind anyway and that he was just plain stupid for thinking it could. To ease his frustration, Arson let himself believe that if he had been caught any other day, her scorn might have resulted in something worse than fixing a leaky roof, which Arson would've had to do eventually anyway.

Grandma's reasons for why she did things, why she treated him a certain way, seemed to get worse with time. It was no secret that she loathed the idea of him diving into the lake, especially if fully clothed. She even claimed there were toxins in the water from pollution that had supposedly killed a bunch of fish years back. But maybe it was a fair trade. He'd returned to the lake all the toxins he'd soaked up with every vile thought. When considered, Grandma's logic didn't seem all that twisted. She probably just didn't want him bringing any of that evil back with him, infected or not. She was superstitious, so Arson made a promise he knew he couldn't keep and said it wouldn't happen again.

The muggy June morning caused his palms to sweat. Arson almost lost his grip on the bucket during the climb to the top but regained his balance before losing any supplies. Spiderman would have been proud. Reading comic books all his life came in handy now and then.

Grandpa took care of the cabin to the best of his ability, had even showed Arson how to repair the roof years back. "If you want something done right, you gotta do it yourself," he recalled. But in spite of his grandfather's hard work, it was clear that time eventually wore away all things, even hope.

Arson worked for about an hour before carelessness got the best of him. A loose, jagged shingle sliced through the palm of his hand. Blood gushed from the wound and onto his leg. He swore as the sting began to overwhelm him. He chucked the hammer and tried to keep pressure on the cut.

"What happened?" Grandma's voice echoed from below. "I heard you cussin' all the way in the kitchen. You know how I feel about that."

"Sorry, Grandma." Arson was glad she left it at that. Sitting on the roof, he turned slightly toward the sun. *It's a gusher,* he thought. Then, as he stared in amazement, he watched the wound cauterize itself in seconds. It burned.

"Arson, are you all right up there?"

He looked down at the remaining scar, struggling to make sense of it, neglecting the mess on his clothes. "Just fine, Grandma," he called down.

"That roof isn't going to fix itself. If I have to spend another night with drops of water hitting my face, I promise you'll regret it."

"All right," Arson said. "I'll get back to work."

By evening, the task was complete. He braced himself and watched the sunset from the rooftop as it melted against a fluorescent sky. Arson listened as Grandma concluded her tea conversation with the man she loved.

Moments later, their time together ended with laughter, and he knew it was safe to come down. Arson caught her while she was clearing away the silverware and china.

"Did you finish the roof, love?" she asked in a pleasant voice.

"Yes, Grandma. It's healed ... I mean, fixed."

"Marvelous. Say, whatcha mean *healed?*"

Arson grabbed the ladder. "I'm really tired. I'm not thinking straight right now. Maybe I just need some rest."

"I think you're right. You're not making any sense at all. Say, do you want a piece of cake before I put it away? Grandpa didn't eat much tonight. He's never been much for carrot cake."

"No thanks. Not hungry," he said.

"Suit yourself. Put your tools away and get on up to bed, then. A growing boy like you needs his rest. I hope you learned your lesson, though. I don't like you spending so much time in that miserable lake. The very idea doesn't sit well with my soul."

Arson nodded with reluctant eyes and put away the ladder and the tools. Then he rushed inside the cabin and up to his room to read a comic book before dozing off. Maybe tonight his dreams would be different.

TWO

It was three in the afternoon when Mandy walked into the ice cream parlor where Arson worked. He felt so unprepared that he found himself wishing something else came out, anything other than a surprised "Hello. How are ya?"

Mandy was beautiful, beyond beautiful. A few years ago, he had let himself believe she was an angel. As far back as he could remember there had been two types of girls: girls like Mandy Kimball, and the rest. During the school year, he avoided encounters with girls like her, that whole crowd, because fitting in always seemed like a challenge, an avoidable one. Besides, the school hallways and lunch tables mandated that conversation with losers like him was the closest thing to social suicide. But for some reason—a reason he couldn't even begin to fathom—Mandy risked her popularity on occasion and chose to notice him.

"That's gotta be the biggest ice cream cone I've ever had," she said, eyes glowing.

"Sorry, I always do that," he said, blinking about a thousand times.

"Do what?"

"Give pretty girls too much," Arson replied, putting his antics on the line in hopes that Venus might actually find him in some way amusing. But in his white and black uniform, covered from nose to neck in a dozen different flavors of Tobey's Sinfully Sweet ice cream, he knew it was empty hope. He held his eyes low, hair curling against his forehead. Then he smiled, feeling like an idiot.

"You get paid to serve us ice cream, loser, not flirt with customers," Mandy's friend said.

Eye games followed while Arson took the cone back. "Stupid me. Forgot the chocolate shots."

Mandy sighed under her breath. "Here you go." Reaching over the counter, she handed him a five-dollar bill.

"Don't even worry about it," Arson said. "We're allowed to give away one free cone a day, compliments of the house, or maybe *lair* would be more appropriate. Always feel awkward telling people this has any resemblance to a home when it has *Tobey's Sinfully Sweet Ice Cream* plastered across the front of the building with big red horns. Either way, consider it a gift."

The friend, whom he'd later remember as Kim from third period biology, piped up again, snapping her fingers. "Excuse me, loser. Does it look like we care?"

Arson handed Mandy the cone again. Luckily, she and her friend were the last customers of the night. He didn't dare get into it with Mandy's friend, even though he wanted to tell her to just shut up and take the free cone. He followed their shadows out the door with interest, focusing on Mandy's. *What does a guy have to do to get a girl like that?* he thought.

Moments later, Arson flipped a switch on the wall, and the *closed* sign illuminated the front window.

"Thanks, Arson. That was real nice," he mumbled to himself, imitating Mandy's voice. "I really like you." His shoulders sank. "Saying it to yourself doesn't make it true, only pathetic."

He locked the door, put his face to the glass, and tried to get a better look at the girls as they walked, but he was too late. Feeling misplaced, another sigh blew out of him. He didn't fit into this world. Nights like these made him wonder if he was simply a manufactured piece of hardware, a mistake in the assembly line of humanity. He felt unique, but in a horrible way.

Arson suddenly started coughing. A sharp pain cut through him. It was the same sensation that had found him on the rooftop. Worse. Sweat dripped from the center of his palms, and they quickly got hotter. Arson raced to the sink, where scoopers sank to the bottom, the colorful assorted residue of a day's worth of ice cream rising to the milky top. Without even thinking, he submerged his hands in the cool water, and the pain went away.

Kay prepared herself for bed, always treasuring the short, fleeting moments at night with her husband.

She cleaned during the day, doing dishes, mopping floors, washing laundry—necessary qualities of all strong women, tasks lost on today's generation. For women, there was no room for something as selfish as a career. But child-raising, pride, and tradition, on the other hand, were what made a woman valuable. Respectable men were supposed to work and provide for their wives, lead. Everybody had their place. It was the way it had always been.

Before bed, Kay often stared into the vanity mirror for a while, gazing into the eyes that had grown so cold over the years. "I'm old," she said, letting her hair down.

The gray static strands zigzagged past her shoulders and across her breasts. The naked woman in her mirror groaned.

Kay looked down and caressed the fatty parts of her skin. The saggy, undesirable folds infuriated her. She didn't want them. Who would? It had been years since she'd felt beautiful. She longed for the days of her youth. Simpler times. She remembered when she first began to blossom, confident with the blessing of puberty and inviting curves. Kay soon learned that the key to a man's heart rested not in his desire for good cooking, like her mother used to tell her, but through his eyes.

Men wanted beautiful women, and youthful beauty, for her, had been easy to lend. From early on, Kay had watched men's expressions melt when she walked into a room. She took their kisses and gifts as quickly as they came, but it was never enough. Deep down, she wanted romance. Marriage and children. After years of empty interests, her wish had come true.

The year was 1969, and Kay was not yet twenty-four. The world was full, free, and reveling. The war and rebellions seemed mere trifles when compared to lonely hearts. It was easy to get lost in a city, transported by its bright lights and sounds. Cambridge was a city that lit up at night, the way she lit up the second Henry Parker stumbled into a downtown pub, looking for a drink to calm an unsettled mind.

A radiant red dress hung off her silky shoulders. Kay's eyes were sparkling jewels. She was exquisite, even in memory. The man she'd come to call *darling* stood yards away when their eyes met for the first time. Slowly, he walked toward her and spoke. "Pleasure to meet you," he said. "I'm Henry. Where have you been all my life?"

A pathetic first line, but she could tell he was trying. Kay had known men before, talked and danced with them, but this stranger's boyish smile showed a calm unlike anything she had ever seen. She had believed herself to be unattainable—incorruptible—until that night. Fluttered heartbeats soon led to long walks and midnight dancing. In time, she fell in love.

Kay knew that Henry Parker held the key to the future she'd always wanted.

But in a blink, it was gone. Kay hated the old shell she now wore, the one that wrapped around her like a coffin. Wrinkles and sagging flesh now corrupted her once flawless cheeks and inviting shape. She was unfit for romance. There was no room for beauty. Passion had fled, and the distant sound of youth called out to her from within the mirror. *You're old, Kay,* it taunted. *You're old.* She began to cry as the young woman continued the ridicule. *A real woman is beautiful. A real woman knows how to love. You're not a real woman, Kay, not anymore.*

"Leave me alone!" Kay screamed back, reaching for a pair of shears and placing them to her stomach. "Get out, or I'll cut you out!"

Henry wouldn't allow it, her reflection answered. *Deep down, he still wants me.*

Kay's tired eyes lingered as she watched young Kay lie upon the bed, gently sliding into Henry's arms. Her Henry. She watched the image press her lips against his mouth as Kay shouted, "Stop! That's enough!" Young Kay glared back from the bed within the mirror, as if reaching through time. An unrelenting stare passed through the portals of then and now, with no way to go back or forward.

Kay fell to her knees, grabbed her face, and wept. She smacked herself twice until blood began to flow. The vindictive critic inside the mirror evaporated.

Quietly, Kay got up, slipped her bathrobe on, and shut off the lights.

With soaked eyes, she crawled into bed. "Goodnight, my darling," she cried.

THREE

He was lost again. No matter how hard Arson screamed and fought to get out, he was stuck. Stretched out before him was a picture, moving slowly, of two young boys. He followed them down the street, the hum of the world surrounding them—tall, condemning lights set against a dark heaven, hopeful musicians and city merchants gambling away life's trifles and gifts, eager to make a quick buck. But no one could see him. No one could hear him.

The boys exchanged comic books, arguing about whose favorite hero was best and how they sympathized with the villains of the stories—those the world called *monsters*. Arson reached out his hand to touch one of them on the shoulder, but his fingers pierced right through the faded flesh, out the other side, as if the boy were not there at all. They continued walking and talking. Arson could see it, though, impossible to miss. The thing Danny was promising would change the way they did tricks; what he said would initiate their evolution from kids to bigger kids nobody messed with. It would be just like the show *Jackass*, he promised. The item was tucked away in Danny's back pocket, sticking out as he danced across their concrete stage, closer and closer to the night's violent performance.

Was Arson supposed to feel his heart beating? He tried waving his hands, begged his body to scream louder. As he turned to his left, Arson noticed a cab moving past, braking farther ahead. His eyes moved beneath the glaze and awe toward the scene about to explode.

Can I save them?

No.

Why?

You're not awake.

Sweat trickled off his brow; the charm of curiosity and nervousness called him to the scene. Images wilted away and folded back. Timeless, careless.

And then he saw it, a spark in the distance. He didn't dare follow closely. No. He'd run again. That was all he could do. *Don't think, don't breathe, just run,* as fast as he could.

Arson's eyes peeled back. He was awake. Sweat cradled his body in puddles as his chest rose and fell. His spine curled up into itself, and he started to shake.

"It's time for breakfast," he heard from below.

Grandma's voice must have brought him to life again. It was Wednesday, which meant scrambled eggs and cheese served with crispy bacon, two slices of rye, and birch beer. Blinking, he took pleasure in what might come if only he could gather the strength to make it out of bed and downstairs.

In moments, he was clean but lethargically moving down the steps that led into the old-fashioned kitchen. It was Grandma's way of keeping the past alive. She was dressed, as always, in her traditional apron and standing beside the morning feast.

"G'mornin'," she said in a soothing voice. "How'd ya sleep?"

Arson found a seat quickly, reached for his fork, and drew the first scoop of eggs to his mouth, not saying a word.

"Well, love, do you feel like talking about what's on your mind?" She set the cup of tea down on the table.

"Good morning," he finally said, lifting his eyes, but only for a second. He couldn't tell her it was happening again. She'd despise him for it. She wouldn't understand sweating so much it ached or hands burning without touching a stove, a fire, nothing. She had never seemed to get it before, and now it would only call out her hatred once more. No. Not today.

Grandma spent several moments absorbed in her newspaper. It used to bother him that the newspaper didn't change. Arson had never believed that reading the same sad news morning after morning could be healthy, but he refused to fight with her about it. No use. She looked at him now and then during breakfast as she turned its faded, crinkled pages.

"Where's Grandpa?" Arson said, hoping that talking about his grandfather might take the attention off him for a bit.

"He's out buying cigarettes," she said. "Marlboro Lights; they're his favorite. It is a filthy habit, though, if I do say so."

Arson took in the moment. He stared into her gray eyes and saw some warmth. The wrinkles on her cheek shaped a pleasant smile.

"You know *him*," she continued, "always up before the sun. Most nights I wonder if the man even sleeps. He's such a hard worker. You know, you might take some lessons from your granddaddy, love." The glow he saw evaporated. "Are you ready to talk about how you slept? I know you didn't sleep well. Heavens! You kept me up nearly half the night. Whatever do you dream about, boy?"

"I'm fine, Grandma. It was nothing," Arson whispered, gulping down the entire glass of birch beer, trying to avoid the subject.

Grandma got up and placed the bottle of birch beer in front of him. "If you don't want me to pry, I won't. I try to care about you, but you don't ever open up. I get so tired of your nonsense, wretch!" Suddenly, he saw her recoil. Arson could feel her eyes slithering up and down his frame.

Then she grasped her cup of tea as daintily as ever and took a sip. In a blink, she was changed. "How's breakfast, love?"

He couldn't understand how she did it, how she morphed instantly. Arson sighed and brushed off the rude remark before replying, "Delicious" with as much phony gratitude as he could muster. He found himself staring at random things around the room, anything to avoid her examination. She didn't mean those words she said, he was sure … he hoped. Unscrewing the soda cap, he listened for the gasp of air escaping. Then he filled his glass with more of the fizzy beverage. He proceeded to down another full glass, every moment more stifling than the last.

"Thank you, Grandma. This is the breakfast of champions."

"Oh, it's nothing, love."

Getting up from his seat, Arson belched. "Excuse me," he said, covering his mouth in an effort to conceal his stomach's grumble. Suddenly, out of the corner of his eye, he glimpsed a spinning plate coming toward him. It whirled and turned in the air so fast, he barely had the chance to duck. Startled, Arson dropped to the floor in a panic as the plate aimed at him smashed against a wall and shattered on the tile. "Grandma, what are you doing?"

"Let that be the last time you welcome foul behavior into this house. You're not some gutter trash from the streets. I expect better manners in the future." In a flash, her lips stretched back into a smile, and she knelt down beside him, picking up the broken fragments off the floor.

Arson reached for some pieces. He could see her face change again.

"Leave it for Grandma, Arson," she said. "You're gonna be late for work. Lord knows those crazy folks love their ice cream as soon as the cock crows. Get goin' and leave the fixin' to me."

Confused, he walked outside. He could feel the morning creeping in, the taste of dew sticking to the inner flesh of his cheek. "Another day," he sighed. Casting his gaze out against Lake Pocotopaug, he groaned with melancholy delight and caught a glimpse of the ripples harmonizing in the wake of restless fishermen.

Arson walked along the rocky path that Grandpa had created, time had weathered, and erosion had ruined before reaching the main stretch of road. Like always, nightfall would come, and the same road would usher him in again, back to the hell he knew as home.

He heard the sound of Mandy's voice. Like music, but softer. "Hey, Arson," she said, walking into Toby's with another mindless clone.

"Traded the last model in for a new one, huh?" Arson grinned. "Anything interesting this one can do?"

Amidst a flurry of people, Mandy exchanged glances with him, not entirely sure what the comment meant. He pretended to read her mind and quickly gave her two scoops of double chocolate chip ice cream in a sugar cone and littered it with chocolate shots. After smiling a few times, Arson reluctantly turned to face paying customers.

Demands from impatient mothers dying to put something into their kids' greedy mouths came at him, as if each ricocheted off the last. Day in and day out, Arson noticed how each mother varied in the amount of her affection toward her child, most far too agitated by the time they stepped inside the parlor to be bothered with any nonsense from an ice cream scooper like him.

So Arson often studied them, observing the way some moms reacted toward their own children, and then he watched how they reacted with others, even complete strangers. In one moment, they were as lethal as black widows and the next as carefree as butterflies. It made him wonder what his mother would have been like if…

Before the thought could put a period at the end of itself, Mandy and the new clone were gone. He was unable to wave goodbye as they made their retreat past a swarm of frustrated housemothers. She and her friend took the free ice cream and escaped without even offering to pay. Not that he would have charged them. Mandy was very dear to him. Arson knew better than anyone that love was rarely fair, that just because you wished away a feeling didn't mean it left you. And he was now sure that no matter what she did or could ever do, he had no choice but to remain corruptibly in love with her.

FOUR

Grandma stormed into Arson's bedroom with a fury. The sound of the door bashing into the wall disturbed him half to death. "Are you some kind of pervert?" she yelled, smacking his face with a newspaper. She must have heard him through the walls. "What's the matter with you, wretch? I raised you better."

She laced each blow with sick pleasure, a mix of disdain and contempt. Arson wasn't sure which he was more afraid of: her eyes or the raw knuckles silencing all feeling within him. What had he done? For the longest time, Arson had believed it was normal. Other kids did it; what else could it be? They were just thoughts, after all. Thoughts he let turn into something more, something passionate. He liked the way they felt. The way he imagined a girl might touch him, kiss him, even love him, if ever they got close enough. It didn't feel wrong. He didn't ask for these thoughts; they just came, and he didn't know what to do with them. But the more Grandma screamed, the more she sank her harsh resolve into his skin, the more the thoughts began to abandon him. It had all been a mistake.

"I'm sorry," he whimpered.

But she didn't seem to care. If only she'd listen to him.

She grabbed Arson by the head and struck him once again. "Those impure thoughts will send you straight to hell, you little demon." Another blow sent bits of black ink and white paper falling to the floor like filthy snowflakes.

When he was younger, kids ridiculed him, as if he were some abnormal freak because he didn't do it. Didn't even really understand what *it* was for so long. Bragging school ground punks, with their pierced ears and ripped jean jackets, exiled him in the bus lines time and time again, played tricks on him.

He used to despise them for their violence and sick jokes. The last days before summer were the worst, with heat so thick teachers focused more on when the bell would ring than noticing the taunts and crimes of adolescent boys. If they didn't see it, it didn't matter. The tormenting culprits found little to fear in suspension anyway. To them, it was all just sport.

Arson hated how sheltered Grandma kept him, entombed in mere existence. She never had talks with him about his body, about the natural and *unnatural* changes. The thoughts. The fevers. The shakes, not quite cold or hot, just miserable. Arson often wondered if this happened because of his dreams. Angry dreams. But it was Grandma who constantly warned him against getting angry. That was unacceptable, and the result of such disobedience would bring devastating consequences. She threatened to leave him forever.

"I never thought you'd have the nerve to do something like that in your granddaddy's house," Grandma said, spitting. "Arson Gable, you've shamed me. You've shamed your mother, God rest her soul. Look at you." He did, staring down at the pants around his ankles. "Animals don't even do that, wretch." Out of the dark came her hard knuckles, sinking into his belly, laced with fury and disgust.

"I'm ... so ... sorry, Gr—," he sobbed.

Grandma threw the paper at him. "Not yet, but you will be. I bet you fornicate to those smut magazines as well. You probably do. Is that why you touch yourself? Because of that filth? Hiding them right under my nose, thinking I'll never find them." She searched but found nothing.

Arson cowered underneath her shadow. So weak, rejected, ashamed, especially to the one who claimed to love him most.

"You ruined my paper. You know how I feel about my newspaper."

"I'm s—"

"Don't interrupt me, pig." She fixed her glasses, scanned the room, and disappeared momentarily. With a towel in her hand, Grandma returned to find Arson on his knees.

"Clean yourself up," she demanded and threw him a rag. "You'll have to think about what you did." Grandma left the room and shut the door. Arson could hear the key sliding into place and then twisting enough to lock him inside. Every click and turn sounded like mad voices, telling him of the punishment and separation to come. "You're just like your daddy," he heard her whisper behind the door.

FIVE

The door was still locked when Arson woke up. Nervously, his hands shook and began to sweat. Hard to believe it had been two days. Hunger warned his body of its need to eat. *It would be so easy,* Arson pondered, *to melt the handle.* Burn everything, not just the room that held him prisoner, but the whole damned house.

"Are you awake, love?" Grandma asked.

At first Arson didn't know what to say. In fact, he didn't want to say anything. He wasn't awake or asleep, alive or dead. He was just there—captive, angry, dismayed. But still he answered, "I am now, Grandma."

"Good. I hope you thought about what you've done, pig," she seethed in a raspy voice.

"Yeah, Grandma, I have."

"You sure? 'Cause I won't be having any more of that wicked behavior in this house, young man, not the house your granddaddy built."

"I built it too," he mumbled.

"Not after what you've done to make us move all the way out here in the middle of nowhere."

His heart sank at her comments. The acid from his belly rose, burning the back of his throat, a pain he was accustomed to. "I know, Grandma. I'm sorry for what I did." Arson shut his eyes. Being separated from her felt strangely sick.

"I wish I could erase you," she said.

Slowly, the door cracked open. The unsettling whine of the splintered wood and rusted hinges scratched his eardrums as it let her in. Her face peered out from the darkness. Squinting, he stood defensively, chilled by her stare.

"Eat some breakfast before it gets cold," she said, handing him a lukewarm plate of scrambled eggs, bacon, and toast. "It's not Wednesday, but I figured I'd make an exception."

Arson reached for the plate in her hand while Grandma placed the drink on his dresser. "Now eat slowly, love. Wouldn't want you to choke." She patted him on the back. "You know, it's not normal for you to go without food for days. Keep those wicked thoughts out of your mind, ya hear?"

Arson dipped his head in shame.

She gently rubbed the back of his neck. He cringed but couldn't bring himself to reject her. The blinds and tape that kept the light out stared with pleasure at him. How feeble and weak he was. He hated being their entertainment.

When he was finished eating, Grandma grabbed his plate and stood up. "Arson, the rules of this house are here for a reason. You must obey them. You must obey me, because I love you. I'm the only one who's *ever* loved you. The only one who can."

Arson's eyes followed her down the stairs. The hummed melody of an old hymn rang through the air, a hymn he had never bothered to memorize.

He reached under his mattress and pulled out a comic book from the pile he'd collected over the years. The pages were thumbed through and worn, but he still got satisfaction from them, even if they were old and cliché. They were splintered fragments left behind from a long-lost childhood filled with heroes and villains facing impossible odds and uncertain futures, a black and white world in which there was no gray. Arson felt more a part of their reality than his own. The stories didn't seem to care who he was or what he could do; it didn't matter. In their world, he wasn't alone. In their world, a freak like them—like him—could become a hero.

Arson could feel the night wrap its fingers around him like smoke. As he raced outside, his face cracked from the heat, and his eyes began to burn. In order to ease the pain, he wet them, blinking rapidly when he could, when he wasn't running. Out of breath, but it didn't matter. Couldn't keep still. *Run,* he thought. *Run. Anywhere but here!*

The air cut through his teeth. Faster he moved, past the abandoned house on his left, through the field of neglected grass and waste. *To the marshes,* he thought, *away from Grandma, away from everything.* It was quiet there, quieter than the lake tonight. Quiet enough to think about what plagued him most, though he hated it.

His breaths were short and stifled by panic. His heart pounded and struggled to keep pace, pumping more heat than blood. He moaned, praying it would stop. But the anger only grew. Violent memories, only hours old, fueled the fire within, begging for release. His skin didn't burn, his body couldn't wilt, but the smell of rotting, bubbling flesh surrounded him, and he could taste its horrible flavor on his lips. Pimples on his face disintegrated and oozed down his cheek. Fireflies sparkled in front and behind him, and he was lost between. Leaves and branches crunched underfoot, and he listened for the sound of summer, of night, but all he heard were screeching tires and the shattering of broken glass somewhere in the distance. Perhaps a few fools had lost their lives in a head-on collision. *Lucky,* Arson thought, clenching his fist tighter as he ran.

By the time he arrived, the veins in his wrists and hands had swelled blood red. Tears slipped down his face only to disappear. He was afraid. Something about the place caused the hairs on the back of his neck to move. Arson never made a habit of coming here, but he was desperate more than anything. He knew it was childish to think a place so calm could awaken such fright, but the dark was good at playing his fears back to him.

Enraged, he grabbed a jagged rock and threw it into the black, hoping it would split the veil of darkness, and then the sky would pity him. Bugs and moths swarmed around his head, seduced by the light from his body. Closer they came. He looked down, taking one wary step into the pool. The grime and soot covered his clothes and stained his hands. He wondered if the cold water could quench him tonight.

Arson then dipped his entire body into the pool and waited. Distracted by roaming fish and water snakes, he held his breath and clenched his eyelids tighter. Grandma stopped hitting him, but Arson knew that beneath the fabricated smiles and almost love, she still loathed him for what he'd done, for what he was. Maybe she was right. Maybe he was a monster, a demon, a pig. He wondered how one person could be responsible for so much madness and pain. He thought back again.

"It's only a dare," Danny said.

"I believe you; I just don't want to do it. I don't like fire."

"Name a hero who's afraid," he heard him sneer.

Silence.

"I dare you, chicken. You'll never be a hero if you're always scared."

"I hate fire," Arson whispered under the current. "I hate what I am."

Danny's words played out in slow motion, spinning amidst chaos and the boom of future horror. "All you have to do is light this piece of junk and chuck it as far as your wimpy arm can throw. It's going to be so cool! You'll see."

Fear moved across their faces, and everything went still, waiting for the world, asking God to step in and save him from what he was about to do. But there was nothing, no one to change it. There it was in Danny's palm, before he handed it over. It was the key to her salvation. Perhaps clearer in reverse, clearer than even that night.

It had moved to his hand now. Nothing would work. Nothing but the fire inside his bones. Frantic and nervous, Arson recalled the anger, the frustration pumping through him, the lack of control that lit his hand. In a blink, it danced across his fingers and disappeared. What seemed like fragments of time was enough to change his world forever. He gasped, and then he saw her face.

Breathe.

No. Not yet.

Breathe.

Arson cried, fighting to be still but knowing this pain was unquenchable. He had to breathe to let it out. In a choking rage, he extended his hands and feet and felt the waters boil. The creatures underneath him and all around him began to die, floating to the surface. He glowed and burned and hated every second of it.

Arson waited for it to end. His senses fought to return to the surface, back to solid ground, the familiar. Swallowing the filth, he shook and swore, breaking to the surface wild and furious. Arson didn't want to commit suicide; he just wanted to die.

SIX

Arson was reluctant to walk into work the next morning. From the second he stepped in, his boss seemed bent on proving a point. The point was simple: time off without the proper notice was reason enough to fire him on the spot, but being the merciful boss that he was, he'd allow Arson to stay on. Punishment began with scrubbing the bathroom floors.

His name was Ray, but nicknames like Murder Breath and Hitler were used frequently. The truth was, he acted as a better dictator than socialite; deep down, he was a terrible human being. His bald spot betrayed him on windy afternoons and on what *he* considered bad hair days. The awkward square glasses framed an unattractive face. Whiteheads soured his appearance, covering his pale-fleshed cheeks and nose. Large, chapped lips accentuated an already helpless mug. Not to mention, dandruff always littered his collar. What kept Arson and the other employees distant, however, was far worse than bad breath or a hideous composure.

Ray smelled. He rarely, if ever, wore deodorant and didn't believe in cologne. Nevertheless, Ray thought that he walked on air. Because his brother owned the ice cream parlor, he took it upon himself to be the world's easiest person to despise. And he enjoyed it too.

"I want the entire stockroom emptied and shelved," Ray demanded after Arson put away the mop. The invisible, murderous mist of Ray's breath invoked obedience. His boss glanced down at his clipboard, checking off the list Arson assumed was created during his back room hours, which, according to Chelsea, his coworker, Ray spent cruising adult Web sites. "After that, I want you to mix another batch of Chocolate Crunch; we're running low, and those mothers can turn into vampires when little Susie doesn't get the flavor she wants."

"Is that all?" Arson said with an overwhelmed sigh.

Ray grinned. "That's nothing, kid. Get started on the boxes." Ray handed him the razor. "Come see me when you're done. I'll be in the back."

"Enjoy the show," Arson groaned while Ray started to walk away. Then he came back.

"What was that? You have something else to say?" He got up close. "No one likes a wise guy," he said, smacking his lips with gum that did little to subdue the wasteland it swam in. After the stare-down, Ray retreated into the back room, slamming the door behind him.

The afternoon drifted. Ray's retribution seemed cruel, considering Arson's co-workers checked text messages while he stacked sugar cones and birthday items customers rarely purchased. After making ice cream, Arson washed the windows. Although not wanting to complain, he thought enough was enough. With every stroke, he mouthed a silent insult. It was then that he caught a glimpse of Mandy's radiant reflection in the glass.

"They've got you washing windows now?" said Venus in all her majesty, a glint in her eye. She came alone this time.

Arson fumbled for words.

"How's it going, Arson?"

"Yeah," he tried, knowing he must've looked hopeless and pathetic. "I mean, okay. Murder Breath, my boss, loves to torture me. He's kind of a head case." Arson stepped off the ladder so he could look into her crystal eyes.

"I've seen him once or twice, I think. He's the one with the—"

"Bald spot? BO? Murderous breath?"

"I was gonna say stain on his shirt," she said, chuckling. Mandy stuck her hand in front of her mouth and exhaled. "But I hope my breath's okay."

"I'm sure it's perfect," Arson said.

They shared a laugh before his eyes fell to her feet. "Nice shoes," he said out of desperation. He had nothing else. What could he talk about? They existed in different worlds. She was too perfect to even be seen with him. It didn't make sense, but Arson could settle for anomalies wrapped in beautiful blonde paper over rejection any day.

Mandy blinked, and he caught a glimpse of the light blue eye shadow painted against her lids. "Thanks," she replied, almost brushing it off entirely. "Most of the time people don't notice my shoes. Guys, I mean. So, I'm curious now, Arson. Just how mean is this boss of yours?"

"It would take way too long to go into it."

"Sounds like a total drag."

"Yeah. So, um, what are you doing here?" Arson said, fumbling over his words. "Not that I don't like your … company, it's just this is, like, your third time in a week. You must really like ice cream."

Mandy squinted and smiled. "I was just in the area. I mean, this place is right on Main Street. Hard to miss if you're driving by. Anyways, something's been bugging me."

The wind stirred, tossing her golden layers toward the center of her face. He swore they were made of rays of sunlight.

"Really? What is it?"

She took a moment to ask. "Is it true?"

"The ambiguity isn't really helping. What are you talking about?"

Mandy whispered, "Is it true you start fires?"

Arson froze, suddenly avoiding eye contact all together. It made perfect sense now—the unexpected visits, the flirting, that mesmerizing smile. "I have no idea what you're talking about."

"Well, rumor has it, Jason saw you melt a ton of ice cream a few nights ago. Does every employee melt a batch or two before cleanup? Why would you do that, Arson?"

"I wouldn't," Arson bit back.

"It's a simple question. What's the big deal? It's not like I'm gonna go running to the Feds."

He bit his lip hard and swallowed. "It's ridiculous. I don't even like fire. Anyways, Jason and Chelsea love to make up stories. They find some kind of sick pleasure in screwing with me." He faked a bashful smile, hands starting to sweat.

"Don't be such a martyr. It's not a bad thing. You like to play with fire. It's actually kind of sexy."

Arson shuffled his feet.

Breaking the awkward tension, Mandy jumped to a softer subject. "So what's the best flavor to try today?"

He was glad she stopped prying, but in the back of his mind, he wondered how long he'd be able to keep his secret from her. He didn't like the feeling of someone looking deeply into him like that, like some kind of specimen. With a sigh, Arson led Mandy inside. The place was dead. "I'd suggest the Chocolate Crunch," he said.

"Sounds like a good choice," Mandy replied plainly. "I'll give it a try."

Arson went behind the counter and scooped two chunks of ice cream into a cone and handed it to her.

She accepted it, eyeing him from where she stood. "Thanks."

"Come back down to earth, you sappy twerp." Chelsea always had a way with words. She began typing numbers into the register and coughed with an open hand extended toward Mandy.

The blonde goddess reached into her pockets and searched for spare change, but her hands emerged empty. "Oh my gosh. I can't believe it. Forgot my wallet." She looked at Arson. "Do you think you can let this one slide? I'll pay you back."

"No, you won't," Chelsea quipped angrily. "Do you stroll into the mall without any cash and hope they'll let you walk out with a nice pair of jeans? You can't just walk into a store broke and expect free ice cream. I'm getting my manager."

Arson stopped her. "Wait a second. What are you doing?"

"Please don't tell me you're buying into her story. We both know she's got it."

"C'mon, Chelsea. Ray's been on my case all day. Let this one slide, okay? I swear I'll put the money in the register at the end of my shift, make sure everything evens out."

"Guys are so weak. Whatever." Chelsea's face was over-smudged with makeup, but it wasn't enough to hide her disgust. She moved to the other side of the counter and started washing tables in order to look busy.

"Impressive," Mandy said. "You're quite the talker."

"Oh, that's me, a smooth criminal."

"Thank you, Arson. I owe you one," she said with a wink.

SEVEN

Arson noticed a moving truck parked outside the property next door that night. The abandoned house had been on the market for over a year. It was eerie, as if clothed in sorrow, its shingles loosed by wind and rain and sadness. Vacant and unredeemed, the structure had turned away many hopeful buyers over that time. He knew the house was ill with something. Grandma had gotten used to its dead glow, its dilapidated, fading, and crippled shape, but somehow he never could.

Arson watched shadows glide across the withered lawn. He paused for a moment on his slow walk back to the cabin to see people moving in. At first all he could make out was the shape of a slender woman. She appeared worn and unsettled by fatigue. He looked closer. Red hair lay fastened in place by a casual pin. The business air she had about her reminded him of those career types Grandma droned on about. The woman worked vigorously but dragged her feet as she walked. There appeared to be something not right with her.

He shifted his eyes for a moment to a green station wagon, an older model with rust encasing the trim, wheel wells, and back bumper. The dent on the front panel was a real eyesore. A rundown sedan sat beside it. What stunned him most, however, was the license plate. Beneath the white and light blue colors by which all Connecticut license plates were identified, read GDBLESU. Whether it was the cynic in him or a sense of faithlessness, Arson was grieved by it. The last thing he expected or desired was a band of religious nuts moving into his quiet corner of the world.

After a moment, he saw a girl. He couldn't get a clear view of her as she emerged from the blood-red front door, but what he did notice was that when she spoke, her voice crept out through strange skin. Twilight soon revealed that she was wearing a mask. *A little early for Halloween, isn't it?* he thought, wishing he had binoculars. Arson fought curiosity while he imagined the girl trapped beneath its tortured, leathery skin; she could be his age.

The screen door suddenly flung open again, and out came a man, moderately built, with the dark shadow of a beard. His collared shirt hung over corduroy pants sloppily, like he'd been hard at work most of the evening. He appeared softer than the woman, gentler. Perhaps he was a philosophy teacher or something sophisticated like that. Arson half-wondered if he sat around smoking a pipe and listening to Beethoven while reclining in a big leather chair.

The man met the woman at the back end of the moving truck. He took a large bin from her, set it on the ground, and started to hug her. She seemed reluctant but hugged him anyway. The man's eyes suddenly drifted toward Arson. With little more than a stare, the man unintentionally made him anxious by standing up to get a better look. Before either of them could spare an introduction, Arson was lost along the dark path toward home.

The man held the woman in his arms for a long moment before letting go. Their embrace was stifled by her hot temper and sour mood. He asked her what was wrong, knowing full well what the answer would be.

"I know you've been worried about this move for the last couple of months," the man said, caressing her cheek. "But so have I. We're going to make it work."

"I've heard that before. That's what you said when Emery was being ridiculed in school by the other kids. You remember her coming home in tears. That's why she was home-schooled. And then a few years after that, because—"

"Rumors started about our family, Aimee," the man said.

"What about Trenton? We were fine there too. You said that would be our home. For a while it was, but…" Her voice trailed off.

"I know it isn't easy, but this is our life. Emery isn't like other daughters. She's someone we've been blessed with."

"Blessed? You call what happened to her a blessing?"

He rolled his eyes. For years he'd tried to convince his wife that what had happened to Emery, though horrible, wasn't the worst thing that could've happened in their family and that he would try to make everything okay. But his wife never could quite see it that way. "Our home is with each other," he said.

"That sounds sweet on a card, but this is real life. I'm not a military brat anymore. I don't want a nomadic life, moving from place to place with nowhere to call home."

The man wrapped his hands around her waist. "This move is going to bring us closer. I promise."

"I want to believe you, but you can't make promises, Joel, because you don't know how to keep them."

The man's face changed. It read defeat and heartbreak. "Listen. We can try, can't we? You have a new, less demanding job, and I don't have to run a church anymore. We'll get to spend more time with each other and with Emery."

"If you say so."

Their eyes met for an awkward moment. He was trying to console her, but she just didn't seem to care.

"Do you even know who she is anymore?" Aimee asked.

Joel's voice cracked with despair. "Of course I do. We've been raising her for the last seventeen years. I love her."

Her nostrils flared. "We?"

"Don't do that, sweetheart. I've tried my best. I've tried hard to be a good father and husband."

The abrupt moment drifted past. Their masked daughter made her way down the porch steps to greet them. "I'm really friggin' hungry," she said. Immediately, her mother stuck out her neck; the gesture was exclamation enough for Emery to reply, "All right. I'll watch my language. You're so strict. You'd think you guys were born in the Stone Age."

"Well, close. But I'm pretty sure Hendrix and Aerosmith might remember it as the *stoned* age."

Aimee shot him a disapproving look, which he knew meant he should have been firmly on her side rather than reminiscing on their youth with an off-color joke.

Joel shrugged his shoulders. "No one can take a friggin' joke around here." He and his daughter shared a chuckle. It had been a while since he'd heard her laugh, even longer since he'd seen her face. Behind the mask, he wondered if the little girl he loved so much was still there. Emery seemed like more of a secret to him now, one that wouldn't be found out. Maybe he didn't have the words or the ability to connect with her. When he reached toward Emery to remove the hideous mask from her face, she accidentally scratched his hand.

"Don't touch it, Dad," she said.

Arson slammed the front door behind him, taking deep breaths.

"Where are you coming from in such a hurry?" asked Grandma, who was sewing at the kitchen table. Too calm.

He filled a glass with water and swallowed it down.

"Well?" Grandma asked expectantly. Her reading glasses lingered above her chest, atop her apron.

"Nothing. Just happy to be home. Long day."

"I'm glad you can still form nice long sentences," she said.

A grin moved across his lips. Arson didn't have time to talk about how his day had gone. He was more interested in the new, unexpected family settling in next door. It was so sudden. Years had passed since they'd had sane neighbors. Arson wanted to meet the strange girl behind the mask.

"Where did those strangers come from?" Arson asked under his breath.

"Who?"

Arson glanced out the window above the sink and dropped the empty glass.

Grandma drew nearer to steal a peek. "I suppose they've arrived. They're a day early, though. The realtor knocked on my door this afternoon, told me they'd be coming. Have you met 'em yet?"

"No," he quickly shot back.

"Look at them. They're so intent on making this their new home. Don't worry; they'll leave us too, just like the poor soul before them. But it is rather curious. Wonder what their story is, love. Everybody's got one." Suddenly, Grandma dropped the blinds and changed the subject. "How was your day?"

"Another day at Tobey's," he responded matter-of-factly, taking a seat at the table.

"C'mon, I'm sure there was something good about it. Something that made *this* day different, hmm?" Her hand brushed his shoulder. He wanted to hug her but didn't know if she'd embrace him back. Was she still angry with him?

"Not today, Grandma." He sighed while she prepared his dinner. He kept Ray's retribution to himself. It would be of no use to let her know. Punishment was punishment in her eyes. Arson considered telling Grandma about Mandy, though, but realized that spilling his guts about a girl like her was sure to only add fuel to an already raging fire. Mandy was the very inspiration for what Grandma called "vile and perverse." To tell her Mandy had dropped by for the third time in a week and that she had even questioned him about starting fires might invoke more of Grandma's hatred. She wouldn't understand. But something about her this evening was unusual.

"It's a shame you work in such a dull environment. Oh, but at least you get to come home to a hot meal." She smiled and placed the dish in front of him. His mind was swimming.

"Now eat up, love. I'm sure you're hungry. I'm going to bed. I'll see you in the morning."

Arson sliced through the roast beef, put it in his mouth, and chewed slowly. It was strange of Grandma to act so kindly, so free. He pondered it. Maybe he had just prepared for the *darker* side tonight. Ever since he could remember, her emotions had been impossible to decipher or even fully comprehend. Her moods could change as quickly as the weather. Grandma smiled often, but there were few occasions when she actually meant it. Tonight he had seen a real part of her, alive for a moment.

As he swallowed, Arson's mind retraced his memories, back to days when Grandma would laugh and briefly find peace with the creature she had been forced to raise. Maybe she had really been happy once, before him. If only Arson could bring back his mother. If he had never been brought into this cruel world, maybe *she'd* still be alive, and the woman he called Grandma wouldn't be so burdened with despair and anguish.

Arson sat in silence, forgetting about the new neighbors for a while and about the job he despised. He was hopeful tonight, reminded now of the person Grandma could be, the person he wanted her to be, and why he loved her.

EIGHT

Walking by that house the next morning bothered Arson. He couldn't shake the eerie feeling that rattled his insides every time he looked at it.

Arson's gaze moved up and down its haunting frame. As he stared at the house's peeling yellow skin, years of old leaves still covering the porch, the missing roof shingles, and the hoary glow in its eyes when the blinds finally lifted, he found himself thinking of the man who had once resided there.

He could remember the loud, unmentionable sounds at night, the tormenting scenarios Arson fabricated after only moments of adolescent imagination. He recalled coming home one day to find the house abandoned, the man gone. Seeing the structure alive again with new souls was beyond emotion or belief. Where had they come from? What did they want with this dull town? Who were they?

Arson wanted these questions answered. He didn't care what the answers were, but he had to know. Strangers didn't belong moving into abandoned houses, not here. They didn't deserve new lives. Soon enough, they'd realize it was a mistake all along, moving here. Soon enough, they'd run away.

He looked down and kept walking. A flood of sadness flushed through his bones. Arson smacked his lips together and sighed. This place wasn't where souls came to find new life; it was where they came to die.

"Rough night?" Joel asked his wife with a groan.

She yawned absentmindedly. Having perfected the art of avoidance, Aimee shut her eyes and leaned over her knees.

"How'd you sleep, sweetheart?" Joel picked his body up from the mattress, placed his feet on the cold floor, and shivered.

"I didn't sleep much, Joel," Aimee finally said, breaking the air. Still tired, she finagled her way into the red bathrobe that hung off the mahogany bed frame and cracked her joints.

"I'm wondering if that's ever going to stop creeping me out," he mumbled.

"You'll probably get used to it when I get used to hearing you snore all night."

Should that have hurt? She wasn't sure if she'd meant it harshly or not; it just seemed to come out that way. Tossing her hair back, Aimee shrugged it off and shuffled into the bathroom.

Aimee wet her hands and ran them down her fore-head and cheekbones. The cold relaxed her face. She rubbed and stretched her skin, pulling back the pale and wrinkling flesh with a number of odd smiles and facial expressions she'd acquired in over a dozen and a half health seminars, the ones her husband bought for her but never got the hint weren't working. Sitting down for an hour at a time, listening to some phony talk about how to lose that excess flab currently resid-ing on the corner of Butt and Hip was nauseating. Those ridiculous self-help gurus claimed to have the cure for aging and debilitation when they looked ten years older than Methuselah himself.

Aimee needed something to distract her thoughts before going into shutdown. Coffee usually did the trick. She hustled around her new kitchen. "Where did I put that stupid pot?" Flurried emotions scattered her brain. She was beginning to regret arranging and rear-ranging the kitchen at four thirty in the morning when her husband and daughter had been sound asleep.

"Now where did I put it?"

Aimee lifted up things and moved pots and pans aside, rummaged through the pantry, but couldn't find it. What she did find were far too many Tupperware containers, containers used to throw potluck dinners for church people they would never see again.

Suddenly, a looming shadow startled her.

"Oh dear. For heaven's sake, Emery, you scared me half to death," Aimee said, flustered.

"Good morning to you too," the voice behind the mask replied.

"You shouldn't sneak up on me like that. I can be very dangerous this early in the morning. Were you trying to give me a heart attack?"

Emery paused.

"That was rhetorical."

"What are you doing anyway?" Emery asked, yawning. "You look like you're searching for the holy grail or something."

"Would that make me crazy?" she said, panting. "I need coffee. Lots of coffee. Maybe that'll fix me. Where did I put that pot?"

"Is this something new?"

"What?"

"Your multiple personality disorder, that's what. It's becoming ever so popular nowadays. When were you diagnosed?" Emery gasped. "How long's it been since the last memory of your *truer* self?"

"Oh, stop it," Aimee said, sticking her head into the deep of the lazy Susan. "Lots of mothers talk to themselves, but you're only seventeen. You wouldn't understand."

Emery took a seat at the counter. "Craziness aside, Mom, do you really think caffeine is going to solve all your problems?"

"Uh huh," she strained. "It sure is. For now, anyway."

"Suit yourself. Hey, did you sleep all right last night? From the looks of you, I'm sensing a little more than the usual first-night-in-a-new-home syndrome got to you."

"What makes you say that?" Aimee echoed from inside one of the cabinets.

"Because as much as I would relish the opportunity to publicly acknowledge your slow spiral into maternal insanity, I remember what you told me our first night in Jersey. You said you couldn't sleep there. So, being the prodigy that I am, I figured first nights in new homes aren't exactly your thing. But I happen to think it's more than that this time."

"*House,* dear," Aimee said, emerging from the dark space. "This is just a house, that's all. This place is temporary. Give your father enough time and he'll find a reason to move us again."

"Everything isn't *his* fault, Mom."

Aimee remembered the long nights alone, wondering where her husband was. She thought back to church functions that took priority over their daughter's birthday parties, the way his job forced him to put someone or something ahead of them, ahead of her.

"Oh, you were so young, Emery. You still are. We just have no real place to call home, and it bugs me."

"You didn't have a real home growing up either; does that mean that you hate your dad too?"

"I do not hate your father. But I don't want you to grow up with regrets. I want you to have a normal life.

Take this mask off, Emery, please. It frightens me. You don't need it. Besides, maybe if you take it off, we can move on with our lives. All of us."

"I'm not taking it off." Emery recoiled. A moment divided them. "By the way, we're not normal. Unless, of course, dysfunctional is the new normal."

Aimee looked at her strangely. How had she and her daughter grown so far apart? She hated the lingering moments during car rides when the air would get so thick you could cut it with a knife, the moments when they both dreaded exchanging words. Or the agonizing and bittersweet disagreements that had spiraled them into separation. So much had changed so fast. When had she become the bad guy?

"Life hasn't been normal since I was a little girl," Emery said, scooting out of the chair and running upstairs to her bedroom.

Slamming the cabinet door shut, Aimee sighed again and wiped her eyes. "I don't even want coffee," she said.

Impatient customers stood in front

of Tobey's. By the time Arson arrived, many of their faces had turned into something sour, their eyes callous and irritated. Was being a few minutes late really that monumental? With a deep sigh, he rapidly unlocked the door and let them in. Avoiding eye contact altogether, he rushed to the back, flipped on the lights, put on his white apron, and raced behind the counter to serve.

The first few orders were simple, cones of this or that. Then they got complicated. Two banana splits followed, both accompanied by mothers who had baseball games to get to, their faces consumed with unease and irritation. "Billy's pitching today," a snarly mother said, "and if he's late, the coach will bench him." Before Arson had the opportunity to ask why any mother in her right mind would buy an ice cream sundae before her son's game, he realized it was smarter to keep quiet. He took the money and picked up the pace. A chocolate milkshake came next, followed by three mashes: a mix of five different flavors, each complete with three extra toppings, whipped cream, peanut butter, hot fudge, and a cherry.

Scurrying back and forth behind the counter, Arson found himself thinking of how pathetic he was. Would he be stuck behind this counter forever, listening to impatient mothers shout orders at him all day? Options like college or a high-paying job weren't exactly in the cards for someone who started fires with his mind. Most of the time, he wasn't even there; his mind often found better, more dignifying places to be, off saving someone or helping an old woman cross the street or in the arms of a beautiful girl. *But it's not real*, his head always reminded him. *It's not real.*

Another rush of people marched in, these even more impatient, demanding, and unthankful than those before. Whether they were headed to mini-golf, a morning sports game, or merely seeking to silence the obnoxious lust for their weekend hot fudge heart attack made no difference. They all raced to the front of the line, spit out an order or a laundry list of orders, and left without leaving a tip. By half past one, there was only one customer left smiling.

She was a sweet, elderly woman who ordered a vanilla sundae. There was something Arson felt when he looked at her that made him think this was how Grandma might have been if he had not come along to disturb her life. This woman was kind and gentle. What Arson found most beautiful about her was the pleasant way she spoke to him, the *thank you*s and *you're so sweet*s she threw in while he took her order. He didn't think people still possessed that kind of goodness anymore. She was special. But he couldn't, for the life of him, even remember her name.

By two o'clock, the parlor had died down, in time for his arm to rest and Jason and Chelsea to stroll in. Neither said more than a hello. They immediately rushed to the break room. After twenty minutes of giving them their space, Arson begged to have a few batches of ice cream made. Jason and Chelsea exchanged frustrated glances and reluctantly completed the task.

While they were in the back, Arson went to the bathroom. Before he had finished washing his hands, he could've sworn he heard someone walking in. But when he stepped out to greet the customer, he instead caught Jason rushing to the back again. It looked like he was up to no good, and Arson had his suspicions.

Trying to ignore it, he created the biggest, most appealing hot fudge sundae in ice cream history for himself in order to relax and calmly relish the few moments of quiet that remained before Murder Breath stumbled in.

NINE

The furious echo of fire trucks beckoned Arson to follow. He was walking home when they passed him. The red and white saviors shortened his breath. The sound of their screeching tires, restless engines, and fierce horns rang through the street and suddenly vanished round an unnamed road. Off to save some weary soul from a burning building, he imagined. Arson's conscience screamed for him to head home, but tonight, intrigue lured him on.

He hustled toward the sound and tried to keep up, staying close behind the sirens and the dim glow their flashing lights sent out into the darkness. He wanted to be there when it happened: the triumphant salvation of a helpless victim. Wanted to watch as some brave soul dragged a barely breathing, soot-covered person out of a fiery grave.

At last he quit running. Distorted shouts and screams muffled the echo of each siren. Loud, unforgiving groans offered up to the dark. The screams came from inside the house. Firemen raced in, some gripping axes, others wrapping their gloved hands around an almost uncontrollable hose as it showered the flames. The fire manipulated Arson's gaze, tempting him to keep watching, while a sudden back draft spit out two firemen. They hurled backward onto the grass and dirt, suits peeling and singed. But their courage remained. Arson's heart leapt into his throat as the same two men abandoned all fear and stormed into the heart of the fiery beast.

He waited. Waited for the heroes to do the saving. Waited for men to save the helpless, to redeem the lost. Arson lamented the empty hope hollowing him from within. He wanted so deeply for it to be true that he felt almost as if he were drowning in fear that everything would burn. In a moment, he imagined himself at the end of a dark road right before the bend. In front of him the world was ablaze, burning with impunity every man, woman, child, and home. Screams erupted from underneath and above. His eyes burned. His hands. His feet. His chest. He was burning along with every soul he watched die. He couldn't save them. He wanted to so badly, but he couldn't move. Torment and gravity were prevailing. Deep sorrow held him still. Arson couldn't save himself. He couldn't save anyone.

But reality burned away even frail imaginings. He stared on. In a violent blink, he witnessed someone bring a coughing woman out from the inferno and down the porch steps. The rescuer fought to calm her panic, but she wouldn't have it. She cried her husband's name, praying the fire would be merciful. It didn't help. She kicked and swore, and tears swelled.

"And what about my son!" she yelled, beating her rescuer's chest.

It was an unholy mess. Seconds later, a smoky figure exploded through the front door, carrying a young boy across blackened shoulders. The boy's skin was still alive, but his eyes looked dead. In fact, they probably couldn't see anything at all.

A deep sound exploded into the night, blasting glass and roof fragments onto the yard. Arson shook with horror. Raspy screams echoed from the woman's throat. With their heads out their windows, anxiously waiting to see the inevitable misery, neighbors oohed and ahhed. Arson noticed that the woman's hair and face were matted with ash and soot, her clothes torn and ripped. She hung there in anguish, in sorrow so enveloping you couldn't breathe. The way the weathered firefighter's stare broke the news of her husband's demise shattered Arson like glass. He was saying sorry without moving his bleeding lips. The woman fought to go back inside. Die if she had to. She sobbed. She clawed. She got down on her hands and knees and threw dirt at the man who refused her freedom, or as they saw it, suicide. There was no hope left inside. The fire had completely destroyed it.

Arson swallowed hard and felt regret. Violent regret. He had done nothing to help them. Was he dead inside or simply dying? At seventeen years of age, what had he gained other than guilt and fear? These men, these simple firemen bound by the limits of their normal skin and bone had more bravery than he did. The fire couldn't hurt him, but still he stayed. A solid stone.

Arson stared at his hands, knowing he could, if he wanted, inflict this kind of violence. One thought was all it would take. In a blink, he could destroy any house on this block. And just then, conviction set in. There was no escape from this curse. Why had he come here? *Get home,* his thoughts commanded, *where it's safe.*

Smoke rose from the ashes, a gray cloud hovering above what was left. Lightning illuminated the sky. Thunder groaned and crashed. And then Arson could feel rain. It was like the tears of God were falling down upon the world and all that was lost.

Arson blamed himself. He wasn't

responsible for creating the fire, but he was responsible for doing nothing. For running away. He pictured the fire eating away at the man's face, the way it must have bubbled and transformed into something ugly and unlovable.

His mother's face suddenly invaded his thoughts, crafted from only photographs he'd uncovered in Grandma's drawer, found a few months ago while she slept. "Couldn't save them...wouldn't save them," he sobbed, his mind swimming. He pulled the photograph out of his wallet, the one he'd kept with him.

Grandma never knew he had taken it, would probably beat him raw if she knew.

"I loved your mother very dearly, Arson. She was my angel. She was my *baby*. My own." That's what Grandma always said right before she cried. On his mother's birthday, Grandma always reminded him of what he'd done. Every October 27, she blamed him for taking her precious angel away. "You cursed little demon," she'd say. "Killer!"

She was right. Grandma had known his mother better than he'd ever had the chance. All he had was a crumpled photograph of Frances Parker, the woman who died because he was born.

Killer! You took her away. Killer! You. Killed. Your own mother.

Arson's nose filled with snot. Sorrow poured down his cheeks. Heavy rain drops hit the back of his neck and felt like knives cutting pieces of his skin off. His hair lay down in surrender in front of his eyes, a gray crystal blur.

Arson reached the end of the street and crossed, ignoring the blinding beams of the car speeding toward him. The wet screech of the tires might have otherwise scared him half to death, but tonight was different. He realized how short and fragile life could be. Life ended at any given moment, like the life of the trapped father who would never see his son again or the mother who had died giving birth to him. Arson knew these feelings well and, tonight, welcomed them.

Hate for himself, hate for the old and gray world that hated him. It seemed like hatred was a gift tonight. It felt good; it felt right.

The road split, and he paused. He knew which way was home and chose the other.

"Watch where you're going!" another incensed driver hollered. "You could get yourself killed!"

Arson began to run. "I deserve it," he whispered. The water felt hot, even though he was sure it wasn't. Maybe it was coming from inside. Suddenly, he stopped still in the middle of the street. Looked around. The world was dead, asleep. Every wandering thought stormed him at once—a childhood he never had, the mother who created a monster, screams of a burning victim trapped in a house without rescue. *Killer!*

His eyes searched the darkness. Still no one. The fire inside begged for release, like a serpent slithering beneath wet flesh. The headache, the numbing rain pouring down from a God he never saw, never knew. In one fluid motion, the serpent took over. It slithered its way to his wrists and spread to the tips of his wrinkled fingers, gasps of fire licking with each twitch. The stop sign to his right suddenly went up in smoke. The telephone pole to his left wilted to black powder and ash. Electric sparks soon illuminated the night. Arson breathed deeply, tears dripping from lit-up eyes. He screamed, unleashing another wave of heat from his body.

The fire felt good.

"I hate the rain," Emery moaned, sitting at the foot of her bed. She toyed with her mask, wishing it were a face instead. She lifted it a bit to feel the flesh beneath while listening to the patter of rain smacking against the windowsill.

"Why do you hate the rain?" Aimee asked with stressed-out eyes.

"It makes me sad and depressed."

As her mother drew closer, Emery remained tense. She hated how her mother looked at her, like a monster. It was obvious her parents had never seen her the same since that day.

"I guess it's normal to feel depressed when it rains, honey. *They* say that weather can sometimes dictate the way we feel. *They* often say that our emotions are fickle, much like the weather." Aimee looked as though she wanted to smile, but her face wouldn't allow it.

"Whatever. You're not as funny as you think, Mom."

"Well, sorry. We can't all be as funny as your father."

Emery saw her mother cringe but ignored it. Instead she tilted her head slightly and stared through the glass window, out into a gray world filled with tears. "I hate the rain," she sighed again, this time murmuring.

A hand brushed the back of her shoulder where the white nightgown Emery let droop to her elbow hung. "What's the matter, sweetheart?"

Emery was silent.

"Honey?"

"What?"

"You seem like you're thinking about something. You were staring out into space. What's wrong with you?"

"Nothing," Emery replied. The last thing she wanted was the possibility of an argument, however small or unprovoked.

"Don't be ridiculous. Tell me what's bothering you." She felt her mother reach to rub her back, but instead Emery coiled up around her pillow. "It's the new house, isn't it? A new bedroom you're not used to. This ugly town feels more like the set of some low-budget horror movie than home."

She focused on her mother, suddenly this opinionated list maker who formed a spreadsheet of all the wrong things.

"God only knows who our neighbors are," Aimee continued. "Gosh, I can't get that creepy boy out of my head. Who sneaks up on people and watches them like that?"

"I don't know. Maybe he was just interested in who we are."

"Yeah, well, I'd like to know what kind of people live around here. There's no telling how bizarre they might be. Heaven forbid we wake up one morning and—"

"Get abducted? Maybe *you* should sit down and talk about your feelings, Mom."

Emery waited for the words to settle in and disturb the living daylights out of her mother.

"Feelings?" Aimee replied. "I'm fine, a little uneasy about this place, that's all."

Emery sank into the pillow, could feel the goose bumps on her arm. It became cold all of a sudden when her mother's hand once more reached out to her. "Why do you keep trying to touch me?"

"I'm your mother, and I love you. You're acting so strange."

Who was she to start making accusations? Did she have to spend seven years afraid of her own reflection? Emery hated how parents and shrinks always thought they had the answers when, in reality, they didn't have a clue. "I'm not acting strange; I just don't want to be touched right now, and I don't want to talk about the rain or this new house. I want you to leave me alone."

"It's perfectly normal to have feelings, Emery," Aimee tried.

Emery's eyes rolled back. "There you go again."

"What did I say this time? What?"

"Nothing."

"No, tell me."

Emery adjusted her mask and retreated under the covers.

"It's that terrible mask. I never liked it, but your father insisted. I can't believe you wear that creepy thing every day. It's awful."

"I know. It's not like your opinions are anything new." Emery groaned. "I'm tired."

"So am I," Aimee spat. "Think what you will about me, but you and I both know that masks can't hide everything."

Emery buried her head beneath the pillow. "You have me all figured out."

A defeated sigh pushed its way out. Aimee turned the light off as she left the room.

Emery could hear loud footsteps outside. She leaned up in bed and stared out the window, noticing a dark figure. The strange boy her mother couldn't stand. Possessed with curiosity, she hopped out of bed and moved toward the windowsill. The blurry figure danced intermittently across the glass. She watched it stretch against the gray world before it vanished inside the neighboring cabin.

"Who are you?" Emery wondered, rubbing her mask, its material more real to her than the skin on her face.

Down the hall, Aimee strolled into her room and quickly got into bed, nerve-wracked. The sound of her husband nestling up beside her never reached her ears. He whispered something, but she didn't respond. She remained in the argument with her daughter.

Joel's hand reached for hers as he tried to smell her hair before he kissed her. But his lips felt unusual and unwelcome.

"I'm not in the mood, Joel," Aimee said under her breath, rolling over.

TEN

Aimee awoke alone. Her eyes had glazed over, and there was a bitter taste in her mouth. Brushing the hair out of her face, she yawned and glanced down. The spot beside her was empty. The imprint of where Joel had lain for the past seven and a half hours betrayed him. Nothing left behind but damp, wrinkled bed sheets. She assumed it was her husband's anxiety back to play the devil after a quiet, loveless evening. Aimee felt somehow refreshed, though. She tried hard not to gloat inside, but it was the first decent sleep she'd caught in weeks. Was it wrong for her to feel some satisfaction?

It amazed her how different they were. How different they'd become. There had been a time when she longed for Joel, even cried sometimes when he left for conferences and meetings. Now, she found herself welcoming the quiet, quite content with the empty space beside her on the bed. Joel was a different man, or perhaps it wasn't until this moment that she'd noticed he hadn't really changed at all.

"You're making breakfast?" Aimee said as she stumbled into the kitchen. Joel was slicing potatoes and stirring eggs when she moseyed past. Anticipation and excitement drew her eyes. He looked peaceable, but forcibly so.

"Maybe," he said, his face glowing with mystique.

"Maybe?" she asked, staring at the countless items and utensils scattered across the countertop.

"Good morning, wife." Joel shook the skillet, the eggs hardening, and then walked over to her. With a deep sigh, he kissed her on the lips.

A stranger's lips, she thought. The way he pressed into her, his palm tickling the soft skin on her lower back, crystallized her veins. "What time did you get up?" Aimee asked.

"About an hour ago," replied Joel. "Didn't want to wake you."

"That was probably a good idea." She pulled away at length and wiped her mouth. "Sorry, my lips are just so chapped when I wake up. Wouldn't want to gross you out."

She could tell his eyes lingered on her. Before they were married, he used to look at her a certain way, not unlike the way he was looking at her now; only this time, his usual grin was now stitched into a tired, aging face. She could almost guess what would come next— something about her figure, how pretty she appeared, at least to him, or the way she said good morning, which today had never actually come out.

"You're so beautiful," he said, looking her right in the eyes.

There it was. Geez, she could practically puke. Could he hear himself? He sounded like a fool, a blind fool far too desperate to see that what she really was, was simple. Ordinary.

Inside she exploded, but on the surface, Aimee rubbed her eyes and said, "No, I'm not." Aimee watched as her husband stirred the spatula into the omelet mix, taking in a whiff of the breakfast steam. He adjusted the stove's temperature then removed the cover on the pan beside the skillet. A smoky mist of potatoes, pepper, and buttery onions filled the kitchen. "Home fries are almost done. Aimee, are you ready for the best thing in your entire life?"

Yes, she wanted to say. *Yes, I am.*

Joel scooped the omelet onto a paper plate, then loaded the other side with sautéed home fries. "A meal fit for a queen. You'll need this in order to impress all your new colleagues at that *prestigious* clinic."

The sheer emphasis he used nearly made her hug her stomach.

"It's a hospital, *dear,* not a clinic."

"Tom-ate-o, Tom-otto." He shrugged.

"Oh no. There's a difference. There is. Ask any nurse, and she'll tell you I'm right." Her eyebrows dipped into her nose, her tone morphing into something grim. Aimee could sense the hot venom begging to come up. She couldn't hold it back any longer.

Months of working hard as a nurse while he lazily tried to find himself again was enough to make any woman want to scream. "That job is the only thing that's going to keep us afloat the next couple of months while you pull yourself together."

Joel bit his lip, beaten.

With numbness in her eyes, she watched his face crumble. "Is something burning?" she asked, flaring her nostrils.

"The toast!" Joel dropped the plate and rushed to the smoking toaster. Jamming the switches up, he stared, defeated, at burnt squares. "It was almost perfect," he sighed, handing his wife the plate.

Those two words described her entire life. *Almost perfect*. Like *almost* getting your chores done before Dad got home or *almost* pregnant. The scares, trials, and, at times, joys of youth seemed to call her again.

Joel dropped two more slices of bread down the toaster's throat while Aimee poked at her food, lost in some fairy-tale ending she'd imagined a thousand times in her head, none of which had brought her here. How did she get here anyway? Playing with the ring that bound her to this failed minister made her feel as if she were a prisoner, and this lackluster rock was keeping her in captivity. Was he just another inmate, or was he the warden, holding the key to her freedom but never letting her go? How could he walk around such a messy, bland, and angry house and act like everything was okay?

Once Joel applied the butter to the two steaming slices of bread, he quickly placed them onto his wife's plate. "Oh," he said. "Almost forgot." Joel then ran the knife down the center of the bread and created four parts, blackened just right. "Thank God for second chances." He smirked.

Aimee chewed her bottom lip, one hand keeping her frizzy mop out of the food, the other cutting a piece of the omelet small enough for her mouth.

"How's it taste, sweetheart?"

She hated omelets. Didn't he know that? When they were dating, she had played like she enjoyed them, but deep down, they reminded her of her father. She loved when he used to make them for her whenever arriving home from months of active duty. The way he'd slow cook everything so that he could spend every precious moment with her, if only to pick up and disappear again. Aimee cherished those moments, ate everything on her plate, just for the colonel.

She was staring into those eyes again, him looking back at her with all the love in the world, and yet she hated him. Hated the way the colonel yelled at her mother whenever he came home from drunken poker games. Used to say he drank 'cause war was hell. If he'd bothered to hang around long enough, maybe he would've noticed home wasn't any different. Aimee rubbed her arms from time to time, checking for bruises that might have sneaked up on her over the years. But instead of rubbing black and blue spots off of her back and ankles, she felt the pain on her heart, the only place she could still feel a wound.

Aimee looked at her husband, but the man looking back at her was clad in medals. The man's gray flattop stuck up from a grim face, eyes worn from staring into the hearts of fearful soldiers, blurred by the notions of right and wrong. She remembered most how his top row of teeth was stained by the grit of tobacco. From head to toe she could see him clearly—the hero of her childhood. Wrinkled fingers placed on his brow, his rocky face a hollowed-out life all its own. But he hadn't changed. His coffee-colored suit matched his skin, as if blended so perfectly you couldn't tell they were ever separated. Then her eyes lingered on his boots, tied to perfection, neither lace longer than the other, and knotted twice. He stood there straight and rigid before her, their eyes once more locked tight. He was *almost* perfect.

As the figure spoke, she could hear her husband's voice coming through. "Are you happy, sweetheart?"

"I hate omelets," she spit out quickly. "I have to go get ready."

Aimee sank her teeth into a slice of toast and rushed upstairs to her bedroom before she could hear Joel say, "I love you."

ELEVEN

Emery eased toward the strange boy lying facedown in the water. Weighing her steps. Counting her heartbeats. *One. Two. Four. No, go back one.* She made a mental note not to get worked up one bit, told herself it was nothing, but that didn't stop chills from racing up and down her body. Part of her struggled to calculate what she might say; the rest of her wondered what he was doing. Was he coming up for air? He was so still. Emery studied him, his back arched against the surface enough to stay afloat. No signs of movement. Who exactly was he trying to impress anyway? Maybe her mother wasn't completely wrong; maybe this boy and whoever else occupied the shack behind her really were from some strange, distant world.

Is he ever coming up? Emery checked her watch, beams of sunlight reflecting from Mickey Mouse's nauseatingly joyous grin. His smiles had seemed like miracles when she was five, but there was nothing funny about a boy drowning himself. This wasn't a game anymore. Perhaps this was a—if he would simply move, kick his leg or something, then she would know he wasn't dead. *Oh no,* she thought. Anything but that.

She never liked to admit it, but watching people die terrified her, right down to her bones. It always made her question what lay on the other side. Heaven or hell? God or the devil? At the thought, Emery fidgeted, thinking back to the time when Tina, her cousin, had been found on the bathroom floor, eyes rolled back in a deep sleep. The panic of that night revisited her now. The slow breaths that followed felt like a spell, a spell that even now forced fear upon her. It was a miracle her cousin had survived. That was more than enough drama for an entire lifetime.

"Hey!" she yelled, flailing her arms to try and get his attention. "Hey, you!"

Alien boy didn't move. He'd been under the water now for over two minutes.

"It's time to come up. Whatever the problem is, I swear you can handle it. It's not as bad as you think." Butterflies swarmed inside her belly, but they felt more like bats, chewing away everything but the anxiety.

"Not again." She winced, diving from the dock headfirst into the lake. As she hit the water, her mask slipped off. Swimming underneath the boy, she fought to bring him up for air. Suddenly, his eyes opened. Paralyzed in fear, she screamed, heart racing, her throat swallowing the bitter water that fought to enter. She sank deep. He noticed her, but she wasn't ready for those eyes.

Immediately, the boy went into a panic. Bubbles popped from his mouth as he emerged. The mask drifted by him, startled him. He reached out to grab it, taking in more oxygen.

Emery's ferocious struggle to breathe outweighed logic. He tried to help her, but she rejected him. Her fingers slid down her face; the rough spots of the scars made her regret diving in at all. What was she thinking? The fate this boy might have endured would have been better than seeing her without her face.

"Who are you?" he asked.

"Where is it?" Emery said, shivering. The cold water stung in spite of the summer's heat.

"What were you doing? Why did you dive in after me?" A black shirt hugged his chest. Jeans clung to his waist and sagged as he started to climb up the dock.

"Are you insane? I was trying to save you from making a colossal mistake!" Emery was nervous, painfully nervous. "Where is my face? Give it back to me!"

"I don't need anyone to save me," the boy spat, brushing back his soaked, ash-brown hair.

"Please, just give it back. I want my mask. If you want to, go back to drowning yourself for all I care, but I need that mask back. Now!"

"What are you talking about? And why are you covering your face?" he asked, staring down at her from the dock, eyes locked.

Emery observed the boy through narrow slits her fingers had allowed. Letting her hair fall down, she said, "What are you looking at?" Emery climbed up onto the ground. *Put me out of my misery,* she thought.

"What is it?" Arson asked her. He should have been more careful, shouldn't have been trying to clear his head, not with new neighbors. New, nosy neighbors like this girl.

"It's a mask." Her voice was muffled because she buried her face in the fabric of her shirt. "What, you've never seen a mask before?"

"I have, but not one like this. It's freaky. You know, for a girl. You friends with Michael Myers?"

She shrugged. "Typical."

"Why do you wear it?"

"What is this, twenty questions?" She seethed. "It's for my safety. Against aliens."

He grinned. "You believe in aliens?"

"Whatever. Look, can I have it back?" she said, reaching. "The freak show's over."

Arson handed it over and stepped away, giving her some room to gather herself. He couldn't imagine why she would need a mask or why she wouldn't let him see her face. In a society where most girls hid themselves behind thick gobs of makeup, she hid behind a creepy mask.

"Thank you," Emery sighed. "Please don't look at me." She turned around, noticing that her clothes were completely ruined. The long skirt, which before the triumphantly stupid rescue had swung at her shins with wrinkled burgundy grace, was now torn in two different sections. Her shoes would surely take hours, if not days, to recoup from the underwater fiasco. Her shirt was covered in grass stains.

As she turned around, she caught him staring at her again. "Quit it!"

"Man, someone woke up on the wrong side of the bed."

"Well, sorry if rescue diving wasn't on my agenda of stupid things to do today."

The girl's slow and spooky breaths were almost haunting. "No one asked you to dive in and save me, whoever you are," Arson replied, hawking a wad of sticky saliva into the dirt.

"You're twisted, you know that? Someone tries to help you and you throw it back in their face. My mom was right." Emery started pacing the spotty lawn, her feet squishing and sliding between wet socks. "All I wanted to do was come over here and cordially introduce myself to the alien."

Arson wiped the water from his face, but confusion remained. "What's with this alien thing?"

She sighed. "It's just my family didn't know you—I still don't even know you—whatever. My mom and

I were talking last night and...forget it. I've finally made contact; that's all that matters."

He stared at her inquisitively. "Mission accomplished?"

"If you call ruining my clothes, losing my mask, and you staring at me like I'm the bearded lady *accomplished*, then yes, it was a roaring success."

There was an amusing mystique about her. In all his life, people had been made up of the sweet and the sour, the beautiful and the ugly. But she was unpredictably unique, somewhere in between, somehow indefinable.

"What's your name?" Arson finally asked, shoulders shrugged.

She paused briefly. "Emery. What's yours?"

"Arson."

"Arson? Okay, weird boy. Weird name. Guess it adds up."

Arson tilted his head. "Coming from the girl who wears a mask."

She didn't say a word.

"I'd invite you in," he began, "but Grandma's about to get up. She's not exactly hard-pressed to meet new people. Usually I'm not either, but you *did* try to save my life or whatever." He said it half-smirking.

"Even though you weren't really drowning," she said, now showing how ashamed she was of it. "Next time I'll just wait it out, read about your underwater tragedy in the obits."

Arson grinned. "Well, I gotta go." As he stared at the cabin, he noticed Grandma's shadow linger over the porch like a vulture in the valley.

"Yeah. We should get cleaned up," Emery agreed, chilled by the old woman's presence.

"Guess I'll see you around," he called out halfway toward the cabin.

A smile pulled her lips up against the inside of the mask.

Grandma sat with prying eyes and disapproving lips as Arson walked in. "You're getting awfully friendly with the new neighbor," she said. Her words held him still. "Awfully friendly indeed." A smug yawn stretched her wrinkly mouth, and her wrists tugged backward, yanking the fabric through the slit her fingers had made. From the looks of the threads in her hand, she was sewing a new blanket.

"I know," Arson said. Shivers slid down the back of his wet neck.

"Would you close that door, love? We don't live on a farm, for heaven's sake."

Arson stepped back and pushed the door shut, the wind escaping from beneath the wooden frames with a soft whisper. He knew what was coming. He never meant to upset her, but he was well aware that he'd already done that.

"Now lock the door, just in case." She looked at him; her eyes were rings of fire on his cold skin. "Come sit by me, won't you?"

Slowly, Arson drew near, apprehensive but willing.

"Go on. I'm not gonna bite you, just wanna talk, that's all." A graceful set of dimples sucked her cheeks in a bit as she made the request, tapping the seat beside her. She looked innocent enough, white hair scaling across her shoulder and eyes that baited him.

He fell into the seat and kept still. Awaiting punishment was a far more difficult task than being honest with his grandmother. The way she looked at him, as if he'd committed crimes unable to be uttered, made his bones want to shatter. Her gaze was inescapable, and her mouth stuttered but didn't speak. Each wrinkle in her face had an opportunity to manipulate and condemn. Each passing second did the same.

"So, what's her name?"

He bit his lip, quickly spitting out, "Emery," before having a chance to even think.

"That's a sweet name. I'll bet she's a sweet girl." Grandma led another line of fabric through a loop with her needle; she looked focused, eyes never drifting from her work.

Arson knew she was playing nice but wondered how long it would last. "I guess. We only talked for five minutes."

"Well," Grandma said matter-of-factly, "five minutes seemed like enough time to get her clothes off and hop into the lake." Her accusing, biting tone sliced through the air like a knife, cutting deeper than metal ever could.

Arson's elbows hit the table, frustrated. Right then, Grandma smacked them both hard with the back of her hand, her diamond ring splitting open a chunk of his wet skin. Tears of red slipped out.

"Like I said, she seemed ... sweet."

"We weren't skinny dipping," Arson pleaded. "We weren't even swimming."

"Of course not, heaven forbid." Grandma's fingers guided her mood, the needle a forecast to the manipulation that would follow. Arson didn't like it. He wanted out of this interrogation, in which Grandma played both good and bad cop. The white walls and manila envelopes, the complimentary coffee and handcuffs, were replaced by condemning eyes, a needle, and bitter speculation. Convicts in movies rarely made it out of such cross-examinations intact. Winning just didn't seem possible.

"I swear. I think she was trying to rescue me."

Grandma stopped sewing altogether and placed one hand on top of his. The bad cop was breathing now. "This little tramp is trouble. I feel it in my bones. Henry feels it too."

Arson felt his eyes roll like marbles inside his head.

"Don't you dare mock me!" Grandma hissed, smacking the table. "And don't you dare mock your granddaddy. You know I don't like you going into that lake. You know how it bothers me. Don't you care about me anymore?"

Arson nodded weakly. He brushed the dark, wet strands of hair away from his face and tucked them behind his ears. She was suffocating him.

"You're not a fish, for heaven's sake. The Lord gave you two feet. You were meant to be on dry land, not holding your breath underwater like some crazy … Oh, what am I going to do with you?" She stood up and sighed, rubbing the crevices on her pale face. Her eyes were cold and condescending, two dreamless windows.

"It helps me think," he replied.

"What on earth could you think about underwater that you can't think about in your own home?"

This wasn't his home. This wasn't hers either. It was only a walled building that kept them inside, dying little by little, waiting to consume them both. She didn't understand that, but he did. Home for them no longer existed. It was a fairy tale, a dream. Grandma needed to wake up.

"I don't know." Arson shrugged. "The lake understands. It can sometimes be quiet underneath."

"It understands? It's quiet." She nodded mockingly. "I'm done listening to this nonsense. Get your skinny hide on up to your room."

Reluctantly, Arson pushed the seat back and got up, the wet stain from his pants dripping off the chair.

With a deep sigh, he marched to her command, like an obedient soldier, told what to do, how to think, and how to feel.

"You'll have plenty of quiet time to think. All by yourself." With arms folded, Grandma followed him up the stairs, angry and militant.

She tossed a towel at him and shoved him into the bedroom. The sound of her turning the key, locking him inside, made his hands burn.

Arson reached for the photograph of his mother. He clutched it tightly until his hands became fists, the face of his mother quickly disintegrating inside his hot grip. Maybe if she were here…

Arson lay huddled on the floor. He'd changed his outfit and had plenty of time to dry off, but he still felt soggy, his clothes sticking to his body every chance they got. Anxious and uneasy, he rocked back and forth. The walls accused and the windows spied. Fury pumped through him. The heat in his hands didn't bother him the way it used to. He practiced lighting and quenching the fire in his palm. Played with it. Let it dance across each line and curve. First a spark, then a red gasp, and then a flame. A smile manipulated his lips. He hated the fire, but it seemed the fire understood him in ways no human could, in ways no human wanted to.

It was then that Arson found a spider crawling amidst the dust, its spiny, intricate legs plotting a vile route with each measured move. Yet the creature appeared insignificant to him. Disgusting and meaningless. The more Arson stared, the more apprehensive the creature became. The spider ceased all movement suddenly. Its dead eyes were black glass. Arson wondered if it had a soul. The spider crawled along, tiptoeing against the back of Arson's wrist for a moment before making its way up unpainted sheetrock. He locked his gaze. The eight-legged acrobat drifted along the wall. Somewhere within this creature's ugliness, there was something painfully beautiful. The room paled in comparison. The boarded windows looked on, but Arson ignored them. A poster of his favorite novel, *The Great Gatsby*, faded away as light skimmed across the filmy layer of web and dust. The web reminded him of Grandma's hair—white, the color of ghosts and winter.

Arson marveled. Seconds turned to minutes and minutes into an hour, and he watched the busy creature spin and twist, carefully unwinding each sticky thread. Jealousy swelled within him. "It's unfair," he snarled.

The spider was done at last. Arson watched it crawl across the web trailing from the bedpost to the ceiling. It was perfect. The dead-eyed spider danced upon the final strand and awaited its prey, huddled in the darkness.

Arson's hand began to burn once more, and this time he let it seduce him. "I hate you," he cried. Frustration and sadness and torment altogether. Arson reached out with one finger and burned the web, letting it fall like ashes at his feet.

TWELVE

Emery liked to analyze, even if she couldn't always understand. People were unpredictable. But trying to figure them out sort of came easy. Even as a child, Emery enjoyed analyzing how people worked, why they did certain things. But long before her thirteenth birthday, Emery had learned the hard way that her thinking needed to change. Her parents had warned her about what a messed-up place the world was, how trusting people always got their hearts broken. They were right. She hated that. Hated how people lied and gave false hope, false acceptance. Hypocrites. Like her family. Like their families. Like everyone else.

In the shower, her mind seemed the most lucid. Perhaps the hot steam or the little stabs of boiling water kept her calm. She let the water sink into her scars, scratching at the bumps and gross craters on her face. But she couldn't stop thinking about him. Emery wanted to know what thoughts found their way into Arson's head. After all, he couldn't possibly be feeling the way she was. Plus, even if he were, it was stupid to even consider because there was no way he could understand what she had gone through as a child, what she was still going through. Who would? She could picture her mother's response. "The two of you could never have a normal life together." But that wasn't enough to ignore the sting of intrigue that found its way into her analytical brain. Maybe this was what girls always talked about. Just a crush.

As flashbacks of the day raced through her mind, Emery recalled coming home to an empty house. The only remnant was a sticky note on the fridge that read: *Had to go out. Be home later. Love you, Dad.*

Cryptic, as usual.

Emery sucked in a deep breath of steam. She could feel her pores, what was left of them, expanding and contracting. The hot needles soothed her muscles and flesh, even the rough parts of her shoulder, which, to the best of her ability, she kept hidden. Those parts of her body would remain diseased, infected. Emery turned the handle and the shower head stopped spitting out warmth. She stepped out onto the cold tile floor, grabbed a towel, and wiped the mirror, where a lost girl stared back at her.

They were only memories; they weren't real. But they still had the power to rip Arson apart.

Danny visited him now and then, but every time Arson tried to talk to him, tell him how screwed up his life was, how he wished they could have remained in contact over the years, the image fled. It stung to be brought back, though. Lingering in the past seemed to constantly breathe new life into the same old misery. It hurt that Danny had never tried to find him. He just disappeared. The years hadn't changed Danny; he was still the way Arson remembered. Sometimes the only thing he talked to was the image of Danny come back to haunt him, come back to remind him of his guilt and regret. Danny always brought the cold.

Arson's teeth chattered. Chilled sweat bled across his forehead. He reached for a comic book to quiet his mind, but it only reminded him of how low he really was. "I'm no hero," he said, grinding his teeth. He hated Grandma for locking him up, hated that key she turned every time she stuck him in here.

It would be so easy...

The more time he spent trapped, the less he believed in heroes. They never came to visit him, only Danny. Only the pain and hurt. Arson had had enough of the haunting spirit, enough of every hero's complacent and fearful silence. Grandma was merely a mortal, weak and vindictive, but beautiful. He knew her footsteps, knew her smile, even knew what her breath smelled like. His hate for her was only equaled by a love he could not explain in ordinary words, not even emotion. But he knew she was right about him. The punishment explained that clearly.

"I am a monster," he whispered to himself, throwing one of his comic books across the room. "I am."

Arson began burning the comic books under his mattress and in the closet. The fire turned it all to ash and dust in minutes. Heroes, like memories, weren't real. They only appeared to be. What was a hero anyway? Did it cry? Did it bleed? It was too hard to be good in such a vile world.

Arson banged his head against one of the walls, chips of sheetrock crashing down into his greasy hair. He seemed to find some sort of pleasure at burning away the heroes he used to idolize, mere casualties of an unfair war.

Arson closed his eyes, and when they opened again, Danny was gone.

"I don't fit," he uttered in breaths not even he could hear.

THIRTEEN

"Arson, wake up! Get up now!" Grandma screamed, banging on his bedroom door with all her might. The walls shook.

Suddenly, the door flung open, and she stumbled toward the bed, frightened and disturbed. Deep, creepy breaths escaped dry lips. "Arson, wake up!" She smacked his cheeks until his eyes opened wide.

He got up, startled, and asked, "What's the matter, Grandma?"

She couldn't stop shaking. Grandma paced the room and stomped. "I can't find Henry."

"What do you mean?"

"I woke up and he wasn't there. He wasn't there!" She stumbled around the bedroom, her stained and threadbare pajamas waving dust from the wooden floor into the light. Bare feet traced the broken floorboards, and a splinter stuck out at the end of her toe. She didn't notice.

Grandma's eyes lit up. "Has he left me for another woman? After so many years, am I not good enough for that selfish ... What more does the man want? Oh, I'm not pretty, am I? He's found someone else." She dropped her hands to her hips. "I went to bed with him and now he's gone. Gone!" Sobs disguised her normal, drawn-out voice. Her eyelids fought to keep back tears.

Arson wiped his face and sighed. "He didn't leave you for another woman, Grandma. Where would you get an idea like that?"

"Then tell me where he went, for heaven's sake. Tell me, you lying little demon. Tell me!" She reached for his neck and started to choke him until her fingernails penetrated the skin.

"Think about it. Grandpa loves you. He would never do anything like that."

That answer didn't satisfy her. "I've been up since dawn, and he's nowhere in sight. Oh, my Henry, where did you go?"

Arson's eyes danced around hers; he couldn't stand to stare into them, not now. She was in pain, and he couldn't bear it.

"Maybe he's out by the dock. Grandpa needs to keep his head clear, right? Always says stress will kill a man."

"Stop lying to me!" she screamed. "I checked the docks, I've checked the basement and the kitchen and the closets and our bedroom. Where is he? Where is my Henry?"

"Maybe he went out for some cigarettes," Arson said, panting. "You know how he has to have a pack in his pocket at all times. Maybe you could give the Quick Mart a call. Yeah, you know how Grandpa gets without smokes. He goes ... crazy."

"Marlboro Lights, they're his favorite," she replied quietly, as peace slipped in.

"Yes, they are," Arson gasped, as he softly touched Grandma's arthritic hand. She was human still. She cried, she missed, and she loved. She wasn't dead like he'd imagined. She still needed someone to cherish, and she needed someone to cherish her. Without love, hearts died.

"Would you lie to me?" She turned again, gripping him tighter. "You wouldn't lie to me, would you?"

"He'll come back to you, I promise. He always comes back, doesn't he?" Arson answered pathetically.

Grandma released him. She turned soft all of a sudden. Her wiry gray hair hung over his shoulder. Arson held her in his arms.

"Grandma loves you," she said over and over again.

Arson sat with his back nudged up against one of the rotted porch pillars, listening to the sound of the lake, when the masked girl from next door dropped by, eager to say hello. He noticed that an obscure band t-shirt covered her thin frame while ripped jeans and Converse classics completed whatever look she was aiming for. Once she got up close, Arson caught a glimpse of what the lower half of her face looked like.

"You look freaked out," she said. "I swear, it's like no one's ever seen a mask before." As if in defeat, she tilted her head, folded her arms, and sat down beside him.

He raised an eyebrow. "Hi."

"You're not planning to drown yourself today, are you?" she said.

"Wasn't part of the plan, no." Arson shrugged.

"You know, the weather guy says this is Connecticut's worst heat wave in years. Figures we'd pick now to move to this crummy town."

They both sighed.

The lake drew his attention. He loved how it looked in the morning with streams of sunlight shining over every ripple.

"You know, you could take a dip without trying to drown yourself. Unless, of course, you can't swim."

"I can swim. It's just..."

"What?"

"Grandma doesn't like it when I go into the lake."

Arson watched her head jerk back, shocked by what he'd just said. "I thought *my* parents were strict," she said.

"Grandma gets upset easy. She's from a different mindset, one that says if you disobey her it means you don't love her or something. I used to get it; now I'm just as confused as every other teenager."

"Parents." Emery sighed. "They should just let us live our lives. Not everything demands their oversight or their approval."

Arson stared.

"Sorry. I just have a weird relationship with the 'rents. Slang, by the way, for parents." Emery began playing with her hair. She looked nervous; he could tell. But Arson didn't know why. "Do you get along with your folks? Is your mom as much of a control freak as your grandmother?"

Arson blinked, silent for a while. "My mother's dead," he slowly replied. "Never met my father. But Grandma told me the kind of person he was. He kind of took off after I was born."

"Oh, that sucks. But you and your grandmother are pretty close, then?"

"She's cared for me ever since."

"Right." Emery shrugged half-heartedly. "I get it. I'm jealous."

The wind blew their hair back and forth. The lake quickly became crowded by boats and jet skis. The stir was plenty loud to distract them from the awkward moment.

"How long have you lived here?"

Who was this girl? She asked so many questions, questions nobody had asked before, questions nobody cared enough to ask. Arson knew nothing about her other than her name, the fact that she wore a mask, and that she had been dead—set on saving his life less than twenty-four hours earlier, when he was sure he didn't need saving. She had just moved in next door and instantly wanted his ear for a conversation.

After a moment, he responded, "We've lived here seven years."

"My family's never stayed in any spot longer than three. Something always happens, and we have to move. Never really had a home, you know? You're really lucky."

Lucky? If there was ever a word to describe him, it wasn't that. Depressed, maybe, or discontented, but never lucky.

"Say, what do you do for fun around here? I mean, you guys have the usual: gas stations and a Mickey D's, but I've never been much for siphoning gas tanks, and I can't stand Big Macs."

Arson stared blankly. He'd never been asked for advice on what was fun. It was always him asking someone else. And had she just asked him out, or was that crazy, masked-girl talk for excessive boredom?

"C'mon, it's July, and summer's already half over. You know, I always wanted to go back to public school ever since the 'rents forced homeschooling down my throat. Said it was better for me. I guess now I'll get my wish. They agreed to let me try it out this fall. I told them I was a senior, for crying out loud. But if I can be honest, the school schedule sucks. I mean, summer just started."

A grin crawled across Arson's lips.

"Sorry, I'm just very opinionated."

"Really?" he said.

Emery playfully shoved him. "I need to do something fun before I go out of my mind. All this unpacking and getting settled in blows. My mom thinks I'm wasting my summer months away. She wants me to start volunteering at the hospital. She's a nurse, by the way. But can you believe that? She's there for, like, a few days and already suggesting I volunteer. I've always wanted to do it but can't stand the fact that she's the one *pushing* me to do something I've wanted to do since I was six. She's probably got everything set up and has me committed."

Arson quietly listened.

"She says it'll be good for me. They always say that, don't they? Whatever."

"Maybe she's right."

"Oh, don't tell me you're on her side," Emery said with a grunt.

Arson raised his hands in defense. "I don't even know your mom, so how could I be on her side? I'm just saying it might be a good idea, that's all."

Emery's mask shook, and he pictured her frustrated beneath its gruesome skin.

"She always thinks she knows what I'm thinking, but she doesn't."

Arson simply nodded, still lost in the insanity of having a conversation with a complete stranger. Well, sort of.

Emery continued, "I'm not sure why I'm telling you all this. I just feel like a geyser, and I've been holding everything down for so long that I just want to pop. You're the closest thing I have to a shrink at the moment, so, sorry, but you're kinda stuck listening."

Arson ran his fingers through his hair nervously. Awkward tension filled the moment.

"Any plans for the Fourth?" she asked, changing the subject. "I'm not keen on the idea of spending the day with Mom and Dad. The way they've been acting, I'd be surprised if they said hello to each other, much less have an enjoyable time. I gotta get out. But I don't even have a car. How lame is that?"

"Really lame," Arson said. "But it seems we have something in common."

"So quit being boring and make a suggestion."

"Hey, you came over here, remember? I never invited you."

"Fine." Emery picked herself up, preparing to walk away. With a purposefully slow pace, she walked, giving him a shot at redemption.

"There's a bowling alley not too far from here," he eventually offered. "We could walk, I guess."

"Bowling? I just sat there for ten minutes and practically divulged my entire family history, and the best thing you can come up with is bowling?" Emery shifted her stance and used her sneakers to make shapes in the dirt. "'K," she sighed. "It's a date. I'll expect to see you at my door at 7:29 sharp tomorrow night."

"7:29?" he asked.

"Yup. Seven thirty is too...normal. Unfun. 7:29 assures me that you actually want to do this. It's inexact, imprecise, and perfect for our little experiment."

"Experiment?"

"First contact's over; it's time for phase two. How does alien boy respond to strange settings? Or perhaps familiar ones? What deep, dark secrets can we uncover? Either way, the results should be interesting. Just promise me a good time, and I promise you won't be forced to endure my *beloved* parents."

Arson stood up, and the porch creaked. He watched her shadow escape as the sunset lit up the sky.

"Pretty," he whispered.

FOURTEEN

A blurry stare fixed Arson's eyes on the gaudy cross hanging from the splintering red door. His palms stuck to the grime on his wrists, some ice cream toppings he'd neglected to clean off. The more he stared at the cross, though, the more the image of a weak and dead Savior stung. It didn't make sense how so much power could be contained and then beaten, left for dead. Where was justice in that? How could God let his own son die? He knew there were those who believed, but it just wasn't that simple. Not for him. He couldn't stare for much longer, eyes now heavy with the weight of the world. They fell to his watch. It was 7:28.

Arson felt a deep throbbing in his chest. He didn't like it. After all, she was just a girl. Just a girl with a mask. He had nothing to prove. "This isn't a date," he repeated over and over.

He couldn't even remember how busy it had been at Tobey's earlier. Didn't really care. But Murder Breath's big, vulgar smile stuck out to him. "Try to stay awake,

Arson," the slob had said. "You look like a zombie, and it's scaring away paying customers."

But the day at Tobey's wasn't total misery. A young boy about seven or eight came in with an action figure practically glued to his hand. The kid wouldn't let it go, not even to enjoy a sundae. The action figure had a creepy face. In some sick way, it reminded him of Emery.

The ticking hand made its way to the sixth dial on the watch, and Arson's hands folded into fists. His knuckles cracked, palms squished together. Was he dressed okay? Suddenly he cared about how he looked. What was the matter with him? This wasn't even a date, was it? But he couldn't help examining what he was wearing: khakis, some two-year-old brand X sneakers, and a hooded sweatshirt.

In the 007 movies he'd watched and studied over the years, he'd always noticed how exact and perfect the couples looked. Bond was handsomely outfitted to reflect his boldness and bravado, an air of mystique. Man, a guy like that could make the straightest men on earth look twice. Bond's mistress always shined as well—precious stones no middle-class American could even spell hung across intricate yet often deadly neck bones, eyes that reflected sunlight, and a figure aching for romance. In every sense of the word, flawless.

But in all fairness, there was no comparison between Arson and them. Bond's idea of fun rarely included rundown bowling alleys.

Each passing second welcomed unease. The watch was a ticking time bomb. The second hand approached nine, then flickered its way to ten. Almost time to gather his strengths, knock, and brace himself. He must have blinked at least a dozen times in the ten seconds that followed, tapping his foot to a beat from a song he'd heard on the radio at work.

Five seconds left.

Four.

Three.

Two.

He took a deep breath and—

"Well, fine! Ground me! I don't have a life anyway! Haven't had one for years, thanks to you!" Emery slammed the door behind her.

Arson breathed deeply again. *Heck of a welcome,* he thought.

"Hi," she said with a long-winded sigh. "My mother and I were having a little discussion about something." She ran her fingers through her hair, tense. "But you were on time. Twenty points."

"Yeah, well, by the looks of things with your mom, maybe this can wait. It seemed very *hostile* in there."

"You should see her when the second row of teeth comes out. Vicious. Besides, if it's so hostile in there, why in the world would you want to send me back? You can't see it, but I'm totally rolling my eyes. Minus five points."

Arson shrugged and stared at the dingy floorboards.

Reaching out her hand, Emery lifted up his chin. "Hey, just because you can't see me doesn't mean I can't see you. It *is* okay to look at me from time to time."

What was this girl's deal? The first time they met, she had practically wanted him crucified for looking at her, and now he appeared insensitive for looking away?

"But if you're freaked out—"

"No, it's not that," he replied immediately.

"Good, then let's get out of here before Frankenstein's bride summons me back to the chambers. We've got some bowling to do. Might as well start raising the white flag, because you don't stand a chance."

Arson shrugged. This girl seemed capable of changing moods at will, like she could shut out her pain so long as it meant having a good time.

"C'mon," she said. "I'll race you there."

An hour and a half at a bowling alley might have been the result of an enjoyable, free-spirited evening on any other night, but tonight the time spent—wasted—was enough to shatter egos. Arson was sick with embarrassment. He couldn't bowl to save his life. Countless gutter balls and misses made the spares and one strike seem like things better left unmentioned. The game was not without its certain elements of fun, but it was time to face the music; he didn't have any kind of skill.

"I don't bowl often."

"Well, that's no excuse for letting a girl beat you in a child's game," Emery said, releasing the ball from a tight grip. She watched with anxious tenacity as it rolled all the way down the middle of the aisle, sending pins flying backward. Another strike.

The sound of ricocheting pins made Arson cringe in his seat. Hoping she wouldn't notice, he secretly entered points in his score rather than hers.

"Don't even think about it," she quipped with a rigid finger.

"Do you have eyes in the back of that mask or something?"

"Or something."

Emery danced back to her seat while Arson moseyed to his spot on the floor. Discomfort crept inside his shoes. He found a ball, feigned a smile with sunken shoulders, and fell in line with his target: a white upside-down triangle consisting of ten ridiculing items braced to shatter his ambition before he even let go. Slinging one hand back, Arson's wrist made a quick snap, sending the ball down the aisle and shattering most of the pins. Victory! Almost. Arson eyeballed the two pins at opposite ends as large mechanical arms began cleaning up the scattered remains.

"Impressive," Emery chimed. "Didn't know you had it in you."

Arson was silent for a moment, unable to absorb the compliment or the sarcasm it was laced with. Instead he glanced around the big, smoky room, noticing how the crowd eyed Emery. He pretended he could hear what they were thinking. Cruel jokes hidden behind awe and bewilderment. It was like their eyes revealed what was in their hearts, their minds. Some sort of disgust or self-righteous contempt. Whispers here and there, puzzled glances from worried parents and punk teenagers. They had no compassion, no discretion; they just stared, like she was a freak. They were the same looks that often found him in the lonely hallways at school. Arson hated them. What, did they expect her to put on a show? Throw on a hat and juggle some fruit? It made him sick.

"We can leave," he said, leaning over, waiting for Emery's reaction. "You know, if you're uncomfortable here."

Emery leaned in and said, "Quit while I'm ahead? Are you crazy?"

Arson waited for her to be still.

"It's cool. The world is always gonna have an opinion about this thing." She pointed to her mask. "It's easy for them to judge."

He nodded. She appeared so strong, almost impervious to each spying eye that found them. At least tonight. Smiling, he decided to get his head back in the game and try to forget about the unkind audience.

When the shoot to his left spit up his bowling ball, Arson slid his fingers into place, took a deep breath, and thrust it down the lane. He studied its revolution with excitement as the ball collided into the right-side pin and then suddenly flipped to the other end. Another spare. Not the best, but he'd take it.

"Could this be a chance at redemption?" Emery laughed, taken aback by what she referred to as obvious luck.

"Brag all you want, but I still have a shot at winning this thing."

"Maybe on your planet, alien boy."

"How do you do that? One minute you're building me up with a compliment, the next you're tearing me down?"

The mask replied, "It's a gift. I didn't know you were so sensitive."

"I'm not."

"Well, don't waste precious time trying to make sense of the female psyche, Arson. That's a game you will *always* lose."

While Emery waited for a new set of pins, Arson went up to the counter at the front of the building to order nachos. There he noticed a big guy with tattoos on both his arms, skin darker than coal. Flashy necklaces dangled from his thick neck and got confused in the threads of unwashed chest hair. "Four beers," Arson heard him say. "And three shots." The bartender replied, "All for you, pal?"

The burly guy just grunted back.

To his dismay, Arson felt like lead had just been dropped inside of him. The big guy bit the chapped flesh of his bottom lip, sizing Arson up with eyes that said, *Don't you dare look at me with that tone of voice.*

Using the last of his cash, he placed the money on the stained countertop, grabbed his order, and brought the nachos back to the table where Emery was erasing like crazy.

"What are you doing? I worked hard at that to get the math right."

"Oh, really? Would that include stealing my points?" She began penciling in the correct score to the best of her recollection.

He sighed. "Guilty." A sad look moved across his face, his lips droopy as they inhaled their first nacho. Instant hopelessness washed over him. While Emery worked diligently to fix the scores, Arson peeked down, trying to get a glimpse of her face. He found himself imagining her as one of the characters he'd read about in the comics. In seconds, her head turned and found him eyeing her.

"Can I help you with something?" she said playfully.

"Nope," he said, defeated.

"Arson, I have to admit that was pretty clever. But very low. What kind of girl would I be if I let you win by cheating?"

He frowned. "What if I said I'd share the spoils with you?" He held out the nachos for a brief moment and then drew them back.

"An ultimatum. Now that's a hit below the belt."

He shrugged.

The sound of his crunching over the next three minutes must have felt like needles in her ear. He knew she wanted them and that it was only a matter of time before she gave in. But instead she folded her arms and faced the other away.

After realizing that in a few minutes they'd have to give the aisle to somebody else, Arson held up a tissue as a sign of surrender. Rolling his eyes, he handed Emery the bowl of nachos. She took them, turned away, and lifted up her mask, but slightly so that he couldn't get a clear view of her face. After swallowing one nacho, she dropped her mask back down and handed him the bowl.

"All that for one nacho?" he said, squinting.

"Like I said, the female psyche is something boys can't understand." She got up and thrust another bowling ball down the lane.

For the first time, she didn't hit a single pin. The ball teetered to the right and sank inside the outer slot. A gutter.

"Sorry, aliens only," Arson chuckled, relishing the moment.

Emery threw a second and only got one pin. She sat down with a sigh and lifted her mask to feed herself another loaded chip. As she listened to the music buzzing through the speakers of the small bowling alley, crackling and staticky, the sound of some pop star she didn't care to remember echoed out. "Man, when's the last time they changed the jukebox around here?"

"Forgive me, Your Highness, this isn't palace bowling. Now, if you don't mind, I need some concentration."

"While you attempt to beat me, even though we both know it's impossible, I'm going to select something with a little more ... anything."

Arson threw the ball down the aisle and didn't really care what pins he knocked down. He was more concerned with following her back to the jukebox with his eyes. Her polka-dotted shirt swished back and forth above skinny jeans. He studied those Converse sneakers covered with scribbled words and that mask that ignited dormant feelings once reserved only for Mandy.

He didn't care about winning the game anymore. Besides, winning was never actually a possibility. Why had he picked bowling anyway? Tons of bum teenagers and old drunks frequented this dump, like the slob at the counter, who was currently checking out his date, laughing with a beet-red face at what Arson could only imagine was her mask. He didn't like it.

Arson wanted to be next to Emery. His hands felt hot as he studied the drunken man's facial structure, wondering how it would look with burns.

Grandma would tell him not to think that way, never to think that way, but he couldn't help it. It was the way he was made. "They'll come for you, love." That's what she'd say. "Don't let that evil outta you, 'cause they'll come, and I'll leave." Those few words might have been the only thing saving that low-life's miserable face.

Arson ran to meet Emery at the jukebox. With a hand on her shoulder, he said, "Hey. I think you might have some competition for first place." It was a complete lie, but it sounded legit.

She selected a song. Some Michael Bolton tune statically echoed through the old speakers. Arson's face shifted from worry to immediate disdain. He groaned and tried to select a song that better suited the evening.

"No, leave it."

"This is terrible. How did it even make it to a jukebox?"

"For this moment. To be different. Every first date in the movies has some lame pop song echoing out a speaker, right? You know it sucks, but you're humming it for days. It helps you remember the way everything was. The way it all felt. So, to enhance the experience, I selected quite possibly the worst song in the jukebox just for us, for our little experiment."

Arson's face changed a bit. "And how is subject 3241 doing?"

"Well, we've discovered bowling apparently doesn't exist on his planet, even if luck permits him a strike or two; his ambitions outweigh his logic and, at times, even his sensitivity. But he knows bad music when he hears it, so he gets twenty-five points for that." She pulled him close and smelled his breath. "He loves nachos, another twenty-seven points. That gives him a grand total of sixty-seven points or something. I'd say subject 3241 was a mild success."

Arson frowned. "Sixty-seven? That's practically failing in some states. Look, you just cleaned the floor with my pride."

"Yeah, I know; you didn't even *let* me win or anything. Pretty pathetic."

"You play dirty," Arson replied.

"I wish you were more of a *challenge*. Why can't you be more like"—her eyes got wide—"Michael Bolton. Ha ha. Just kidding."

Arson's head jerked from side to side. She was playing him.

"I'm not really serious. Michael Bolton's a tool," she said. "But he writes a mean love song, doesn't he?"

There it was again, her beautiful sarcasm. He could stay in this moment forever if he had to. A sudden sense of happiness sparked inside, his heart racing for a reason he didn't quite understand. And it didn't matter. Emery was staring at him, but he was too stunned to look back. He turned to the bar, where the drunken slob had either fallen asleep or passed out. Nothing to worry about anymore. Flying to Emery's rescue a minute ago had kind of felt good.

But it all faded suddenly as the sound of exploding fireworks miles away carried Arson back to a cold autumn night. He was standing in the middle of the road, his hand hot with fear. The scared little boy who ruined beauty. Every sound seemed louder. He began picturing each device exploding one by one, shattering sight and sound. In his mind, he imagined the voices dying and every smile turning to disfigured horror, while he fought to shut out the booms and echoes of the holiday celebration. *Turn it off,* he prayed. *Enough!* It was then that he heard it again. A scream, shrill and violent, traveled through time and found him again. He swore it was real.

"Can you hear that? It's so loud." Panic crawled up his body.

"Yeah, barely," Emery said. "The fireworks are going off a mile away. What are you, part canine?"

His eyes wandered. *Killer!* It thundered within him, almost numbing. He was lost, brought to a place in his mind he didn't want to go. Not now.

"Arson, are you okay?"

A glaze covered his eyes.

"Snap out of it." Emery nudged his shoulder.

The firecracker pops transformed again and again into the screams of a little girl.

"Hey, come back to earth."

Back to reality.

"What happened?" he asked her in between gasps.

"You started freaking out when you heard the fireworks."

Arson looked around to make sure nothing was burning.

"Are you all right?" Emery asked.

Arson checked his hands. A chill fell over them. "What? Yeah, I guess."

"C'mon. Let's go outside. Maybe we'll still be able to catch some of the fireworks."

"No, that's okay. Never been much for firecrackers."

"These are the big boys, dummy. Fire*works,* not the lame firecrackers you can pick up at Wal-Mart. C'mon, what are you so afraid of?"

"I just don't want to go outside, that's all, okay?"

"Fine. Why would we want to have fun? It's not like this is a date or anything."

"It's not, is it?"

"Oh, right." The mask looked down. "Whatever. PacMan will cheer me up. I don't want to see the fire-works anyway."

He heard *firecracker.*

"Let me know when you're ready to take me home and brave the darkness." Emery walked toward the arcade games. "Happy Fourth of July," she mumbled.

Arson retreated to the bathroom to run cold water down his face. Regret flooded in. He didn't mean what he'd said. He liked her, a lot, but admitting something of that magnitude in his current state was too much to bear. A moment of contemplation made him question if he'd ever have the guts to tell her. Perhaps silence would prove the lesser of two evils.

But if he never unveiled his feelings, then she wouldn't be able to reject him or hate him for who he was. For what he was. That way he wouldn't have to explain what he could do or the sin of a past that haunted him still. Then Emery couldn't forget him, because it would be like he had never existed at all.

FIFTEEN

Joel closed his eyes and breathed deeply. He thought about his life before the move, before the accident, before he'd made a complete mess of his marriage. The thoughts came in slowly and found a way to drag with them the bitter moments of his twenty-two-year failed endeavor. The times when he'd come home late, too tired to even greet Aimee with a kiss. Like their first anniversary, when he told her he didn't have time to be the husband she needed him to be. She'd get so angry if he didn't eat dinner with them or if he was out taking care of the elderly in his congregation or counseling some couple too horny to push back the wedding date but hard-pressed to remain virgins until they exchanged vows. He'd bless the marriages but deep down always thought they'd fail.

The things that scared him the most were nights of wondering. Questioning. The way Aimee really felt. How Emery might react to everything around them. Those members of the congregation who'd never accept her. Did they have any idea what it was like to raise a monster?

No, she wasn't a monster.

He begged forgiveness for even thinking it. He loved his daughter, his wife, but for some reason feared getting too close. Wanted to, but never crossed the river to reach them. Instead Joel filled his schedules with writing long-winded sermons, playing paintball with the youth group, and planning mission trips while he watched his family shatter to pieces—pieces he couldn't pick up or even find.

What a failure I am, Joel thought, clenching his teeth. *I miss my wife. I miss my Emery.*

Joel stared down at the ring in his hand, the new ring he'd sized for his wife. He'd searched for hours and hours to find it. It had been in the back of his mind for so long. It was like one he'd told her on their wedding day he couldn't afford to buy her. It had always been Joel's intention to someday recommit himself to their marriage, renew their vows, and perhaps he'd finally have the chance. Maybe his wife could learn to love him again. Maybe this ring was hope. Maybe it was redemption staring back at him. He didn't care which as long as it fixed everything. He didn't care for how long.

"It's perfect," he whispered to himself, almost crying.

Joel tucked it away in his jacket pocket. The time would come when he'd give it to her. Not yet, but soon.

He rubbed the back of his head, wondering if bashing his skull into the dashboard could erase the man he'd been for the past few years. But he knew that wouldn't placate a burdened conscience. There was only one thing that could. He could taste the flavor in his mouth, longed for it, even now.

He swallowed hard and eyed the clock glowing on the dash. It was getting late, but he still had time before Aimee grew suspicious.

Emery walked ahead most of the way back to their street. The evening had gone better than anticipated, the first part, anyway. Then the fireworks came and ruined everything. It had been a long time since she had felt safe, so able to lower her guard, if only for one night. This stupid boy had something about him she couldn't quite put her finger on, but whatever it was brought her warmth. This stupid, inconsiderate, and pathetically cute boy called Arson.

Their driveways rested right around the next street corner. Emery wanted to speak. Enough was enough.

"I forgive you," she mouthed, her voice coming out muffled.

"For what?" Arson snapped. "I didn't do anything."

Did he just say that? Clearly this whole forgiveness thing was flawed. Because if he couldn't see himself being a complete blank, then maybe it *was* all hopeless.

"What is it?" she asked, frustrated.

Arson kept walking, saying everything with his eyes and nothing with his lips.

"What is it about me that you don't like?"

"Other than that hideous mask or those nerdy-looking shoes—"

"These are classics, but I wouldn't expect you to know anything about fashion."

"Ouch, that one stung," he said with a smug grin.

"Good," she said. "How does it feel?" Immediately, regret sank in and forced her to apologize.

"I guess I made a bad second impression," Arson mumbled. "I'm sure you'll go home and write about me in your little diary."

"Why are you being such a jerk?"

Arson walked faster.

"Wait, I didn't mean that." She jogged toward him; her house stood only yards away now. "Well, you are being somewhat of a jerk, but would you just wait up and talk to me?"

"You're not making any sense."

"I know. Sometimes when I meet new people … it gets complicated." She couldn't believe what was coming out of her mouth. What did she have to be sorry for other than honest feelings? *He* was the one being unreasonable. Where was his apology? Nevertheless, whatever this was, it had gone too far. She wasn't ready to forfeit the subtle connection existing between them. "I had fun tonight, and it looked like you did too—even though I was totally kicking your butt—and that awful Michael Bolton song was playing, and you had your arm around me, and … I thought for a split second—"

"What?" he said, rolling his eyes.

"You might like me, I guess."

"It's a little early to start throwing around your feelings like that. We just met. I barely know you, and you—you don't want to know me." He looked at her as her shoulders sank. "Besides, what can one date really show you about somebody?"

As they neared her porch, Emery fixed her looming posture and turned to him. "So it *was* a date."

"Wait a second."

"Nope. You said it. It's out there. Can't take it back."

"Goodnight," Arson said, walking away before the moment demanded an explanation.

"That's it? Goodnight? Missing fireworks on the Fourth of July wasn't enough? Now you're bailing on me?"

"What were you expecting? I don't know the first thing about how to treat a girl, much less a girl like you." He paused to rethink. "Look, that's not what I meant. It was just one date, and a crummy one at that."

"Keep digging."

"Tell me you don't want to see me again," he spit out, shrinking back. "That's what we both want, right? Then we can pretend like this disaster never happened."

"Why would I want to do that?"

"I thought you said I was a jerk."

Her voice lifted suddenly. "You are. But what if I let you make it up to me? Volunteer with me tomorrow."

Arson shuffled his feet. "Yeah, as fun as that sounds, I have work."

"All day? I told my mom anything before three just wouldn't be possible. C'mon, Arson. Promise I won't be a nagging girlfriend ... friend ... I mean, neighbor," she tried.

"Fine," he reluctantly agreed. "But this is a one-time thing."

"Deal," she replied.

"Goodnight."

"Bye." Emery entered her house, pressing her spine up against the door as it shut. *Third time's a charm.*

SIXTEEN

"I'm not covering for you!" Chelsea spat once she and Arson were without an audience. Arson had asked her to cover for him upon arriving at Tobey's earlier in the morning, and Chelsea had agreed to have a sensible conversation about the matter when she had a sec, but according to her, talking and maliciously hollering at each other were one and the same. And both resulted in spiteful, resounding nos.

"Why not?" Arson asked with hung shoulders. "I cover for you all the time. And that goes for you too, Jason." He flared his nostrils, eyeing them both. "Look, you guys hate me; I get it, but it's kind of an emergency. I need coverage. Besides, Ray's waiting for any excuse to fire me."

Chelsea placed one arm inside the other and glared at him with beady eyes.

"Arson, this isn't some lame high school elective. You can't blow it off and hope for a passing grade. This is the real world. Don't expect everyone to always cover your back." Leave it to Jason, a kid who barely passed phys-ed, to try to mix morality and real-life ethics in order to defend a crappy minimum-wage job.

"Thanks for nothing." Arson grabbed a broom and started sweeping; Jason went to the bathroom, as was his routine when there was work to be done.

After Chelsea removed the chocolate sprinkles from her fingertips, she said, "Why do you need coverage so badly? What, do you have plans with your grandma? Is the old bat finally ready to come out of her cave and face the real world?" A vindictive laugh followed.

Arson ignored her.

"No, seriously, Arson, what could you have to do that is so important on a Saturday afternoon? It's not like you have friends or anything."

He chucked the broom against the wall and walked outside. Studying the busy street, his eyes hopped from plaza to plaza, careless passersby to speeding cars, one with a bumper sticker that read, *Proud parent of an honor student.* Arson tried to imagine what it would be like to have Grandma driving around with that statement, true or not, stuck to the bumper. But he didn't dare dwell on what it would've been like to have proud parents, ones who drove Volvos or spoke highly of their freak child.

Suddenly, a pewter-stained pickup raced by, wildly swerving in and out of traffic. The maniac pulled into a Citgo station, a recently remodeled building that sat beside Governor's Tavern, one of East Hampton's most lucrative Main Street restaurants. After shoving a pack of smokes into his pocket, the guy in the dilapidated pickup sped off, and Arson noticed a number of tacky bumper stickers obnoxiously bombarding his rear windshield. He managed to only focus in on one of them. It read, *How's my driving? Call (1–800) Eat-Crap.*

"Figures," Arson said under his breath.

Maybe Grandma was right to keep to herself, smart not to venture out this far. Maybe her fear of escaping the cabin was justified because of the way the world was, its lack of empathy, even compassion. How it revolved around the coldest natures. Oblivious sidewalks littered with souls who walked up and down it without a care in the world. Restaurants catering to fleeting cravings and insatiable hunger. Drug stores sedating the lost and the numb. Arson was starting to see more clearly the colors of cruelty and malice, ways of getting ahead and stealing time. The human painting was filled with splashes of menace and impatience and blind ambition. Drivers too calloused to consider those around them. Co-workers managed by spite and unkindness.

A cold world. The real world.

The afternoon drifted past. Arson's

gaze shifted to the dusty clock on the wall. He watched its skinny fingers tick and tock. *Funny*, he thought. It was a merciless machine, doing what it was designed to do, and it could silence his cravings, his wants, with a mere flicker of time. There wasn't much to be grateful for during the hours stuck behind a sloppy countertop with an ice cream scooper in hand. But beyond the occasional smiling customer and the stupid tasks of the parlor, the afternoon granted him one unexpected thing worthy of stealing his eyes away from trivial musings, if only for a few moments.

"Arson, I didn't know you were working today. How've you been?" The inflated buoyancy of Mandy's voice weakened him, but he took pleasure in it. No matter how often he heard her speak, her voice somehow always possessed a sliver of seduction.

"Oh, I've been busy."

"Working?" she asked, swinging back her hair, allowing the sunlight to reflect each golden strand.

He nodded, still captivated and still nervous.

"That's cool, I guess. You're braver than I am. Wouldn't be caught dead working in a place like this. So, what flavors do you have today?"

Just then an impatient man behind her—a bald, odd-looking Wal-Mart employee type—tapped her on the shoulder.

"Excuse me," he barked. "I was in line first." He sought to chew her up as if he were a pit bull or something.

She pretended not to notice him, seemingly able to find gratification in watching Arson melt.

"Hey," the pit bull barked again, "I'm a paying customer, and I've got someplace to be. This isn't a beauty pageant. So step aside."

"Sir, I'll be with you in a minute," Arson replied forcefully. "Mandy, what would you like?"

"Oh, I don't know." She blushed. "There are so many to choose from."

Arson shrugged, noticing Chelsea and Jason spying on him from the break room, refusing to offer any help. He could hear snickering but was too captivated to care.

"I always do this," Mandy said. "I guess I'm indecisive." Her illustrious white smile shimmered behind wet lips. Every time she licked them, his neck hairs stood up.

The pit bull was starting to show teeth. "Would the beauty queen mind hurrying up? I don't have time for this. I came in here for an ice cream sundae, not to hear *her* talk about how indecisive she is. If you're looking for an emotional audience, miss, call Oprah."

Mandy's bright eyes drew Arson in like morning sunlight. He didn't hear a word.

"I'll take a soft serve chocolate ice cream cone, please, with extra chocolate shots. Thanks so much, cutie."

Arson didn't know what to say, so he simply got to making the cone.

"Do you have any plans for tonight?" she asked after a moment's hesitation, while he shuffled around behind the counter.

Arson remained tight-lipped. His smile faded as he ignored the unease crawling up his spine. He knew he should tell her. Wanted to. But he couldn't get the words out.

"No, I, uh, I don't have any plans. You?"

"Really?" she said, licking her ice cream, letting some slip onto her chin.

This was his chance to recant that stupid lie and suddenly remember that thing he had to do with that girl he'd just met.

"I'm free tonight," he said rapidly enough for it to sound rehearsed. "Pathetic, huh? I mean, what kind of kid doesn't have plans on a—"

"So, Kim, you remember Kim, right? That flighty little brat blew me off to go hang out with her new boy toy, and all of my other friends made plans, so forget them. But I'm curious... Did you want to come over?"

Arson froze. This couldn't be happening. No, it wasn't happening. *Wake up, Arson, you're dreaming.* "Um... how does this work?"

"Well, the process usually involves me writing my number on your hand," she answered with a chuckle.

"Uh huh." Arson nodded, hands in his pockets, confused by what had recently come out of her beautiful mouth.

Mandy rolled her eyes. "Or I could use a napkin."

That smile, those eyes, her perfect body.

Mandy began writing her number down. Awe and disconcertment rushed him all at once, followed by exhilaration and a nervous stomach full of rats.

"Here you go. That's my cell. You can call me or just stop by at five."

She was flawless. He watched her playfully bite her lip. He didn't even care that he wasn't supposed to clock out until five. But it wasn't every day that Venus walked into an ice cream parlor looking for a scrawny, ash-haired firestarter to have dinner with.

"O-okay," he managed.

"'K. Ciao."

"Okay." Arson knew he sounded like a stuttering idiot.

A stuttering idiot with a phone number.

SEVENTEEN

Years had come and gone since Grandma Kay had been on an actual date. Decades. She didn't really understand anything Arson conveyed during the hectic moments when he'd rushed through the screen door, dripping with sweat from the bike ride home.

He quickly found the best thing he owned, sprayed his body with cheap cologne, and brushed his teeth. Ready just in time to be a half hour late.

Grandma was on the recliner with the remote lodged between her fingers when Arson was ready to leave. "Where do you think you're going?" she said.

"Out. It's a Saturday. I already told you. I have a da ... dinner, with a friend."

"So what's the day of the week got to do with anything? And since when do you have friends? What's with all the mingling? Last night you left me here alone and took off with that strange girl from next door. The freak with the mask."

"Please don't call Emery that," Arson said.

"All I'm saying is that you seem awfully busy lately. Don't even have time for your old grandma." She stared up from the recliner, her arctic eyes outlined by plastic, ancient frames.

"It's nothing, Grandma. Maybe a movie or something. That's all. I'll be home before you know it."

"When did you become Mr. Celebrity? I can't remember the last time you went out on a Saturday night. Especially this late. God only knows what kind of riffraff is out this time of night."

"Grandma, it's five thirty in the afternoon. And it's not like this town has hook men running around. I'll be fine."

Arson stood in front of the mirror, the one affixed to the wall. It hung beside the doorway beneath the cabin's only staircase. He checked his shirt, wondering if it was the right one. Then he breathed into his sweaty palm, assuring himself it smelled minty enough for one of those kisses he'd only seen in movies, the kind that provoke entire body movement—tongues, hands, and deep breaths in between.

Arson reworked his hair and settled for a brushed-back look, keeping the seditious strands away from his eyes. And the random spots of acne now exposed weren't as bad as he'd imagined. Within his reflection, he could see Emery's mask grimacing at him from all angles. The sound of her voice seemed muffled, and Arson focused his intentions on tuning both the image and its voice out of his head; nothing could ruin this night.

Grandma's raspy voice continued. "You see that, love? Some poor soul was lost today because of a drunk driver. I don't want you driving."

"I don't have a car, Grandma, remember?" Arson replied. "But *you* do. God forbid we ever use it."

"What's that you're mumbling over there? Oh, heavens. I could never forgive myself if you were to leave me. Automobiles will be the death of us. Promise me you'll never leave me."

"I have to leave sometime. I'm gonna be late."

"Promise!"

"I promise. Now, I have to go."

Her lips pursed into a frown as she rotated in her chair, using the remote to turn up the volume. "What's so important about going out tonight anyway?"

"Everything." Arson leaned down to kiss her on the cheek.

"I suppose your grandfather and I can survive this night alone. We've made it this long."

"Sure thing, Grandma," he said, rolling his eyes. "I'll be home later."

Mandy's house stood on the other side of the lake. Arson rode his bike to get there. He didn't mind; the weather was nice, not to mention he would've walked if he had to. He'd seen her driveway once from a distance but never had the courage or the invitation to dare walk the long and winding road up to her doorstep. Its windows looked more like eyes, and its door was one that, when he walked through it, made him feel like he was getting eaten. Most girls dreamed of being treated like a princess, having everything they wanted and more, but for Mandy it wasn't a dream; it was reality.

When Arson entered her bedroom, he noticed that dolls of every variety covered much of the floor space. "I know it's childish," she said, "but I think they're still pretty cool." Posters of Orlando Bloom and Brad Pitt covered the pink and white walls. A king-size bed with floral arrangements sat in the corner of the room atop a pastel rug and next to that, a six-foot-tall vanity and a closet the size of his entire bedroom.

"I guess that's the problem with being an only child. I always get what I want."

"That was never *my* problem." He shrugged.

"I mean, *they* love me. Like, because I'm Daddy's little girl and everything, I think he feels obligated to shower me with all the stuff he never had."

Arson shoved his hands into his pockets. A nervous sweat trickled down his brow. He looked at Mandy.

"I never got to properly thank you for all those free ice creams you gave me, Arson Gable."

"Oh, don't worry about it. I make enough."

"No, you don't." She shut her bedroom door and leaned in close.

He was paralyzed once he inhaled her sweet, inviting breath. His heart drummed. "I've never been in a girl's room before."

Mandy smiled and kissed him. "I'll bet you've never done this before either."

He couldn't help but stare at her, noticing her eyes were closed and focused while his wandered to everything in the room. After seconds, he closed his eyes and started thinking with his lips. Was he doing it right? His mind wouldn't let him believe this was happening. It couldn't be. Was she trying to make out with him? Did she even really *like* him?

But then it came with a whisper. "Freak," she said.

"What? Why did you call me that?"

"You're acting crazy," Mandy denied immediately. "I didn't say anything."

"You called me a freak."

"Arson, don't be stupid. I thought this was what you wanted. Your mind must be playing tricks on you. Now quit it, all right? I could easily think of about six other boys who would give up a spot on the team to be where you are right now, so let it go!"

She leaned into him once more, and he didn't resist. Couldn't. With one hand she massaged the back of his neck. It felt soft, delicate.

"What about your parents?" Arson panted. "Won't they come up eventually?"

"Eventually."

"Mandy, what is this? Why all of a sudden? You never liked me before." He breathed short, nervous breaths, hands still shaking. "I don't get it."

"What's there to get? I'm a girl who has everything she wants. Except you. You're dangerous, unpredictable. Kinda cute."

"What's so dangerous about me?" Arson felt another rush of anxiety and unease bleed down his spine.

"I know what you do, Arson. Rumors spread quickly around school. But you don't have to deny them. I know you're not like everybody else. Besides, I've had the ordinary, boring guys. I want something more, something dangerous. Don't you want me?"

His throat quivered.

Mandy kissed him again on the lips. "Just relax. I know what I'm doing."

"Mandy, your parents are downstairs."

"I know," she said, nudging up against him. "Forget about them. They won't mind."

Arson's chest felt like it was going to shatter into a million pieces. It ached with each heartbeat. Sweat dripped into his eyes and down his face. Heat started at his fingertips and spread to his body slowly.

"You're warm." Mandy smiled.

What was this? He'd dreamt of kissing Mandy for so long, wondered what she would smell like up close, what her hands might feel like wrapped around his neck in an embrace. But he couldn't touch her. All he could do was lie still.

Images of Grandma beating him with a rolled-up newspaper and spitting in a fit of anger ruined the moment. In a flash, Emery appeared, as if out of thin air. She stood right in front of him, looking at the scene through a creepy mask. Arson could sense she was hurt. He tried to close his eyes and make the imaginations disappear, but they wouldn't. Instead the fear dragged him away.

"Mandy, I—"

"I want this, Arson. I always wanted my own firestarter."

"Look, I don't know what you're thinking, but I'm a normal kid, okay? I work in a lame ice cream shop. I live with my grandmother, and I have no friends. That's the extent of my existence."

"Hmmm, normal? Right."

"I'm not what you think I am. I don't start fires. I hate fire."

"Liar."

"I'm just an average teenage boy. Nothing more."

"Whatever you say, freak," Mandy said, leaning into his lips.

Arson was numb to the word, its meaning slipping from consciousness. Everything about this moment seemed forced, an unwilled vindication for abandoning Emery to volunteering alone, he imagined.

The strange sensation lingered in his mind. He was motionless. Weak.

"Still want to watch that movie?" Mandy whispered.

Arson didn't reply.

"Me neither."

He lay there for a while, his shirt messy, his soul somewhere else, where he couldn't be judged or ridiculed by guilt. *She's not Emery,* he kept thinking. *She's not Emery.*

"What is it?" she asked.

"Nothing." The truth was unutterable. In all the futures he had created to perfection inside his head, this seemed so unfamiliar. Now wasn't the time to think about her or even about love.

Arson abandoned his turbulent thoughts and left them on autopilot, not caring if they crash-landed or wound up somewhere in oblivion. He swallowed hard, succumbing to the fevers of a lonely heart, unquenchable and always longing. All Arson knew, all that seemed to matter this very moment, was that he was finally getting what he thought he'd always wanted.

EIGHTEEN

Aimee Phoenix felt stretched in ways she had never thought possible. Worn out. Lost. One week down, a lifetime to go.

Her husband had perfected the art of procrastination. Part of her wondered if he'd ever find work. He came up with every excuse in the book, reasons why he couldn't find a job, or at least not something dignified. She supposed the noble wife in her should've been more supportive and encouraging, but he really didn't have a clue how much he shamed her, their family. How hard it was to carry on, knowing that a past life was gone and may never return. There was no handbook on how to react when things spiraled out of control, only on how to cope once they did. And she wasn't ready to cope just yet, not while the failure on her living room sofa lamented his mistakes, waiting for his next epiphany.

Things weren't okay. Couldn't he feel that? She didn't know when exactly she had begun viewing her husband as a stranger, but it had happened quickly. A few hard months had shaken her to the breaking point. Ever since she was six years old, Aimee had wanted to be married, to be loved. She knew that being a good wife, a good mother, required her to deal with pain and work on keeping the family inside the boat, even if the boat was sinking. But maybe she was the one who was drowning, and there was no boat, no one at all in a sea of questions. She just wanted to breathe again. Needed to.

Aimee stood uneasily behind Dr. Pena's door, reluctant to knock. She thought she'd be prepared enough to face him after five minutes of heavy breathing. But once she relived in her mind their parting words years ago, she was certain not even an eternity would be enough time. She reached for the handle and stepped inside the office.

"You asked to see me, Dr. Pena?"

"Hello. Please have a seat, Aimee." Dr. Pena signed a document and then removed his reading glasses. "Or should I call you Mrs. Phoenix?"

"No, Dr. Pena, please don't be silly. Aimee's fine."

"Okay. Long week?"

"Long life. Normally that's a good thing, but not for me. I mean, never mind."

"No, please go on."

He was precisely as she remembered. The way he opened people up like diaries, sometimes coercively, other times gently. They used to joke that he'd one day become a shrink—a career path she'd later discover he thought was his passion until a cute medical doctor had convinced him to reconsider. When looking at him in the light, she could tell he still had the same boyish profile, soft and discreet, offering enough to make a girl feel secure. His hair was dark still, sprinkled with snow around his ears and forehead. Seeing him again transported her to their prom night. How handsome he looked. But before she had time to dwell on it, she found herself staring at his left hand. No wedding band.

"As you probably have heard, my family and I have recently relocated," Aimee said. "We bought a shack in East Hampton. Ha, you know, when my husband told me, I pictured gold staircases and fancy cars. The little girl in me still likes to dream, I guess. "

"I'd hardly call it a shack, Aimee. I've seen the house, and it's not half bad. Needs a little sprucing up, though. I'm sure you can manage that. But these are all peripherals. I know you recently moved and that it must feel strange coming back after so many years. Perhaps that's why you are working at this hospital, for some familiarity, right?"

"Maybe. I mean, I like my job."

"Of course you do. We all do. We're crazy, I suppose. It's a calling. We do it because we have to. We feel that somehow we're doing our part in this sick and dying world." He leaned in with a grin. "And the pay isn't bad either."

She laughed but avoided his glances.

"You don't have to lie to me, Aimee. If anyone knows you, I do."

"I know. I can't thank you enough for letting me work here. I know the staff must be on your case about it. Norma says applications usually take weeks, sometimes longer to get processed. You made it all happen in a matter of hours. You really are a miracle worker."

"Don't mind the secretaries. They think they know when God sneezes, but there's a lot that goes on behind this office door that goes unnoticed. Besides, it was nothing." He stretched back in his chair and placed both hands behind his head. He seemed at ease with her. "Seriously, you're starting to bore me here. It's been such a long time. Too long, in fact. I'm dying to know what's really bothering you. What deep, dark secrets are you hiding behind those eyes of yours?"

She didn't want to answer. Sure, she had answers and even more questions, but now just didn't seem like the time or place for a confession. Aimee coughed, letting her eyes survey the office. A framed picture of Dr. Pena and a woman sat affixed to one of the walls beside a rather large fish tank and a nightstand with a fresh bouquet of flowers that added a unique and pleasant aroma to the stagnant office air.

"You looked happy then," Aimee said, pointing to the picture. "Pretty autumn day. Lucky girl. Were you?"

"Was I what?" Dr. Pena replied.

"Happy. Is that your wife?"

"Ex-wife," he said.

"Yeah. Couldn't help but notice you weren't wearing a ring. But with doctors and bacteria and operations, you can never be sure who's married and who isn't. Sorry."

"It's quite all right. Many people make that connection when stepping into my office for the first time. The photograph is magnificent, though, isn't it? She was an excellent photographer, a true artist. It'd be a shame to dispose of such a work of art, don't you think?"

"Yeah," Aimee said, trying to avoid eye contact with him.

"Oh, who am I kidding? I suppose part of me is still holding on in spite of it all."

"What happened?"

"She wanted more. More than I could give. My job, it requires so much of me. But don't let this turn into a pity party. After all, it's been eight years; I should be over it by now."

"Does it get any easier? The separation, I mean."

"What kind of a question is that?" he replied. "You're perfectly happy in your marriage, aren't you?"

"That depends on what your definition of perfectly happy is, Doctor. I'm not happy being married to a failed minister. I'm not happy with the way my relationship with my daughter is going. And I'd be lying if I said this job brought me any kind of bliss." What was she doing? Opening up to him was a big mistake. She had sworn she wouldn't.

"You've finally let the cat out of the bag. Now we're getting somewhere. How does it feel to be honest with yourself?"

"I feel like throwing up. What happened to me?"

"You know, I'm not quite sure, but you were looking awfully plain in comparison to the good old days," he said in a joking manner as his eyes panned her from head to toe. His wink let her know it was okay, bringing her once more to their prom night so many years ago.

"You're such a riot. You and my husband would probably get along well."

"Ahh, your husband." His fingers folded into a pyramid. "I've never had the pleasure of meeting him."

Aimee coughed and sighed.

"Everyone has marital struggles. Have you ever tried talking to the man?"

"Believe me, I've tried. But Joel can be so thick sometimes. I feel like there's no way to get through to him."

"Well, it sounds to me like you need to work things out with your family. I know you just started here, but do you want some time off?"

"I can work. I'm not an invalid. I've got a backbone."

"Aimee, I'm here to listen. You can be candid with me. I thought that our history together would've been enough for you to feel safe in this place. Don't think of me as your boss, please; think of me as your friend."

"Thank you, Carlos. But you've already done enough to support the Aimee Phoenix Foundation. Besides, pity sponsorship is not the same as friendship."

He frowned. "Pity? Don't insult me. I don't pity you. If I can be perfectly honest, I envy you. You've lasted over twenty years in a loveless marriage. I couldn't make it past seven months. And you've got a beautiful daughter, although you'd never know it."

"Please, don't even get me started on that hideous mask. Emery thinks I'm the antichrist for suggesting that it's time to let go of the past and move on with her life without it."

"You always were so up front with your feelings. But you shouldn't be so hard on her. Not everyone can move on as fast or as easily as you can." Carlos stood up and walked around the office. She had forgotten how tall he was. "Why didn't you call me when the accident happened? Her procedure should have been done by someone you trusted, not some Boston hack. I know many professionals, far better than even myself. You should've—"

"I couldn't simply call you up out of the blue with an emergency request. How would that make me look?"

"Like a concerned mother."

"We hadn't spoken since college."

"You had my e-mail address and my personal cell. A phone call to an old friend wouldn't have killed you."

"Maybe not. But my husband wouldn't have exactly been thrilled either."

Carlos bit his lip. As he moved past her shoulders, the breeze from his swaying white coat lifted up the hair on the back of her neck. "It doesn't matter. You found your way back."

Aimee stared up at him for a moment. "So, what is this, Carlos? Did you ask me in here to say that it's been a long time? A lot's changed since the old days? I'm not ready for that."

He sat on his desk, folded his hands, and collected his composure. "If you need time to yourself, for your daughter and your husband, I understand, and I will make plans for someone else to cover for you."

"No, you've already done enough."

Carlos fell into her eyes. "I could never do enough."

Aimee clutched her purse and avoided eye contact as best she could. It felt wrong to look into his eyes again.

Suddenly, there was a knock on the door.

"Come in," he said.

"Oh, I don't want to intrude," the voice replied from behind the door. "I'm looking for my mom."

"Oh, your beautiful daughter has come to rescue you from me. You know, Emery, I don't usually bite."

Carlos grinned, facing the door. "Say, how was your first day of volunteering? Was it everything you hoped for?"

"Sure, there's nothing quite as exciting as spending the day watching people mourn how life basically sucks now that they're alone and how they wished they'd done so much more with their time, you know, right before one of them passes out on you," Emery chimed sarcastically. "But it was all right, I suppose. Wasn't complete boredom; I met one really solid guy named Abraham."

"What you're doing is great, Emery. A lot of the people in the hospice unit don't get many visitors," Carlos said.

"That's me, a good Samaritan. So have you seen my mom, or was this an excuse to talk my ear off?"

Aimee rolled her eyes. "Emery, why don't you come on in and talk to the man instead of hiding behind a door?"

"Aiding and abetting the enemy, Dr. Pena? I should've known."

He whispered, "At least she knows my name. It's a *solid* start."

"Anyway, Mom," Emery continued, "my stomach is ready to, like, eat itself. And didn't you promise Dad you'd be home by seven? It's already quarter after."

Carlos squinted with amusement. "She's quite the pistol, isn't she?"

"You have no idea," Aimee said. "I'm coming, sweetheart. See you Monday, Dr. Pena." She rushed out of the room.

"Aimee, please think about my offer. I'm here if you need anything," he said as the door closed behind her. "Anything at all."

NINETEEN

"So it wasn't as bad as you thought, was it?" her mother asked on the ride home.

"Don't put words in my mouth, Mom," Emery said.

"Well, I didn't think you'd be so offended by my saying so."

"I'm not... It's just... I don't know."

"You don't know, or you don't want to tell me?"

Emery touched her mask, feeling the rigid, bent corners. She liked the way its texture slid between her palms and fingers. At least it was smooth. Her mother didn't get it. She probably never could, even if she wanted to.

"I suppose I could pressure you into telling me what I want to hear, but I'm guessing that'll only instigate another argument. And I've had enough of those lately."

"Could've fooled me," Emery spat.

"What's that supposed to mean, young lady?"

"Oh, I don't know. Maybe the fact that yesterday you called me a defiant little witch because I wanted to go out with Arson. Oh, his name is Arson, by the way. Our alien from next door. And let's not forget what a nag you've been around Dad."

Emery watched her mother get heated, blinking rapidly, the way she did any time they started to disagree. "Don't pretend to know what married life is like, young lady, because you don't have a clue. It's difficult. Sometimes people fight. But it's between your father and me. So if that's what your little attitude is about—"

"It's not only that. It's..." Emery's voice trailed off.

"Let's leave your father out of this one. You're upset at me for arguing with you last night. Well, sorry for being a mother."

"Mom, you told me I wasn't allowed to date after I told you that it probably wasn't even a date. At least, *he* didn't think it was." She glared out the foggy window. "You thought that somehow it was your decision to make, and it wasn't. I'm almost eighteen. Get off my back and let me live my life."

"I'm your mother, Emery. My opinion, whether you like it or not, matters. Besides, someone's got to remind you that hideous mask isn't a face."

Emery was good at blocking arrows, word bullets too, but that one stung. "My *real* face isn't a face either."

"You look so awful in that thing, dear."

Emery locked her arms inside each other and stewed in frustration. Did she honestly think adding the word *dear* onto the end of her comment was going to make the situation better?

"There you go again, shutting out the world, shutting out your own mother."

"Remind me the last time you were a mother."

Before the comment finished coming out, Emery's head jerked. Her mother swerved off the main stretch of Route 66 in Portland, the next town over, slamming on the brakes. Emery's forehead bashed against the dashboard, and she swore while frantic speeders off the Arrigoni Bridge raced past.

"You could've warned me you hadn't been taking your meds, Mom. Are you insane?"

"Maybe I am. But you need to start showing me some respect. And watch your language!"

"Fine!"

"How many times have I told you to buckle your seatbelt when you're in *my* car? It's another reason why you're not ready to get your license."

"Dad paid for the car," Emery groaned, trying to recoup from her recent make-out session with the dashboard. She could see her mother's face take a turn for the worse, her eyes lit.

"Now buckle up."

"All right!" Emery screamed back, fastening her seatbelt.

"Let's try to have a conversation, shall we? With some civility." Her mother pulled back onto the main road. "How was the first day of volunteering?"

"My first day was simply peachy. Is that what you want to hear?"

"You're transparent, Emery. I can tell when you're not being honest with me."

"Oh, really, Mother? How perceptive of you. Shall we discuss it over tea? Perhaps a dinner on the veranda?"

"Charming. But I asked for us to be civil. Could we, for two seconds, act like a loving mother and daughter?"

Emery didn't take her eyes off the glaring window, focusing on the world outside instead of her own. Passing cars and flashing traffic lights. "Well, forgive me for ruining your little charade, but I can't pretend like something isn't the matter when it is."

"Your father and I will—"

"The spotlight isn't on you right now, Mom. Remember me, your daughter? I've got problems too." Emery could see her mother's face flush with relief and surprise. But she made the observation appear discreet and nonchalant. "When did life get so complicated?"

"How is *your* life complicated? You hide behind a mask. One of these days you're gonna have to face the world."

"Easy for you to say," Emery said. "It didn't happen to you."

"I have tried to be as supportive as possible."

"Give me a break. You have no idea what this is like. How it feels to be different. To feel like some freak. You and Dad are both too busy for my life. Maybe the two of you can coexist inside your own little bubble, but I'm sick of living with this. I hate the girl I see in the mirror every day. And for the record, I hate you."

A long moment spread between them.

"Emery, you're different, that's all, not a freak."

"Different doesn't even scratch the surface, Aimee."

"You're right. I don't know what it's like. But you won't let me in. I want to be your friend, but I'm a mother first, Emery. I care about you. And I don't want that mask to be a crutch for the rest of your life." As the confession left her lips, Aimee began swerving in and out of lanes, like she couldn't focus on the conversation anymore.

"Way to go, Mom. You missed the turn."

Her mother sat quietly, thinking about something, perhaps wondering what had become of their relationship.

"Where are you going?" Emery asked.

"I'm taking the long way home, okay? Are you in a rush or something?"

"If you're asking me if I want to sit around and talk about how much we disagree about *everything* and how you don't understand anything I'm trying to tell you, then maybe I am. Look, even now we can't discuss something about me, about *my* life, without you making it somehow about you or how disgusting you think my mask is. What an embarrassment I am to you. Forget it."

"So you met Abraham?" her mother added, ignoring everything Emery had just said. "He's quite the character, isn't he? You know, he has a granddaughter; I think she's about your age. She's sick, though. Poor old man. He's stuck in some hospice unit, and he has to worry about a beautiful granddaughter in Michigan."

Emery noticed the way her mother described the little girl, someone she'd never even met but seemed to care about more than her own flesh and blood. The way her lips formed the word *beautiful* was almost painful, hand motions and everything. Aimee Phoenix, a regular performer, art at its finest.

"I feel sorry for him."

Dear God, Aimee was more of a mother to complete strangers. Emery suddenly felt nausea creep up her gut. *Get me home,* she thought. *I don't want to be with you, even near you. I want to be with Arson. I want to run across that lawn and pound against his door until my palms bleed. I'll know I'm alive.*

But the more Emery dwelled on the mysterious boy, the more she was reminded of how he too had abandoned her, today of all days. How he had made a promise he couldn't keep. She wondered if he had ever planned on showing up at all or if this was simply a game to him, the way other kids used to play. She could feel a tear sliding down her nose as silence took her heart away.

"Are you crying?" her mother asked, seemingly sympathetic.

"No," Emery lied. "I just don't wanna talk anymore."

Joel sat in front of the blank computer screen, watching the blurry cursor appear and disappear. He took a sip of beer and placed the bottle beside countless books, ones that read, *Overcoming Your Demons* and *Kicking the Habit Old School: A Guide to Cold Turkey Freedom.* Their covers looked almost as uninteresting as their titles, and it didn't help matters much that he didn't believe half the trash he read. Much of it he forgot almost instantly, and whenever Aimee asked him to recite to her a passage that moved him in some way, he usually recited verbatim the first line of each book. Lame.

He could feel his eyes glazing over. Why on earth was he in front of a computer screen when he should be out hunting for a job? Securing his family. Trying to type out a sermon after months of isolation and self-judgment proved complicated, to say the least. All inspiration seemed lost. Was that his conscience or his wife's scratchy voice piercing his eardrums, spilling words of disapproval?

Oh, to be young again. To be in love. In a time when life was easier, when Aimee's mouth tasted of sweeter things than deprecation. Joel took another sip. How long had it been since they had embraced for real, how long since they were intimate? Perhaps it was too painful to recall. It might as well have been failure plastered across the screen in big block letters. It belonged on a billboard with his worn-out face beside it. Writing sermons had never been this hard. But he couldn't keep a stray thought, even if he focused. First, he tried to bullet them, using coherent notes. He had enough mental baggage to write twenty volumes of self-help jargon, but nothing seemed to come out when he put pen to paper or finger to keyboard. Emery's often gentle suggestion that he start taking a deeper interest in technology had revolutionized the way he put a sermon together. In fact, with her expertise and his... *Forget it, Joel.* It was another lifetime, another world. Not this one. Here he couldn't even get a simple paragraph down. Nothing.

Joel stared at the cursor of the document until it became his own thoughts, wandering, disappearing, and reappearing again only for a moment. He longed for something of meaning, anything. He typed one question out. *Do better men exist?* He saved it to his desktop and powered off the machine.

Cracking his knuckles, Joel reclined and took a long swig, frowning at the taste. He'd made such a mess of everything. Nearly ruined a marriage he'd spent years trying to build. Aimee, she was still so beautiful. He loved to watch her from the bed while she was in the shower, her shadow dancing against the glass with the bathroom door creaked open. But maybe he'd be stronger if she were more supportive. If she didn't critique everything he did every day. Didn't he love his family? He'd made his mistakes, but he was a good man.

"I just want a second chance," he muttered, almost in tears. He swallowed the last sip of alcohol, coming to grips with the harsh truth: he was not a minister anymore. He was Joel Phoenix, failed husband, bad father.

Just then, light broke into the dark room. The sound of car doors slamming shut echoed through the windowpanes. Nervously, Joel opened the bottom drawer to his mahogany desk. Inside he saw two old bottles he'd never gotten rid of. The smell of stagnant beer floated into the air. Careless. Joel stashed away the empty bottle in the drawer beside the other would-be culprits to his inevitable demise. *Like Peter,* he thought.

Before closing the drawer, Joel caught a glimpse of the ring he had planned to give Aimee. *Don't even think about it,* his mind snickered. *Your breath smells, you look pathetic, and you're still waiting for a believable lie to sell her. What else could she do now but throw it right back in your face?*

Joel slammed the drawer, misted himself with cologne, and reached into his pocket for a mint. He approached the door with a smile on his face, studying the two silhouettes awaiting him on the other side. As the door opened, he found a soft, unspoiled part of his daughter's neck and kissed it. Then he turned to his wife and threw his arms around her. But he knew there was more than space between them.

TWENTY

Emery fought to keep the morning light from reaching her eyes. It stretched its long, yellow fingers past the terribly painted windows in her room and onto the bed, where she lay sprawled out and covered. It always came to wake her up, but even though the sun came out from hiding, it didn't mean she wanted to.

"Wake up, Emery," her mother said. "You'd think that sleeping for twelve hours would be enough."

Emery groaned and rolled over.

"I found this under the door when I woke up." Her mother dropped a torn and folded piece of paper onto the bed before rushing out of the room with a basket of laundry nudged up against her hip.

Emery yawned and felt her warm face, the skin like play dough beneath the mask. With a deep breath, she staggered out of bed. She hated Sundays, always had. She hated living a lie. The lie of going to church, the lie that everything was okay when it wasn't. Her parents had become skilled actors in the stage that was their life. She was glad they had a reason to stop going to church, even though part of her missed God.

Emery unfolded the page and mouthed the only words: *I'm sorry. From, the alien.*

Those two words could have been written in blood permanently. A beautiful stain. But what could be said in just two words? Was Arson sorry for not coming the night before, or was he just saying so to appease a sleepy conscience?

The uncertain paranoia was killing her. Emery dug her fingernails into the flesh of her palms. She wanted to know the truth. She had to know.

Emery gathered herself, made a fist, and knocked on Arson's door.

"What do you want?" a voice said as the door finally creaked opened. An old woman with a haggard appearance squinted, the sunlight glistening against her leathery skin.

"Good morning," Emery said, hands folded, the note crumpled inside. "Is Arson around, ma'am?"

"You nearly scared me half to death, child. Who are you?"

"I'm sorry, ma'am. The mask is kind of frightening. I'm one of your new neighbors. My name is Emery."

"What on earth are you doing knocking on my door at this hour on a Sunday morning? Doesn't anyone go to church anymore?"

Emery rocked back and forth. "I'm sorry for disturbing you. I never meant to scare you. Should I just come back later?"

"What good would that do?" the old woman said with a rasp in her voice. "You already woke me up, for heaven's sake. I suppose I'll go and make some coffee for me and my husband. Now that I'm up, I can't possibly go back to bed."

The door pinched open farther. Emery noticed the old woman's pantyhose dangling halfway down her sun-spotted legs. With darting eyes, she saw that the woman's clothes consisted only of a gray bathrobe with stains on the lapel. The knot keeping each threadbare piece of fabric in place hung loosely toward the right side of her sagging backside.

"What's your husband's name?" Emery asked.

The old woman's face lit up all of a sudden. "Oh, his name is Henry, dear. You would fall in love with him, surely. He's so lovely, simply a dream. Why don't you come inside? I'll introduce you."

"Arson never mentioned a grandfather."

Suddenly, a shadow appeared out of the kitchen. It scaled along the wall and stopped at the sunlit doorway, stretching out before them.

"Arson, what are you doing up, love?"

"Couldn't sleep, Grandma." He stood rigidly, one arm extended to the doorpost, the rest of his body placed between Emery and his grandmother.

"Hi," Emery said, almost in a whisper, revealing the note.

He stared down at her. "Oh, hi." Arson turned to his grandmother. "Thanks for getting the door. Could I talk to her alone, please?"

"Sure. She really is delightful. Perhaps I'll introduce you to Henry another time," the old woman said, heading toward the kitchen, her bare feet dragging behind her. "Do come again."

Arson shut the door and found a spot on the porch in the shade where they could talk. "How are you doing?"

"What were you doing yesterday?" Emery said.

Hesitating, he replied, "I told you I had work."

"All day?"

"Pretty much. We were slammed. I was very busy."

"Oh, really? And I can see how a phone call is too much trouble. I don't even know why I came over here," Emery said, getting up from her spot but leaving the note behind.

A silent wind lifted the page and carried it onto the dead grass.

"I said I was sorry," Arson said. "What else do you want from me?"

"Did you mean it?"

"I wouldn't have written it if I didn't mean it. I wanted to be there yesterday; I really did."

"Then why weren't you? What was so important?"

He didn't speak.

"Look, I get it if you don't want to see me," Emery said. "But don't lie to me."

Arson got up and moved toward her. She could hear her heart booming. Hands clammy, mouth dry from spitting accusations. Her fingernails chipped and painted in certain spots, the polish cracking at the tip. He was right behind her now. She could feel his breath lifting up the hairs on her neck. Emery turned around and noticed him holding onto the crinkled note, sincerity in his eyes.

"Emery, I am sorry," he whispered.

Her icy tone melted when he uttered the words she had marched over to hear for herself. Words that meant maybe, just maybe, he felt something for her too.

"I'm volunteering again tomorrow at two o'clock. Should a girl get her hopes up again?"

Arson bit his lip and sighed. "Count me in."

TWENTY-ONE

The hallways of Middlesex Hospital were white tunnels with no ends. There was light, but it was scarce, most of the darkness contained in small rooms. Doctors skulked around. Nurses checked for bad mechanical readings or stutters in heartbeats. Once or twice Arson covered his ears and just tried to watch everything in silence. He watched everything with cold eyes, and cold eyes looked back. It was like for a second he glimpsed a soul. It looked sad.

The sound he heard when he tried to shut out the world was unlike any other sound. It was quiet, similar to breathing, faint, and with secrets all its own. He tried to hear the heartbeats of patients in hospital beds, but he couldn't because the drum of reality called him back.

For a few hours, Arson and Emery wheeled around a cart filled with medications and prescriptions he'd never heard of and various snacks no one in a million years would willingly eat. But the patients ate what they were given, most without incident or complaining, because they had to. Some refused, some too in pain to even think about a meal, but everyone eventually ate. Over the hours, it was hard not to picture Grandma lying in a hospital bed, replacing one old soul with another. He wondered if he would look like that kid he had noticed three rooms back, so sad he was sweating and not crying. So cold he was almost blue. The boy couldn't have been much older than ten. Maybe children were stronger than they knew. Maybe they had the power to keep people alive or kill them just by how much they loved or got angry. But places like this didn't seem to host animosity or ill will, only the good that was left in people. Only the parts they usually kept hidden until it was too late.

The gloom didn't appear to bother Emery the way it bothered him, like a thousand hateful spiders dancing along his shoulder blades. Arson tried to see the good in what they were doing, tried to see a point to it all, but it didn't make sense how fragile people were. It was painful walking by those rooms filled with AIDS patients, those with disease-rotten faces, the limbless cancer victims, tons of people who were already dead. Arson pitied them. The world could be so cruel and unfair. The more he looked at each victim, the more he presumed it was him and not them who was dying. Supplying them with medicine, food, and water seemed futile. What right did he have, what right did anyone have, to give these poor souls false hope?

"What's the matter?" Emery asked, scrubbing her hands with disinfectant. She'd said she needed a break. He didn't want to say anything. "You look weird. Are you sick or something?"

"No, it's ... What's the point? I mean, what are you doing here?"

"I'm not doing anything. *We* are doing something. And what kind of a question is that?"

"It all feels so meaningless," Arson said. "We live, we get sick. We get old, and then we're forgotten in places like this."

"I try to think of this place as a last chance. One final stop before the end. It's kinda hopeful if you think about it like that."

"Maybe. But these people in here make me feel so drained. They're empty shells, machines that stopped working. It just feels like we're lying to them."

"Never knew you were such a cynic," she concluded.

They didn't talk much after that, not for a while.

Emery wheeled into a room with a yawn sometime later. Arson looked at the name affixed to the plastic panel hanging up against the wall outside the door. Genevieve D'Angelo, age forty-seven.

Emery leaned toward Arson and whispered, "She has leukemia." Then, with a smile, she said, "Hi, Genevieve. You remember me, don't you? So good to see you up and awake."

Gray light outlined the woman's pale face, a virtually motionless body stuck with needles and wired to respirators and other machines Arson didn't even have the name for. The woman's eyes fought to stay open, while dry lips begged to speak. Withered hands sought the affection of his masked partner fearlessly. It was weird how this dying woman didn't seem to care that Emery was different or looked frightening. This stranger, drowning in layers of white sheets, seemed only to care that someone was here to listen, even if they shared but a few words. The obvious deterioration of her face and skin ripped Arson apart inside. How long did she have?

During the hectic afternoon, Emery's mother had only run into them once. She bumped into Arson as the two of them were exiting the hospital café, spilling a cup of soda on his white volunteer scrubs. He could tell that the moment was beyond awkward for Emery, who made certain to clean up the mess by dabbing his shirt a hundred times, grunting, and tossing a pack of Wet Ones at her mom. The remainder of the embarrassing meeting was short-lived, consisted of the cliché *hi—this-is-the-boy-I've-been-telling-you-about* and the *goodbye—nice-of-you-to-interfere-with-my-life* conversation.

"So that's my mom," Emery said as they rounded the corner.

Arson knew it was best to leave it at that.

"Back to saving the world," she said. "Come along, Robin."

"Robin?"

"Yeah? Is it too early for sidekick nicknames?"

Arson shrugged. "Whatever. Lead the way to Gotham, Dark Knight."

He could tell Emery wanted to talk, might have been aching to, but a conversation was the last thing on his mind. They moved down the hallway and entered room 219. Arson hadn't even checked the information hanging on the wall outside the door.

"Look who it is, my daily pain in the butt." The voice belonged to a tired-looking, elderly man perched up in his bed. "And she brought a friend."

"Hello, Abraham," Emery replied plainly. "It's a pleasure to see you too."

"Now, I'm not dead just yet. Come on over here and give an old man a hug."

"Don't mind him," she said, turning to Arson. "I'm guessing he didn't get a whole lot of action when he was younger, so now he's kind of a flirt."

"She thinks she's got me all figured out, son. Don't they all? My name's Abraham. Abraham Finch."

Arson reached out to shake the man's hand. "Arson Gable."

Emery handed the old man some crackers.

"So what brings a young, strapping boy like you to a dump like this?"

"Abraham, watch what you say," Emery said, noticing the old man smirk.

He glanced up at her, mocked her while her back was turned, and continued. "How long have you two been ... canoodling?"

"Abraham, you're a bum, you know that?"

"What? It's an honest question. What's a boy gonna be spending his summer volunteering for if he ain't at least dating you? Shoot, I think hell would've frozen over before I stepped foot in a place like this at your age."

"Well, fortunately for you, everyone's not so ornery. You know, it's only my second day, and already you're acting fresh. Besides, this boy and I aren't together."

"That's not what it looks like to me."

"Well, maybe I should buy you a new pair of glasses."

"Ouch! This one doesn't go quietly." Abe's eyes got big and wide.

Arson stepped a little closer to the bed, intrigued by the man, who appeared as threatening as a stuffed animal, wrapped inside the sheets, soft, buoyant cheeks puffing at the surface. His coffee-colored skin seemed loosely draped around sagging muscles and brittle bones.

Emery got up and poured Abe a cup of water.

"Didn't I ask you to bring me something with a little more flavor?" he said.

"The powers that be won't let me sneak alcohol into room 219 or any other room, for that matter. I guess you're gonna have to stay sober."

"Fine. Living was hard enough. Didn't think dying would be this hard. Man, oh, man, somebody could be dying and they won't even give him a drink to help ease the pain."

"He's good at making you feel guilty, but don't fall for it, Arson. He just wants some booze."

"Okay, suit yourself. But when I come to haunt you from the grave, you'll know why." The old man removed his glasses and made an attempt at trying to creep her out, but the wrinkles inside his brown mug made him look like more of a snarling pug than anything that was supposed to scare her.

"So have you kissed her yet? By the time I was your age, I'd kissed four gals." Abe held up four fingers, as if he were trying to make sure he could still count.

"Oh, Mr. Finch, that's fresh."

"I know, but I'm trying to have a little bit of fun before I check out of this place. It kinda feels like purgatory. A waiting place before, you know, the afterlife crapstorm."

"Abraham Finch, keep it down. Don't get so worked up. I'd bring some sun-tanning lotion at the rate you're going."

"I'm sorry I'm not a pale-faced, virgin priest, but I seen some things in my day. I lived my life. Spent too much time being modest and not enough time saying it like it is."

"Well, say it like it is when other nurses and volunteers are catering to you."

"Like your mother? She's a pretty lady, Emery."

Emery didn't respond.

"Soft subject," Arson whispered.

"So, Arson," Abe continued, changing the direction of the conversation, "you have quite a unique name. I like it. Say, I'm a bit curious, do you like matches, kid?"

"Abraham, if you can't behave—"

He folded his lips together and replied, "You'll what? Pass on over to room 220? Lord knows I'm a dream compared to Peggy the hippo."

"Mrs. Yeshur is not as mean or as plump as you think she is. What's gotten into you?"

"Depression, constipation. In case you couldn't tell, I'm in a hospice unit. Have some compassion, for crying out loud!"

"Please. You and I both know you're going to outlive us all."

"What good is that if I ain't got nothing to numb the pain of cruel and unusual volunteers?"

"Here he goes," Emery said, rolling her eyes. "Abraham, what would your mother think?"

"Momma wouldn't play, but even Momma knew not to be stubborn all the time."

A smile crawled across Arson's face as he said, "I don't think she's gonna budge."

"Tell me about it."

"I suppose you think you're funny, huh? Fine." She prepared to take the cup of water away.

"Wait a minute. I'm not finished with that, thank you." He wore a sly grin, showcasing what decay and nicotine had left behind.

"Oh, now he's content with water," she said.

"Don't have much of a choice, do I?" Abe answered, his voice throaty and wet.

"Forgive me for caring about your health," Emery said.

"Sweetheart, those uppity white suits say my number should've been up days ago. But I've been here for weeks, and I'm still kicking, ain't I? If anything's killing me, it's this place, this bed. I don't think a sip of gin is gonna send me to the grave now. Besides, if it does, I'd welcome that black-hooded fool with open arms. Heck, I'd give him a sip."

"Look, Abraham, it's my job to help you, without booze. I happen to care about you," Emery said. "I'm not sure why, but I do. Guess you're like the grandpa I never had."

"You never had a granddaddy?"

"Or a grandmother. They all checked out before I was born."

"What a shame." Abe was crestfallen. "How about you, kid?"

"I have a grandmother," Arson said. "Her name is Kay."

"You love her?"

Arson hesitated. "Yeah."

"Good. You gotta cherish the ones you love. Don't leave her in a place like this to rot. It's downright cruel. Why haven't any of my babies come to visit me? I paid my dues in this world, Emery. Loved a good woman, raised beautiful babies, fought them blasted fools in Korea. Maybe it wasn't enough. Maybe I'm paying for all the abuse I did to this big, black carcass of mine. Lung cancer ain't exactly a walk in the park, you know." His voice quivered with a deep rasp, and he started to cough.

"I'm sorry, Abraham. I can't imagine how hard this must be for you." Emery rubbed his shoulder. "But you have me and Arson here to keep you company. Whatever you need."

"Some gin would be nice."

Emery breathed deeply, ignoring the request of the old man. She punched Arson in the chest. "Come on, Robin. He's never gonna quit asking. Besides, we've got our rounds to make before we head home. Gotham needs us. Goodbye, Abraham."

As they left the room, Arson felt strange. Maybe it was relief; he wasn't quite sure. For the few moments he'd spent with Abe, he wondered if there was any hope left. But then he turned back and for a split second focused all of his attention on the frail man lying in the bed, a bed that might as well have been his coffin. He saw Abe looking out the window with a vacant stare in his eyes.

Heaven seemed so far away.

Joel lay sprawled out on the pull-out sofa

when Aimee and Emery arrived home. She paused and stared at him drooling away on the living room rug. She couldn't stand how unpleasant the room looked, how dated and uninspiring the walls were. The least he could do was spruce the place up. It was hard enough getting her and Emery to move to this hick town, but if he thought for one second she'd help him dress up the rooms, he was mistaken. This was temporary, she told herself every morning before work. Moving here had been a stupid thing to do.

"Temporary," Aimee said under her breath, using a tissue to wipe her husband's drool off the sofa pillow.

She removed her summer coat, felt the strap of her purse slip loosely down her arm, and kept eyeballing him. On the table beside her leg lay the culprits of his daily crimes: empty cartons of Chinese food, crumbs cluttered about the floor, the ring left behind on the coffee table from a glass of water he'd forgotten to finish. "We have coasters for a reason," she seethed.

Aimee ran her fingers across his stubbly jaw. She noticed him twitch in his sleep. What was he so tired for? Aimee started grinding her teeth. It wasn't right. Joel wasn't right. His worn-out clothes reminded her of their worn-out love. What happened to the man she had married? Joel Phoenix, Harvard grad. She swore she didn't know this man. Didn't want to know him. Swore she hated him. Aimee rubbed her eyes. *I want to run,* she mouthed. *I just want to run.*

The stranger continued snoring away like she wasn't even there.

"Joel, get up!" she said, tugging at his hair.

He rolled over in his sleep with a groan.

"Get up. You're drooling all over my sofa." Aimee grunted and went upstairs to take a bath.

TWENTY-TWO

Arson didn't understand why he was so compelled to return to the hospice unit. Didn't know what it was exactly that drew his mind back there when he should have been focused on making hot fudge sundaes and milkshakes. His daily mishaps at Tobey's caused Ray to drop by unannounced—and more than once. Routine checkups, Ray called them.

After his painful shifts were through, Arson rode his bike to the hospital. He never went inside. Didn't seem right going there without Emery. Part of him wanted to check himself into the hospice unit. He'd know exactly what he'd say if they starting asking any questions too. "I'm ready to die, ma'am. Put me on the waiting list." It sounded so depressing, the words rotating like a squeaky wheel inside his brain. He realized Grandma would never fit in there, but maybe he would.

A grouchy nurse walked outside suddenly. She noticed him but refused to acknowledge his presence. Her hands reached into her purse for a lighter, a match, anything to light the cigarette pinched between her jaws. He heard her curse, not just at the lighter or the cigarette, but at random things like a babysitter at home, a boss she couldn't stand, her lack of ambition, and that jerk who took her spot in the parking garage this morning. Arson listened to this stranger go off about everything that was wrong with her day, with her life.

He thought he could help her. Deep down he really wanted to. All it would take was a snap of the fingers. One rage-induced thought, and he could make it all okay. The one thing he hated about himself seemed like the only thing that could grant her peace.

When the nurse finally found that book of matches, her world seemed different. The thought that at any point this dark and wiry-haired nurse could self-destruct over something so small and insignificant made his stomach sink. Yet her desire seemed simple enough. And Arson found himself wondering what changed a person so quickly. All she wanted was release, a release she got from a rolled-up hunk of tobacco. The cigarette would stain her mouth, ruin her gums, and most likely kill her one day. But even she was doing her part in the world to help, to heal, to fix what this world had left broken.

Now that he thought about it, Arson remembered seeing her rush down the hallway past him the other day. How infuriated she had seemed, frantic and pressured. The sickest part of it all was that he envied her.

Even this foul-mouthed, jittery addict could do what he didn't know how to do. She could be a hero.

The weekend finally arrived. Arson
had the day off. He hadn't slept all night from mere anticipation. He didn't know whether it was excitement or that awkward feeling you get right before an interview. *Today will be different,* he told himself. This time he *wanted* to volunteer. So much so that Grandma even had her suspicions.

"That girl isn't dragging you into some cult now, is she?" she said at breakfast.

Arson pretended not to hear her as he rushed out the door.

The heat wave didn't let up. It was in its third week, which meant he sweated much more than usual, an issue he was rather embarrassed about but one he hoped Emery wouldn't notice. It was about noon when Arson started tossing pebbles at her window.

After going at it for a good five minutes with no response, someone called out from the side of the house. "What do you think you're doing?" the voice said, deep and forceful.

"Hello? Who is that?" Arson replied. He dropped the few pebbles he had in his hand immediately.

"I'm the guy who lives here. And you're the kid trying to break my windows." The voice came with a face, a scruffy-looking one. The man's hair tapered off into moody curls. He wore a white *Kiss the Pastor* t-shirt—most of which was covered in paint—a pair of cutoff shorts, and sock-stuffed sandals.

"Normally I don't introduce myself to vandals, but I've been reading this book, and it's been telling me for three chapters straight why I need to start going out of my way to talk to new people, even people I don't like—not that I don't like you or anything—but anyway. What are you doing throwing rocks at my window, kid?"

"I'm looking for Emery," Arson said abruptly.

"Emery?" the man said, as if he didn't recognize the name. "What business do you have with my daughter?"

A sudden nervousness slipped inside Arson's skin. "She volunteers at the hospital, and I usually"—he felt his eyes wander—"go with her."

"Really?" the man said. "Do you have some kind of agenda with my daughter?"

"Agenda?"

"Do you ask a lot of girls out just for kicks? You like leading them along until you get what you want?"

"Excuse me, sir?"

The man eyeballed Arson.

"Okay. Your name's Arson, right?"

Arson nodded his head.

"You'll have to forgive my apprehensive nature. I love my daughter very much, and she's not exactly like most daughters."

"No, sir, she's definitely not."

"My name's Joel." He shook Arson's hand but failed to mention it was dripping with paint. "Sorry about that."

Arson winced at the sight of his gooey palms. "Is she here, sir?"

"What? You're just gonna leave me here to paint a house by myself?"

Now Arson was confused. "Do you need help, sir?"

"If you keep calling me sir, I'm gonna start feeling old."

Arson sighed.

"Aren't you a little early for volunteering? My wife doesn't leave for work for another hour and a half or so. Emery rides with her."

"Oh. I guess I could lend you a hand, then."

"Both hands, preferably," Joel said, hopping onto the ladder.

Arson could hear the rickety ladder squeal with every step. Joel was a lean man, but he put a lot of pressure on his heels while he climbed.

"Have you been in a relationship before, Arson?" Joel asked, dipping the paint brush into the bowl and sliding it across the dingy boards of the house.

"Not exactly."

"Ever had sex?" Joel stared at him for a second. It felt like forever.

"Um, no?"

"Is that a question or an answer?"

"An answer, sir. I don't have a lot of experience with the opposite sex."

"Good to know." Joel continued to paint, almost absentmindedly.

"Look, I'm new at all this. I was never the kid with a lot of friends. Emery is a unique person. I just want to get to know her. I'm not like other kids."

Joel nodded, eyes locked.

Arson could feel the sweat pouring from his face. His neck stuck to the back of his shirt. The tension built upon itself with every unmeasured word.

"So, Arson, who's-not-like-other-people, do you plan on helping me at all, or are you just gonna stand there?"

He was thankful Joel changed the subject. "Do you have another ladder I could use? Yours doesn't look all that safe."

"Not that I'm aware of," came the reply.

"I suppose I could use the same ladder and get up there and paint with you."

"Two guys on a rusty ladder isn't exactly the safest thing in the world."

"You're right. That was a stupid idea." Arson looked away for a moment, wishing Emery were out here to save him from this miserably awkward conversation. "That spot seems a little hard for you to reach, sir. Why don't I get it? You can take a break for a while."

"Nah, that's all right. I've had to paint two churches in my lifetime. I think I know a thing or two about—"

It was then that Joel twisted his leg inside one of the ladder's jaws. He screamed in agony and lost his balance on the step. Seconds later, Arson stared in shock as Joel's body thudded against the ground.

"My back," Joel groaned, eyes shut.

"Sir, are you okay? Is it broken?"

"It hurts."

"Well, try to move it," Arson said.

Joel adjusted himself on the ground and found that he could move if he did it slowly and without much effort.

"Aimee! Emery!" Joel yelled. "Emery!" He breathed deeply, fighting the pain.

Arson listened for approaching footsteps. Emery ran to her father's side and held his hand. "Dad, what happened?" she asked.

"He fell off the ladder," Arson said. "I warned him it wasn't safe."

"Yeah, says the guy who wanted to come up there with me."

"Enough, you two," she barked. "How did you fall?"

"It's not that big a deal. I was up there painting and talking to your new friend. Went to reach for a spot and got my ankle twisted in one of the steps. Then I slipped, and like magic, here we are."

"You know, you're not twenty anymore, Dad. You really need to be careful."

He furrowed his brow. "I *was* careful. And I am not that old, for crying out loud. Just help me up, will you, sweetheart? Where's your mother?"

Emery and Arson lifted him up slowly. "I don't know. I heard you scream and ran out here as fast as I could. I think she was upstairs."

"Try and relax," Arson said, the three of them walking into the house.

"I think you should go see a doctor, Dad. What if you broke something?"

"I'm not going to the emergency room to wait for three hours so they can tell me I need to take it easy for a while. I'll be fine."

"Dad, you just fell, like, fifteen feet."

"Sweetheart, thank you for caring about me, really, but I'm just going to lie down for the afternoon. If I feel worse later, I'll call a doctor."

Emery reluctantly agreed and brought him to the pull-out sofa where he'd spent the last few nights.

"Could you get me a glass of water?" Joel begged.

"Yeah, be right back."

Aimee came down the stairs and found Arson standing next to the pull-out sofa. "Oh, hello, Arson. Are you planning on volunteering today?"

He nodded.

"I can drive you, if you'd like." She turned and looked at the man on the sofa. "What happened to you, Joel?" she asked.

"He lost his step and fell off the ladder," Arson answered.

"You really must be more careful in the future," Aimee said, brushing her hair back.

Emery entered the room. "Here you go, Dad," she said, handing him the glass of water.

"Thank you," he replied feebly.

"Are you kids ready to go? I was thinking I would go in early today." Aimee grabbed her purse and walked out the front door. "Meet you in the car."

Emery turned to Arson and shook her head. "Bye, Dad," she said, following her mother out the door.

TWENTY-THREE

Abe was in the middle of a coughing fit when they walked into room 219. But when he saw Arson and Emery, his chapped mouth danced back into a frail grin, almost like joy was rebuking his pain, at least for one moment. Arson figured this was his soft side being exposed.

Abe said the nurses had been hassling him all morning and that he was glad to have the new recruits drop in and save the day. He looked terrible, though. His brown skin seemed to show age more and more each day, worn and manipulated. The black hair that once occupied his forehead was swallowed up in scattered white bunches. Abe pulled the sheets close to his chin, trying to get warm.

"It's cruel of you guys to leave me here alone for almost a week. The white suits are getting sick of me. I think they wanna euthanize me or something. Man, I could've gone cuckoo." The old man's eyes glowed, and the wrinkles in his cheeks flushed along the surface of his face when his stained gums came out of hiding. They could tell he was hurting.

"Sorry, Abraham. I've been busy with the house and moving in and stuff," Emery tried. "Arson and I try to make it here as often as we can, you know that. But there are other volunteers. Why don't you try being friendly to some of them?"

"I'm not really all that friendly to you guys, and I *like* you. Those other young punks ain't got a shot." He struggled to breathe.

Emery poured him a glass of water and told him to take it easy, but he wasn't in the mood to comply.

"Maybe if you weren't so pretty I could find it within myself to befriend some of the other volunteers. But I'm afraid Cupid has done his magic already." Abe winked at Arson.

"That's really sweet, Abraham, and so Hallmark it's almost disgusting. Didn't know you had it in you."

"I'm insulted. I've always been a gentleman to you, my dear."

Emery burst into laughter that could be heard down the hall.

"Keep it down, girl. Just trying to pay you a compliment. See, Arson, this is why you don't compliment women; it always comes back to bite you."

"Don't listen to him," Emery said, handing Abe some Jell-O. "Women love to be complimented at the right time."

"And when do you suppose that is?" Arson finally piped up.

"I don't know. But if the man's a real gentleman, he'll know."

"After all my years of living on this earth," Abe began, taking another sip of water, "I've learned it's a whole lot easier to upset a lady than it is to get one of them to smile."

"Say what you will, Abraham, but men can be fickle too. And cruel. And scummy. And pig-headed—"

"All right, all right," Abe said. "It seems I've underestimated you once again, my dear. You continue to make me ever wiser and even more ornery. Congratulations."

They all shared a brief laugh.

Abe turned to face the boy in the corner of the room now. "So who are you, Arson?" his lips fired off. "Tell me about yourself; I don't know a thing about you."

Arson stared blankly back.

"I don't want to know your name, per se. I know what they call you, and that's not really important. That's not what makes you who you are. You could be called Jim or Travis or Loser for all I care. What matters most is who you are deep down in your soul."

"If I have a soul," Arson sighed.

Abe was taken aback. "Don't be silly. Everybody's got one, kid. Do you believe in God, Arson?"

"What?"

"You know, heaven and stuff?"

It took awhile for him to answer. "I'm not sure. Still waiting for proof."

"Maybe we could call you Thomas, then." Abe bit his lip and chuckled. "I get it. I was waiting too. But you know what I figured out after all my years of waiting and getting angry at the world? I realized that you only waste time that way. Waiting for something good to happen to you. Waiting to get out of the mess you're in. No, that ain't the way to be, kid. You gotta be the hero. You gotta stand, even when you feel like quitting. Forget about your proof. If I was waiting on proof, I'd still be waiting."

Arson looked at Emery with confusion. Who did this old bat think he was, telling him what to do? Like he had all the answers? The lung cancer patient who had smoked himself to the hospice wing was giving him answers on how to live. The very thought was ridiculous. Today felt like an interrogation. First, Emery's father had treated him like some potential fiend trying to deflower his only daughter. Now here Abe was sucker-punching him in the gut with random philosophy. Was the room actually shrinking, or was that his imagination?

"Thanks for the advice," Arson said, rolling his eyes.

"You ain't gonna listen, but I suppose that's all right. I didn't listen either when some old fool told me the same thing. Man, oh, man, how much time I missed in this life, bitter at the world. To them, I was just another minority loser. But I told my mother I'd be somebody, be something. Do something. The world didn't take too kindly to me for a while, but things change. They always do. And I did, Momma, I tried."

It was the first time either of them had seen Abe cry. He'd looked sad before, like he'd wanted to, but today he threw caution to the wind.

"I'm sorry, Mr. Finch. This world can be pretty cruel."

The old man cleared his nose and said, "But it's got life too, kid. That's what I'm saying. Even this messed-up place got a soul. It ain't perfect, but it needs saving, just like I did, just like you do. Everybody needs help sometime. Everybody needs love, but no one's got it to give. Man, oh, man, if only I knew then what I know—"

He started coughing again. Blood and phlegm came up on his sheets. Emery panicked and paged the nurse.

"Take it easy, Abraham," Arson said.

"You still haven't answered my question, kid."

Arson fired off the first set of answers that flooded his brain. "My name is Arson Gable. I live in a cabin in East Hampton, and I work at an ice cream parlor."

Abe leaned against his pillow and collected his composure. Emery helped get the spit off his jaw. "Give me something to chew on!"

"Maybe twenty questions is something we should save for another day, Abraham," Emery said.

"I suppose you're right, my dear." Abe cracked his neck and leaned his head back against the pillow drenched in sweat. He pulled the covers over his chest and started to shiver as the nurse walked in. She asked if everything was okay, and Abe told her to get lost.

Once she left in a fit, Emery whispered, "That wasn't very nice."

"She was bothering me," Abe said in a raspy voice, as he closed his eyes. "Think about what I said, Arson. Life's too short to become a cynical old fool like me."

Arson's gaze was far away. He hadn't been able to buy what Abe was selling. The old man didn't live in the world as Arson knew it. He didn't know what high school was like now, didn't know what waking up afraid felt like, or the lingering fury he possessed when starting a fire with one stray thought. There were no rallies for his kind, because no one else was like him. There were no fire-starting professionals or compassionate politicians for Arson to look up to. People didn't like those they couldn't understand. And how could he ever expect them to like him when even *he* hated what he was? Abe seemed smart enough to get by in a hospital bed, but he was wrong. Dead wrong.

TWENTY-FOUR

Emery should've knocked. She made the mistake of walking into the bathroom unannounced. There she saw her father, tired and unkempt, leaning on the bathroom counter. He was chugging a beer. The look on his face read guilt and shock as he swallowed. Her father told her she shouldn't be barging in on people without knocking. Then he put the beer down and asked her to talk to him for a moment.

"I wasn't expecting you home yet," he said. "I could've sworn it was locked."

"Mom's home too. Dad, what are you doing? This isn't what it looks like, right? I mean, tell me that isn't beer in your hand and that you're not drinking it in front of me. Tell me I'm crazy. I'll believe you if you say it."

Joel hung his head low. "Would you keep your voice down, please? That's all I need is another fight with your mother. She's so ... "

Emery shut the door and leaned against it. As much as she wanted to be sympathetic to whatever it was her father was going through, she was still stuck in that hospital room with Abe and Arson.

"Look, Emery, I want to talk to you. For real. Once you hear me out, then I'll let you judge me, hate me, whatever you want."

She watched him scratch his head frantically, panicking and sighing and flaring his nostrils. It wasn't just stress on his face or even the loss of a job. It looked like failure.

"First of all, tell me why you've been lying to me," she said.

"This life. I never wanted it. I thought I was so sure about things. I wanted to tell you, I really did, but it's not that easy for me."

"What's not easy, Dad? The fact that you moved us out in the middle of nowhere or that you swore you'd never take another drink again?" She felt her vocal cords crack. "Or what about Mom keeping this family afloat while you cope with a mistake you made almost two years ago. We lost everything because of you. They hated us. And I couldn't blame them."

Joel bit his lip. "*I* lost the church."

Emery grumbled and folded her arms. "Grow up, Dad. How could you do this to us? To me? I believed you. We can't go through this again. My father's supposed to be stronger. You were my hero, Dad. Now, you're going to be another loser in rehab."

"I'm not going to rehab, sweetheart. Look, I'm try-ing to stay calm, okay? It's not like I need alcohol to survive or anything. This is a one-time thing."

"You've said that before. Do you actually believe yourself when you lie?"

Joel clenched his fists and banged his head up against the wall. "I just need to get my mind out of this mess. Having a drink helps me forget about the mistakes I've made to you and to your mother. I love that woman, but she doesn't even recognize me. I don't recognize me, Emery. This isn't what I want, but I'm hurt. I'm in pain."

For the first time in a long time, she could tell he was being honest. She'd hated him before for the lies, for the mixed-up priorities. But this time, the man who used to be a minister was telling the truth, and he meant it.

"Dad. I thought when it happened—"

"Just say it again, Emery. When *what* happened?"

Dead air crept into the room.

"I thought when you lost the church things would be different. I mean, they called you a drunk, a loser. Don't you think that hurt me?"

"I know it did, sweetheart. It nearly killed me. I wish I could change everything, but I can't. This is the way our life is now. Things *are* different. But your mother isn't making it easy."

"Can you blame her?" Emery grinded her teeth. "I hate you for making me side with her."

"I never asked you to pick a side."

"You never had to; it just happened. And news-flash, it's starting to happen between you and me too. Is this what you want?"

"Emery, try to understand."

She had problems to call her own, and she didn't need his dumped on top. Didn't he care that people were worse off than he was? People like Abe or Gen-evieve. "Understand what? You lied to me. And to Mom. Most of all, you lied to yourself."

"Emery, it's only a beer."

"No, it's not only a beer. It's everything. It's you, Mom, our screwed-up family."

"Our family?" Joel said, smirking. "I lost our family long before I lost the church."

Emery stared at him awhile and saw him as the weak and fragile human being he'd become. The way his failure glared out from his eyes. She shut her own and thought of a time when he made her smile or held her while she slept. Few memories like those existed, but she held tight to them because that was the man she wanted to remember, that was the father she needed now.

Emery grabbed the bottle of beer from the bath-room vanity and walked downstairs to the kitchen, leaving her father to sob on the toilet seat. The lights were off. She could see shades of the moonlight sliding along the countertops and cabinet space. Outside the window, she saw a sky full of bright light and unity.

She closed the blinds and wept. *Be strong,* she told herself. *Be stronger.*

Emery began pouring the bottle out into the sink. The slow chug as it emptied brought back images of her former life as a quiet pastor's daughter with a perfectly flawed family.

The suds oozed out the lip of the bottle. But before it was empty, an idea crept into her head. She'd wasted enough. Immediately, she looked for another container, one a little less conspicuous. Once the bottle was empty, she rinsed it out and placed it in a bag in her room. She'd dispose of it in the morning. No need for her mom to freak out too. Not yet, anyway. Maybe her father needed more time.

She rushed upstairs with a plan and prayed for tomorrow.

TWENTY-FIVE

Arson arrived to work late again. He swore he'd woken up on time, remembered setting his alarm clock, but it never went off. Normally, he didn't rely on the alarm to wake him up, but volunteering with Emery was taking its toll on him. Ray's threats to have him fired had become routine. Arson tried not to let them bother him. Instead he remained quiet and simply did as he was told.

He brushed his hair to the side, rushed to the back, threw on an apron, and got to work. "Can I help you, ma'am?" he asked a middle-aged woman, holding the scooper in hand. His face, still sweaty from the swift bike ride, was glowing red.

"I'll take one scoop of chocolate chip ice cream in a sugar cone, please." She had a Julie Andrews type of accent. Despite having to wait more than ten minutes to get her cone, she still managed to call it magnificent.

The next customer paraded down the line rudely and then asked for three scoops, all different flavors, complete with the works, and two vanilla milkshakes to go. "I'm on a tight schedule," she gasped, her cheeks so plump he thought they'd pop if he didn't complete the order before she counted to five.

Arson noticed Chelsea and Jason moving purposely slow, taking one customer for every three he helped. Arson knew what they were doing but ignored it. The two of them made remarks like, "Pick up the pace" and "Why are you always late?" between serving sundaes.

During lunch break, he worked. Scrubbing up sticky residue off the tile floor, washing windows, and rearranging the merchandise items were among the few tasks he completed while Chelsea talked to Ray about a raise due to her impeccable attendance record. Jason had to make an emergency call. But the minor setbacks didn't stop incoming customers. Arson dropped what he was doing to serve them, and Ray took pleasure in watching him panic to get everyone taken care of.

Once he had a moment to breathe, Arson dropped his eyes into the sink, where he watched his reflection drown with the soap and the ice cream toppings he'd cleaned off from his hands. When he looked up again, he was startled to find a mask staring him in the face.

"Good afternoon, kind sir," Emery said. "You're not still getting scared because of this thing, are you?"

"No, of course not."

"So this is where you work?"

"You found me," Arson said.

"Don't sound so excited to see me."

"Sorry. I've had one of those days."

"Looks like you need a break. I know you weren't planning on volunteering today, but I've kinda got this thing planned. Wanted to run it by you. When do you get off? Maybe we could volunteer together. Or, you know, we could wait 'til tomorrow if you're too busy."

Mandy walked in suddenly and made him nervous. Her skin shimmered in the afternoon light, and with every step closer, Arson felt as though his heart might literally leap into his throat. More panic rushed in.

"Hey, Arson," she said, avoiding Emery altogether. Her lips toyed with the wad of gum in her mouth. She tilted her head, letting most of her golden hair cascade down onto the mask.

Discomfort climbed up Arson's spine.

"Excuse me!" Emery said.

Mandy turned toward the mask. "Sorry, I didn't see you there."

"So, Arson," Emery began, stepping to the right, "when can you help me volunteer again at the hospital?"

"Hospital?" Mandy said, arching her toothpick eyebrows. "Since when do you volunteer at a hospital, Arson?"

"Oh, I'm really confused right now," he said, avoiding eye contact with either of them.

"Since I asked him to," Emery replied quite matter-of-factly. "We've been doing it for a few weeks now."

"Oh, that's nice," Mandy said. "I never understood volunteering for things. What's the point of doing something if you're not getting paid for it?"

"So what flavor do you want, Mandy?" Arson said, jumping in before a catfight broke out.

"Oh," Mandy replied, "I'll take two scoops of double chocolate chip, handsome."

Arson felt his cheeks fill with blood. All Mandy had to do was mention their bedroom rendezvous and everything between Emery and him could be ruined.

"What do you do when you volunteer anyway?"

"We take care of people in the hospice unit," Emery sneered. "It's got something to do with being compassionate."

"I was talking to Arson," Mandy said.

"It's not that bad," he interjected. "We've met a really cool guy."

Mandy recoiled, apparently offended by their constant use of *we*. "I couldn't go near my grandfather after they moved him into one of those homes. Spending time with old people who are about to croak freaks me out."

Emery couldn't hold her mocking laughter at bay.

Arson looked down whenever he could. But Mandy's pink shirt, half unbuttoned, made him sweat. He felt guilty for being curious.

"Here you go," Arson said, handing Mandy the sundae.

"Thanks, Arson," she said, taking a lick of the ice cream. "You really know how to do it."

He folded his lips together. "Um, five fifty," he mumbled. It seemed awkward charging her for the ice cream, but he noticed Ray's vicious glare out of the corner of his eye.

Mandy had a shocked look on her face but began digging into her Prada purse, looking for change.

"Arson, I feel like such a ditz. I left my wallet in my other purse. Is there any way I could pay you back? You know I'm good for it." She winked at him, slowly licking the top layer of the ice cream before it started to melt.

Arson swallowed hard. A lump hung in his throat. He glanced at the back office, looked at Emery, then Mandy. His hands felt sticky and sweaty all of a sudden, and in the back of his mind, he could hear his own conscience, in all of its teenage wisdom, shouting *Mayday!*

He caught another glimpse of Mandy's thick lips and her pencil-thin features he imagined might one day grace the cover of *Maxim*. His mind wandered back to the night he'd spent with her.

"Okay," Arson sighed. It was inevitable. He was weak. Practically paralyzed. He couldn't refuse her even though he wanted to. Even though he knew he should. His shoulders sagged, exposing the weak boy that he was, a boy who cared more about his hormones than his job or the girl whose feelings he knew he had just crushed.

Mandy left quickly. Reaching into his pocket for a five-dollar bill and some change, Arson heard Ray call out his name from the back office.

"And the Lord shall smite the wicked," Emery sighed, seeming more disappointed than angry.

"Pray for me," Arson replied before rushing to the back to receive retribution. Part of him wanted her to wait until he returned, but as soon as he blinked, she was gone too.

TWENTY-SIX

Grandma was walking on glass, her feet cut up and covered in blood. Arson couldn't tell what it was she was doing or why, only that fear was written on every wrinkle and crack in her face. Blood and life itself completely drained from those white-washed pores. Stone-cold and heartless eyes. Tears streamed down her chin, and as soon as he arrived, she began trying to fix the mess she'd made of the kitchen.

Wine glasses and splintered wood littered the floor. Her gray, wiry strands of hair stuck to parts of her face like thick pieces of burnt thread. White lines created boundaries between her nose and parched lips. She was cloaked in bed sheets and rested her head on the antique hutch that stood perpendicular to the kitchen entrance and the hallway.

Arson looked around the room with shock. The crunch beneath him gave off an eerie feeling, which rested right at the center of his gut. He swallowed and observed Grandma for a long moment. It had been a while since he'd seen her like this. He'd seen bits of fingernails stuck in the wallpaper where she'd scratched and then bled. His first instinct was to help her clean up, but Grandma started to attack him.

"Get out of my house!" she demanded. "You're a villain. A creep trying to steal from an old woman. You should be ashamed of yourself."

"Grandma, don't you know who I am? What happened to you?"

"Oh no," she kept saying. Her eyes were like a child's. "Unhand me, you pervert. What would you want with an old woman, pig?"

"It's me," he said frantically. He blocked her incoming strikes, shutting his eyes when her fingers weren't stuck in them. "It's me ... It's me!"

She was stronger than usual. Every time their eyes met, Arson was afraid. Grandma had lost the sense of perspective, of reason. This was the creature Arson feared the most, the one without conscience or feeling. The dead one who lived inside of his grandmother, imprisoned for a time. The one who beat him and said hurtful things or took pleasure in ensuring his pain. A woman ruled by fear and bitterness.

"Grandma, I want to help you." Arson fought her as best as he could without hurting her. The sheets slipped off during the struggle, revealing a naked body underneath. Weathered skin dripped off her bones. Sun spots plagued certain areas of her flesh, and countless wrinkles fell over her kneecaps and thighs. His eyes noticed things he'd never seen before. Tortuous veins running down her legs like green spider webs. Teeth missing and the cracked skin of old age. He tried to cover her up, but she refused him with strikes to the face.

"Grandma, it's me. Please let me help you. What's the matter?"

"Why bother? Take a good look, pig. Take a photograph while you're at it. The whole world out there is full of perverts like you. Henry? Henry?" she called out.

"Grandma, it's me. Don't you recognize me?"

"Go ahead, get your jollies out." She made a fist and struck him on the nose. Her eyes lit up when blood poured out.

"Please just tell me what's wrong."

"Why do you keep calling me Grandma? I don't know you. Henry?" She walked around the kitchen, glass and ceramic plates slicing into her heel. "Henry, come save me from this . . . this menace."

She swung a piece of glass at Arson, but he ducked down to the floor, cutting up his palms. "I'm not a criminal. I love you. Can't you see that?"

"Henry, this pervert means to harm me. Save me from this place, Henry. Save me."

Arson tried holding her, but she wouldn't let him. She reached for a piece of glass from the floor and threatened to cut him. "What are you doing, Grandma?" Arson said, moving backward.

He watched Grandma shake, blood from her hand slipping out onto the tile. "I swear, I'll cut you if you don't tell me who you really are."

"Arson Gable. I'm your grandson. Remember your daughter? She died giving birth to me because I'm different." Arson could feel the rage pumping through him. He was angry enough. With painful effort and struggle, the fire obeyed him. A spark lit up his palm. "Remember?"

"You're lying," she spat.

He moved closer, trying to get the glass out of her hand. His heart wanted to explode. The thought of life without her made him nearly sick. His grandmother screamed, exposing the jagged shards of metal that were her teeth. Carefully, Arson took another step toward her. "It's okay," he told her. "I'm here for you, Grandma."

Quickly, Arson quenched the small spark and rushed her, stealing away the piece of glass. She yelled and fought him. He struggled as she seized his wrist with her teeth. It stung, but he suppressed the pain. Grabbing the bed sheet off the floor, he collided into her frail body and wrapped her in his arms. She hit her head. Signs of bruising appeared above her eyebrow, beneath the strands of gray wire. She was a ghost.

"Stephen?" she asked softly.

Arson stared into her. He hadn't heard her call him that in many years. In fact, he swore he didn't even recognize that name. He moved away from her, partly afraid, partly uncertain. Relief traded for questions.

"Stephen, it's you. My daughter's child. I remember you now."

The fire hadn't worked to convince Grandma who he was. It wasn't enough to show her he wasn't a villain. *She had to see it in my eyes,* he thought. *She had to know it was me, if it's me at all.*

Arson fought to look away, but everything inside of him led him back again. "Yeah, it's me, Grandma." He still couldn't believe what he was saying. Still couldn't believe that was his name. She called him Arson, but his name was Stephen. He remembered now, but he prayed he could forget.

"Where's Henry?" she said, clawing at his shirt. "He didn't save me. Where's my Henry?"

Arson gathered his wits. He had sworn he would never say it. Sworn he never could. But in this moment, he knew it was the only thing he could do. "Grandma, he's dead."

"No, he can't be." Her voice cracked. "I went to bed with him last night. He's up there waiting for me right now. I'm sure of it."

Arson struggled getting the words out. "No, he's not. Grandpa died two years ago. Heart failure. 'Some hearts just aren't strong enough.' That's what you said when he died, Grandma. Remember?"

She sobbed and fell into him. "He's dead?"

Arson held her close and never wanted to let go. The image of his grandfather lying lifeless in his bed returned for the first time—a rush of pain, bitterness, and grief storming the shores he'd kept guarded for two years. Embracing her made him recall what it had been like touching the dead body before the medics carried it away. He remembered the cold and dreary day of the funeral; he was the only one standing beside a lonely grave. Grandma was too broken to bear it.

"He's dead," Arson said again with tears in his eyes. And it became real to him.

Arson laid her in bed and listened to her breathing for a few moments until she fell asleep. He hid his face in his hands. The blood from his nose had already begun to dry at the top of his lip, so he grabbed a towel. With hands still trembling, he walked downstairs in silence.

As he stepped into the kitchen, flashes of his grandmother so weak and angry flooded in. He tried hard to reorganize it the way he remembered, but his memory was a mess. The picture frames, the hutch with broken china inside, the table covered with newspaper shreds. He wanted this scene placed back in the dark of his mind where it belonged, but it wouldn't stay. He watched his grandfather die over and over again.

He went to the closet to get the broom and the dustpan. While Arson swept the broken dishes and glass fragments into a pile, he wiped away hot tears, but they kept coming. *This is me,* he thought, *broken dishes and shards of glass.* It hurt, but he had to be strong for her.

Much of the glass from the hutch had been shattered. Fragments still stuck inside the oak frame came loose with enough pulling. As he ripped and struggled with the wood, the thought of losing his job earlier that day hit him. He wouldn't tell Grandma, couldn't. She'd freak out. The money left over from Grandpa's life insurance would have to be enough, at least until he could clear his mind again and fix things.

Arson rearranged the picture frame within the hutch, the one that held the three of them at Mystic Aquarium. He remembered that day. But even then he hadn't smiled. None of them had. Maybe none of them could. Nevertheless, a picture like this let him forget for a brief moment in time what he was.

TWENTY-SEVEN

Arson didn't like Emery avoiding him. She seemed so skilled at it. It was all still very strange for him to believe that it even bothered him. Some chick with a mask threatening to cut herself out of his life.

Good, go ahead.

No, it wasn't that easy. It wasn't just cut and dried, sever the ties and be done with it. He didn't operate that way. He couldn't let go of Grandpa that way, couldn't remove even someone as vindictive as his grandmother from his mind. He had never been so consumed about anyone or anything before. Part of him wondered what it was exactly that he felt for Emery. Was it love? Tolerance? Ridiculous, blind hope? He seemed so desperate and pathetic.

You've gotta grow up sometime, Arson, he thought. *Be a man, not a boy, and get past her.*

But he couldn't do that. He didn't want to.

He'd told himself again and again that volunteering would be a mistake, especially after what she'd seen him do at Tobey's. Man, he could be so stupid. He'd tried to talk to her, but she had headphones in her ears most of the time and barely even looked his way.

It was awkward walking around the hospital without direction or a clue of what to do, apart from taking orders from a mask. Filling up cups with water and dropping snacks off upon cranky requests was enough to make him go nuts. The fact that he had even showed up was a miracle, but it wasn't like Emery knew that. Wasn't like she had any idea that he'd spent hours of the morning depressed in his bed, sweating.

Arson followed behind her. Well, it was probably more like stalking. She'd divided her shift with another volunteer so that she'd see less of Arson during the day. Said she had nothing to say to him. During lunch break, he found her in the café and tried to strike up some semblance of a conversation, but all attempts ended in her ignoring him.

"I don't understand why you're so mad," he said, rushing up behind her. She tilted her head toward him but said nothing.

He could tell she was enjoying watching him squirm, her satisfaction and delight apparent by the way she carried herself down the hallways—blissful, like nothing was the matter even when it was.

Emery continued rolling the cart down the third-floor hallway. All he wanted was forgiveness.

He rolled his eyes, sighed, coughed, and watched her walk deliberately fast. But if she picked up speed, he picked up speed. Arson hated these childish games, but it seemed like the only chance to get closer to her.

She stopped all of a sudden. Abe's room. Arson had spent so much time trying to get Emery to talk to him that he'd forgotten about Abe altogether. He put aside pride, ambition, and all hopes of a conversation and just followed her shadow inside.

"Good afternoon, you young lovebirds," Abe said, attempting to hide the bloodstained handkerchief.

"Abraham, don't start!" Emery said, taking out her headphones. "The last thing I even want to think about is being with someone like him."

"What did you do?" Abe said weakly, looking at Arson.

"He acted like a complete love-drunk sap bag."

"Love-drunk sap bag?" Abe said. "That's a new one. If I were you, kid, I'd start with flowers and chocolates, after begging for forgiveness. Soften her right up."

"Abraham, just pretend he's not even here. My mom gave him a ride today, even though I told her not to."

"Man, oh, man, for someone so young and charming, you'd think you would be happy."

"You're right, Abraham, but I really don't need a lecture right now, okay? Now, do you want the surprise or not?"

Abe turned once more to Arson and whispered, "It's like I just ran over her cat or something."

"Don't feel bad," Arson said. "At least she's talking to you."

Emery pulled out a plastic container filled with what appeared to be apple juice.

"See what I mean? She won't even acknowledge me. It's like I'm a ghost."

Abe laughed. "What I wouldn't have given for a relationship like that back in my day."

Emery stood with her hand on her waist.

"Oh, what? I'm old-fashioned. The pretty gals are best seen and ... oh, I always forg—oh, right, not heard."

"Are you old-fashioned or sexist?"

"Is there a difference?" Abe roared in amusement, but soon his laughs turned to throaty coughs, deep and mixed with red phlegm. "I'm only having fun with you, Emery. Take it easy."

"I'm sorry. I'm being rude. You didn't do anything, Abraham. It's not your fault. I should just know better than to trust other people."

Abe smiled and told her to laugh more. Arson wanted to understand Emery, but didn't she see that he was human? That he made mistakes and wasn't perfect? It wasn't fair, her treating him this way. It wasn't fair that Grandma could have a mental breakdown—several—and he was just expected to keep running things as normal. It wasn't fair that there was a flame inside of him. It wasn't fair that he was falling for such a fun—at times emotionally complicated—girl like Emery.

She started to pour the beverage into a cup.

"Don't get old like me," Abe said, sinking back into his pillow.

"I'll try," Emery said with a certain cheer in her voice. "Abe, do you remember the one wish you asked me for a few weeks ago when I started volunteering?"

"Of course I do. The wish ain't changed."

"Well, consider this my chance to make an old man happy one last time."

Emery handed him the cup, and he took it with shocked eyes and shaky hands.

"My little dynamite. I hope I've not corrupted you. I mean, what would your parents think of me?"

"I hardly think they'd care at this point. Forget about them. I just want you to be happy. And I know I'm not your granddaughter, but hopefully you'll remember me. I care about you, Abraham."

"Don't get all sappy on me. We don't have enough tissues for the both of us." His lips spread out into a warm grin.

"It's probably flat, but it's the best I could do."

He smelled the drink before sipping it. "Where'd you get it? It's not exactly easy for a preacher's daughter to get a hold of stuff like this."

"You'd be surprised. You have to promise to keep this between us. If anyone finds out about this, I'm officially d-e-a-d."

"You don't have to worry about me. I'm no snitch. Thank you, baby."

Abe took a long sip, rolled his eyes back, and relished the moment. Arson stared at the stretchy flesh that made up Abe's throat, watched his Adam's apple bob up and down as he swallowed the sweet new taste of an old desire. It was peaceful.

Emery waited for Abe to finish his cup and wrapped the contents covertly beneath the Jell-O tray.

Aimee wanted him so badly. She'd imagined making love to him in her sleep and even while she was awake. The way Carlos might kiss her. Would his lips taste the same? Or had they been jaded from twenty-five years of listless lovers? The thoughts had taken her away from much of what needed to be done around the hospital. During her shifts, patients were put on hold, and other nurses were asked to wait until Aimee finished reapplying makeup, ruffling her hair, anything to catch Carlos's attention when he passed her in the hallways. She could get a smile out of him in public, but she craved more.

She was the one who had changed, after all. Trading a life of mystery and fun for an organized one secluded in churches and lonely bedrooms. The man she loved was in love with other things, like congregations and beer. Was she really all that guilty? After all, there were plenty of times when Joel glanced far too long at choir directors or cute ushers during a morning service. Long hours spent during the week *counseling* and *ministering,* as he said, while she and Emery ate dinner cold.

Aimee had always wondered if this would happen, used to fear it. Most girls spent their wedding nights embracing their husbands. Aimee had been held, but she couldn't help thinking that one day she might break Joel's heart, like she'd broken Carlos's heart and others before him. When they hugged or got romantic, she'd get the feeling, and it would consume every waking breath. She had been just strong enough to keep stray thoughts at bay these long years. But she'd always wanted to look, wanted to dream again of something sweeter, more right, of a love uncorrupted by family ties or religion or friends.

"So, how have you been adjusting to the environment, Aimee, since we spoke a few weeks ago?" Carlos asked, breaking the silence. His voice gave her chills.

"Better." Lie. Could he tell? "I'm only here to make ends meet for my family." Okay, that was at least partly true.

"Really?"

No. She was here for him. It had always been Carlos. It should have been Carlos.

"Coming back to work hasn't exactly been easy for me, but it's nice to get away once in a while."

"Get away?" he asked.

"From my life. Joel and I aren't exactly talking right now. We're going through some hard times. My husband especially."

Now he would understand that this wasn't just about her and her family but about him. She was thinking about him, dreaming about him, longing for him. It had taken her weeks to finally be honest with herself. Maybe now she could be honest with him.

"So remind me again what happened." Carlos stroked his chin and twitched his lips a certain welcoming way. Aimee remembered him doing it often when they used to date.

She smiled and then paused, not sure if she was ready to share something so personal. But the sound of a ticking clock at the back of the office provoked her to speak. "My husband's church kicked us out when they found him drinking in the office. It was a Tuesday, I remember, when we got the news that he was out of a job. The last thing they wanted was an inebriated fool for a pastor. They called us heathens."

"Ouch. Whatever happened to love in the church, huh?"

"Well, I can't say I blame them. Joel came home drunk one night and I nearly had a heart attack. But it's not exactly catching-up conversation, is it?"

"Well, we've been catching up for the last couple of weeks, haven't we?"

A pause.

"I so wish we'd kept in touch, Aimee. Think of all the time we've lost. All the memories we might have shared."

Aimee's fingers cut through her hair, as she leaned up in the chair. "It wouldn't have been right. I am a married woman."

"The girl I used to know went out of her way to bend the rules. I'd hate to see a little church ruin that free spirit."

"Free spirit? Is that what they're calling promiscuity these days?"

"C'mon." He shrugged. "Don't be so hard on yourself. I'm not throwing any stones here. We had fun in the past, didn't we?"

She leaned back and tried to sit up straight but couldn't quite get comfortable. "I was young and naïve."

"But we were in love."

"It was a long time ago, Carlos. We're different people now." Goosebumps chilled her forearm. "It was a different life. We were just kids. I didn't know what I wanted."

"If you ask me, you still don't."

An arrow she wasn't ready for. His words pierced deep and left a scar to prove it. "I don't remember asking for your two cents."

Carlos raised his hands in defense. "I crossed the line, didn't I? Please forgive me, Aimee. You're absolutely right; we have changed. I'm just glad one of us has found happiness. That's rare in today's world. I can only hope that one day I, too can find it." He got up and courted her out of the office. "I've got to go in for surgery soon."

"Yeah, and I've got patients to attend to. Carlos, I'm not sure these visits to your office in the middle of the day are the best thing for either of us. I don't want to ruin your reputation." She wanted him to say something, anything. She loved to hear his voice. The way it cracked through the air. She could smell his breath when he got up close. Still sweet.

At length, Carlos replied, "Don't worry about it, Aimee. Like I said, you were never one to play it safe. Look, if you need anything, you know I'll always be here for you."

She nodded. An answer she needed.

The door to the office closed behind them. They went off in opposite directions down the hall, but Aimee looked back.

TWENTY-EIGHT

The ride home bordered on agonizing. Arson had his head up against the window when Emery started blasting loud music through the back speakers, right next to his ear. The front speakers, she argued, didn't get the sound right. Ignoring her mother's comment to lower it, she continued humming along to the song's chaotic jam. Arson tried to talk to her above the noise, but she said she couldn't hear him. He knew it was a mistake after all to think she could forgive him.

As soon as they arrived home, Emery made a run for the front door.

"Can we call a truce?" he asked, frustrated.

Emery stopped at the foot of the porch. "Why?"

"Because I'm sorry, Emery," he said. "I know I hurt you. And I'm so sorry."

"Oh, right. When you decided to give that slut a free sundae. Is that what you're talking about?"

Aimee turned off the ignition and rushed inside, leaving them to quarrel in peace.

"Do you hate me?" Arson asked, the distance between them like miles of empty space.

"Right now, yeah. But you can't take it back, so I guess you're gonna have to get used to it."

"Emery, it was a stupid ice cream. This is ridiculous!"

"Not to me it isn't. I thought you were different."

"I am different."

"No, you're not. You're just like every other guy I've met. Why don't you just get outta here? Go be with her if that's what you want. You two deserve each other."

It wasn't what he wanted. In fact, if he could write in the stars, it would be Emery's name next to his. Arson wanted to tell her how he felt about her, tell her that she was the only thing he could think about, that even when he was with Mandy, *she* was on his mind.

"I don't want to be enemies, Emery. I want us to be better. I made a mistake, and I'm begging you to forgive me. I'm thankful that today happened. We got to do something special for Abraham. Man, did you see him smile?"

"*I* did something special for Abraham. You happened to be there."

Arson grunted.

"You know, I wanted to tell you about it. I walked all the way to your lame job just to tell you. But yesterday's performance proved you really don't care about me. I still can't believe you let her manipulate you like that."

"I can't even talk to you. You're acting crazy."

"Maybe I am crazy. Maybe I'm a freak."

Arson shook his head. "Whatever. For the record, I got fired. Hope you're happy; justice is served."

Emery ran to him, her mask rushing toward his face. "You just don't get it, do you?" She staggered around the lawn, throwing her hands up in surrender.

"Emery, I don't know what you want. I said I was sorry. I spent the whole day trying to somehow earn your forgiveness. Maybe you don't want this to work."

"What?"

"Whatever this is. Us."

She began to cry. "So what? Now I'm supposed to believe you actually care about me?"

"Maybe. Look, I thought...I don't know. I guess we were both wrong."

"Now I'm going to lose you too?" she said.

Arson glared at her, confused.

"Maybe I'm jealous, Arson. Okay? My life isn't picture perfect. My dad is a failed minister, and my mom is a nitpicking control freak. I have a family that's falling apart. I thought that if I reached out enough times, people might see me as something else, something other than a girl with a mask. When I volunteer at the hospital, that's what those dying people see. They see a person. I don't have a pretty face, but I'm still human."

He watched as she crumbled.

"Mandy's manipulative. And you're blind if you can't see that. She probably has everything in the world, including you, wrapped around her pretty little finger." She sobbed. "I wish I were beautiful. I wish I could make you look at me the way you look at her. But you wouldn't like what's underneath."

Arson couldn't believe how cruel he'd been. Insensitive and unsympathetic. He swore it wasn't intentional. But he had problems to deal with too. At least she had a family, a mother, a father. Arson never had the chance to meet his parents. Instead, he had a mother who died giving birth to an unnatural creature like him. And a father who walked away. He didn't even know his name. Could she understand what a burden like that was?

Arson quieted his mind and gave himself a moment to think. He wanted to see Emery happy. Staring into her eyes, Arson reached toward the back of her head and began untying the mask. At first, Emery was reluctant. She put her hands up and tried to resist, but Arson had already unraveled the string. The mask slipped off in his hands, and he could see her clearly for the first time.

The two of them remained still and quiet.

Arson counted his heartbeats and watched her eyes dance around him. Sections of her skin glistened with a pasty pink color. Bumpy scar tissue perverted the upper right side of her forehead, the front of her scalp eaten away. Scars littered her neck and chin. Arson wanted to break as she looked up at him with eyes that could hold oceans.

"You're looking at me weird. Like I'm a monster," she said.

He gently touched her cheek. "This is what you were afraid of?"

She slowly nodded.

Arson licked his chapped lips and let the flutters inside him subside. "You're beautiful, Emery."

"No one has touched my face since I was a little girl," she said, still crying. "Sometimes I wish I were dead. Every day I have to look at this mask. I hate the way it makes me feel. I hate the fact that I can't change it. This creature is what I am now. I wish I could go back—"

"Emery, what happened to you?" Arson whispered, his voice changing from sympathetic to concerned.

She wiped her nose with the back of her hand, tears streaming down her blood-red cheeks. "Nothing. Just stupid boys."

Arson was silent.

"I hate them for what they did to me. I know I shouldn't, but they turned me into this freak."

He lifted her chin and looked into her eyes. He began to drown.

"I was ten. The last time I remember being happy. I can still see that blinding light as the fire hit my eyes. Right before everything went black." She sniffled between breaths. "I don't want to think about it anymore."

"Emery?" A wave of realization rushed over him. "Oh God."

"I was a good girl. I would've been pretty. Then you might have loved me. Maybe they'd love me too." She grinded her teeth.

Arson's hands went cold, dead. He was ice. He was regret.

"It doesn't matter anymore. It was an accident that changed my life. They were just stupid boys playing with fire."

The image of the exploding firecracker forced Arson's eyes shut. He was running again, always running. Cambridge. Night. Cold. Deep breaths. No breaths. Fear.

Suddenly, Arson felt a tingling in his palm, and then it turned hotter, more painful. He panted, the images of himself as a ten-year-old boy like flashes of lightning. Then the screams came, silencing everything. Arson pushed her away.

She quickly put the mask back on. It seemed to glare back at him with sinister pleasure, scraping away the darkness.

She drew near, but he was a statue. His molars ached, his knuckles cracked. His heart boomed in the pulse.

"What is it?" she asked, as he started running away.

Emery dangled her head over the toilet bowl, puking out regret. The sick feeling in her stomach expanded and expanded until all viable space was devoured. She imagined herself as somebody else, somebody hung over from the greatest party she'd ever crashed, the kinds of parties she'd heard other people her age talk about. The ones she never got invited to.

Bile poured out of her, stinging as it bubbled up the back of her throat. She watched in a dizzy haze as drops of what she had eaten for lunch sank into the pool and then floated back to the top. The smell made her hurl even more.

After a few minutes of self-condemnation, there was a loud knock on the door. It was her father. She told him to go away.

Emery didn't know why, but it felt like spiders were crawling across her skin. Big, hairy spiders with no sympathy for an ugly girl. They wanted the mask. They wanted her. The haunting sensation made her take off the mask and throw it across the bathroom floor.

"I'm so stupid," she slurred.

Emery flushed the toilet, brushed her hair back, and sighed. Empty. She stepped into the shower with her clothes on and turned the faucet. She'd seen Arson drown himself in the lake. Maybe it would help her too. Maybe it could help her forget how stupid she was for letting him see her.

Within seconds, hot needles began trickling out the steel lip, licking her skin as it rained down. The water disguised her tears, red circles swelling around her cheeks and eyes. She sank down in the tub, tucking her head into her knees. The dreaded mask glared back at her from the tile floor, its haunting grin sending a new chill through her bones.

Emery cried awhile, constantly scratching her face and wishing that for one moment she could be beautiful, for real.

TWENTY-NINE

Arson's ears boomed as he sank into the lake, waiting for the currents of sorrow to pull him down.

He listened for anything other than the screams, something quieter than the mayhem of an exploding mistake. Under water, he could see Emery's face. It waved and floated away with the tide. He screamed, but the drone of boats cutting through the water stole away the lake's sympathy. Air bubbles popped in and out of his nose, his face a red balloon filled with turmoil.

His eyes burned; everything burned.

Emery looked out over the lake and the body that lay within it. It was like déjà vu. Just a few weeks ago she had been here, standing in the same spot, fearing for the life of a complete stranger. What did he find underneath that dark blue current? Was it peace? Or hope?

She watched him diligently. Any minute now he'd come back, right? There wasn't a chance she was diving in after him, not this time. She just stared. Emery didn't even know she was studying the shape of his back while she did it or the undersized muscles that formed the lower half of his triceps, that little bit of ash occupying the flesh of his elbow. She folded her arms, unable to look away as his moppy hair lapped the water slowly. She reminded herself not to panic.

"What are you, part fish?" Emery mumbled to herself.

Enough. She had to talk to him. She huffed, untied one of her shoes, and threw it at his back. The body suddenly jerked. She imagined the expanding and collapsing of Arson's lungs, while he wiped his face and pulled himself up onto the dock.

"Is this yours?" Arson asked, tossing her the beat-up sneaker.

She shrugged and placed it back on her foot. Not a gasp, not even a look in her direction. Was she that hideous that he couldn't even glance at her for a moment? Emery ignored the wet and squishy feeling that slipped around between her toes.

"What do you want?" he said, barely audible.

"Do I need an excuse to come by and see you?"

He told her he didn't want to talk, but that wasn't a good enough reason for her to quit. She wondered if he'd actually practiced such a dark, reclusive stare.

"Was last night a mistake?" she asked after a short pause.

Arson chewed his lip.

"I mean, you tell me I'm beautiful, and then you just run away. Are you trying to hurt me? I was vulnerable, Arson, and you took advantage of that."

"No, I didn't. I mean, I didn't mean to."

"Try to understand. Underneath this mask, I'm safe, and I don't have to worry about jerks like you running away in the middle of a conversation. I feel like it was a mistake letting you see me like that."

"I'm sorry." His eyes were far from hers.

"You can only say it so many times before it loses meaning, Arson."

Drops of water slid from one side of his face to the other. Dragging his unclipped fingernails across random spots of facial hair, Arson squinted from the sunlight and started walking toward the cabin. "I can't do this right now," he said from a distance. "I'm sorry. I just can't."

Emery didn't move for half an hour. She cried, though more out of frustration than a crushed ego. She'd had a lot of practice getting treated badly, people looking down on her, if they bothered to look at her at all. But it was different when Arson did it.

Cracking her knuckles seemed to alleviate some of the tension building up inside her. But once that ran its course, she remembered she hadn't yet tied her shoe. The sudden distraction of tying a shoelace seemed to make a lot of sense at the moment. Memories flashed back of when she was six and finally mastered such a simplistic art form. What a marvel it had been back then. How pathetic it seemed now, when everything she had ever wanted was about to slip right through her fingers.

Emery checked her pulse. "I'm still alive." She breathed, almost reluctantly. Marching up to Arson's doorstep and telling him off seemed impossible. *Don't be a baby,* she thought. *Just walk up to him and demand some answers. This world's too small for two weirdos.* She took a step toward the cabin.

What if he says he never wants to see me again? Frozen in place. After a second to think about it, she said aloud, "No, that's not gonna happen. Pull yourself together, Emery."

A drop of relief came. Or maybe that was a little bit of sweat sticking to the hair on the back of her neck. Anxious, she took another step. She was a goner; she was sure of it. For a moment, she started walking the other way but suddenly redirected herself once more toward Arson's front door.

Taking a deep breath, she rushed up the porch and knocked. "Arson, I know you're in there. I haven't moved from your lawn for the last half hour. That may sound sketchy, but I need some answers. Why won't you talk to me?"

Footsteps approached. Suddenly, a thousand wilting flowers began to bloom inside of her. Then an old woman opened the door.

"Henry's dead," the old woman said. There was a brief pause. "Who the devil are you?"

"Um," Emery began, startled by the naked old woman in front of her. "I'm looking for Arson. I need to talk to somebody."

"Then get a shrink. Didn't you hear me? My Henry's dead. Now, who are you?"

"My name is Emery Phoenix. I live in that house over there." She pointed, trying to blot out the image of saggy skin, the wiry gray hair in awkward places. "We've met before. Don't you remember?"

"Oh yeah, the freak with the mask."

"Grandma!" Arson yelled from the kitchen. "What are you doing?" His shadow rushed toward them.

"Hi," he mumbled weakly, looking at Emery.

The mask nodded.

"Grandma, please go put some clothes on," he suggested, trying to cover her up with his body.

Kay formed a smile and began walking away but turned back to say that Henry was dead one last time.

Arson waited for her to disappear behind the staircase. "I told you I can't do this right now."

"Is she all right?" Emery asked.

Arson sighed and answered after a long moment. "I think it's finally starting to settle in."

"What?"

He leaned on the door, half his body inside, half outside. "The fact that my grandfather passed away. It's been two years. I guess everybody crashes and burns sometime, right?"

"Whoa. Your grandfather's dead? But she said—"

"It's a coping mechanism. Her mind never really accepted it, I guess. Grandma's been denying the truth for so long. I just couldn't take it anymore. I had to say something."

"Arson, I'm so sorry."

"Yeah, well, life happens. Look, Emery, this isn't really a good time."

"When would it be a good time?"

"I don't know. Never?"

"I know you're avoiding me, but we need to talk. Last night … you just took off. What got into you?"

"As you can see, I've got a lot on my hands. I lost my job, my grandmother is freaking out, and now you. Maybe we shouldn't hang out anymore."

"Arson, what's wrong with you? I'm sorry for being slightly overbearing. But if you weren't so sensitive, we could talk this out like rational people." She paced the porch floorboards. "You know, for someone who so desperately wants redemption, you're not very quick to offer it."

Fear dripped down his spine. "I think it might be better for both of us if you forget you ever knew me."

"I can't do that. We live next door to each other, for heaven's sake. Besides, you've kind of grown on me."

Arson's eyes were distant.

"Look at *me*. Why won't you look at me?" Emery shoved him in the chest. "Am I disgusting? Am I that hideous? You can't even look at me."

Arson grabbed her by the arm and pulled her close. "You couldn't possibly understand. Every time I look at you, I'm reminded of it. My regret."

"What are you talking about?"

Arson finally looked deep into her eyes. "Seven years ago, we lived in Cambridge. My friend and I were bored, and we wanted to play a game. He dared me. Emery, it was an accident. I swear we never meant to hurt anyone."

She listened but was confused.

"I was just a stupid kid who should've kept to himself. I never thought … It was only a game." He looked out over the lake. The current moved violently. The sky bled gray.

Arson turned around. "It was a firecracker, Emery. I didn't want to do it. It all happened in a blink. I'm there again. I can hear it. I can hear the little girl. You, Emery, it's you. No one was supposed to get hurt. You believe me, right? It was an accident."

"Arson, I'm confused."

He locked gazes with her.

"Look, that's terrible what happened. Was the girl okay?"

His eyes were wet, his mouth dry, and his body rigid. "I don't know, you … Wait, what?"

"The girl. What ended up happening to her?"

"Emery, don't you see? I did this to you. Your face. I hurt you, and now I can't bear it. I jump in the lake sometimes to try to forget, try to cope. Hoping that one day I'll find forgiveness somehow for what I've done. What I am."

Emery whispered something to herself. Looking up at him, she placed her hands inside his. "They're warm," she said.

He didn't respond.

Touching his chest, she could feel his heart beating. "It's a little crazy inside too, huh? Arson, I'm sorry that you had to suffer that conviction for so many years. It's simply awful what happened to that little girl. But it wasn't me." A faint smile split her lips. "What happened to me wasn't your fault."

"Yes it is. I was stupid. I was afraid. I don't deserve to know you. Not after what I've done."

"Arson, it's not your fault. I'm sorry for the girl in your story, but I swear it isn't me."

He stepped back.

Emery walked toward the bench at the far end of the porch and sat down. "This is crazy. I never thought I'd have to tell you this. My cousins and I decided to have a bonfire behind my house one night. They were much older than me. My parents went out for the evening; they hadn't been on a date in months."

Her voice broke into pieces as she tried to laugh. "They left my *responsible* cousins in charge. Didn't know there'd be drugs. So Kyle and Tyler invited their girlfriends to the house, and then they got stoned, while I tried to amuse myself for three hours. I just wanted s'mores, you know?"

Sobs invaded her thoughts. "They were playing football near the fire. Suddenly, I see Eric rushing for the ball, and in no time he's crashing into me. I couldn't see much of anything, except the fire. I remember the way it felt as it burned my skin."

Arson wasn't sure if words were enough. Thoughts sure weren't. He still couldn't wrap his brain around the idea that when it came to Emery, he was innocent. He wasn't responsible for ruining her life. But he hated seeing her so distraught and torn. He wanted to make it right, fix the broken parts of her if he could. If she'd let him.

"The next thing I know," Emery continued, "I'm waking up in a hospital bed with bright lights and gauze on my face. After that, it felt better to just keep it all hidden. My parents knew it was an accident, but they were a mess. Never trusted me alone with any-body. Our families became estranged. It's funny. One night can change everything."

Arson blinked. Suddenly, it was air in his lungs that he was breathing and not regret. He pulled Emery close and held her tightly. He could've held her forever.

THIRTY

Emery had never heard her mother say the word *divorce* before. The word meant an end, a separation, a mistake. It opposed everything they believed, everything she was holding onto. Her mother wanted to end things, wanted something better.

The fights Emery often overheard before bed or the ones her parents tried to keep discreet by passing vindictive glances across a dinner table rarely led to cursing. But the fights were taking on a whole new shape. Nothing said "welcome home" like screaming parents. Every room she walked into told of a fight, betrayed the afternoon's disagreement, spoke of discontentment and depleted love.

Emery cradled her head in her hands, waiting for her father to say something bold, something right, anything to calm the situation and make sense of it all. But he didn't.

She counted the minutes, the seconds, the milliseconds. When would it stop? *Divorce* kept playing in her mind like a bad recording. Repeat. Stop. Repeat. *Divorce.* Rewind. Repeat. *Divorce.* It was real.

Emery moseyed up the stairs. She crawled to the corner of her parents' bedroom door, beside the dust collecting on the floor moulding. Emery found a place to listen and to cry.

"Sweetheart, what is so important? I'm trying to talk to you, and all you care about is checking your voicemail. Expecting someone special to call?"

"Don't be ridiculous, Joel," her mother snarled. "Get away from me. I can't talk to you like this."

"Can't or won't? Aimee, what's happening?"

"What do you mean?"

"I mean, what is happening to you, to this family? I make you breakfast, you refuse to eat. I try to spruce up the house, and there's always a reason why you can't help me or a piece of furniture that doesn't quite match the décor you had in mind. It's like we're finding new ways to avoid one another. I want what we had before all of this."

"Please. What we had before wasn't all that special either."

"You're like a stranger, Aimee. Can you even remember the last time we were intimate?"

"So that's what this is about?"

"No, that's not what this is about."

"Yes, it is," she said. "You're upset because we haven't been intimate enough with each other. How can you expect me to be intimate with someone as self-ish or as stubborn as you?"

"Selfish?"

"I'm not some object, Joel, put on this earth to sat-isfy your every need. I can't help it if I'm not always in the mood."

"It seems like you haven't been *in the mood* for a long time," he said with air quotations.

"Maybe you're right," she spat.

"Baby, that's not the point. I love you. All I want is for us to try. Can we talk for five minutes?"

"Talk? You want to control me. I know this game. You want to spy on me in the middle of the night, check my phone calls, my e-mails. Imagine your inno-cent little wife in some sort of manipulated conspiracy. You're not my father, Joel."

"I never wanted to be. I love you. Why would I want to control you? I want to be with you, hold you. You're my wife."

She cringed. "All you do is preach. Don't you see, *baby?* Your church didn't want to listen to you. They were sick of being lied to. No one likes a hypocrite."

Joel sank into himself. A look of defeat ran across his face. Brokenness. With a lost stare, he wandered the room. He glanced at the half-painted, naked walls, the nightstand photograph of a happy couple turned on its face, the cardboard boxes they never unpacked, pieces of a past life buried inside.

"I feel like I don't know you anymore," he said. "I'm lonely when I'm not with you, and even lonelier when I am. Baby, I just want to talk. Let's work this out. I can be better. I can change. We can change."

"I don't want to listen anymore. For years I've listened, putting up with all your garbage, your lies. Watching you break promise after promise, forcing us to move because you screwed up."

"Aimee, how did we get here? We're a family. Is it too much for me to ask my wife to stand by me?"

"I was only ever there to absorb the blows. Emery and I are done taking the blame for you. We're drowning, Joel. Can't you see that? This isn't a marriage."

He gasped. "After everything we've been through, how can you say that?"

"It's *because* of everything we've been through that I can say that. You're a better liar than a pastor. A better drunk than a husband. You have loved everyone and everything more than you have loved us. More than you have ever loved me."

"That's a lie," he denied emphatically.

"Oh, really?" She rushed to the vanity and opened the top drawer. She pulled out three empty beer bottles. "Found these in your study, along with countless others scattered around this dump."

"I can explain," he said, raising his hands.

"Why don't you put it in that sermon you've been working so hard on? You know, the one taking time away from you getting a job. Relive the glory days.

Maybe one day, someday, you can lie to another con-gregation, manipulate them for a while. That's *if* they can't smell your breath."

Emery wanted to grab both of them by the necks and shake them until they loved each other again. She wanted to throw herself in and tell them how stupid and childish they were being, tell her mother how lame she sounded. Scream in the face of that once—preacher and let him know that her dreams died too, that this wasn't only about him, and how weak he came across.

But there was no use. Nothing she could do. She decided to go get changed. The pressure inside of her was filled to the breaking point. Any longer and she'd explode. Emery swore under her breath and rubbed her face. Listening to them fight made her body ache, the shrill sound of her mother's voice cutting through her.

"Once a drunk, always a drunk. You know, they say you marry someone just like your father. I guess the world was right. He lied to me too. What's next, Joel? Are you going to start hitting me?"

"I would never hurt you!" he screamed.

"Too late." She walked around him, one hand on her waist, the other on her hip. "Do you want to know what's happening to this family, Joel? It's dying."

"I made a mistake! For heaven's sake, can't you for-give me? I've done my best for you and Emery. I've always supported this family."

She grinned. "Would eating leftover Chinese food in the living room count as your husbandly contribution? What about getting drunk in the middle of the afternoon?"

"You want the truth!" Joel hollered. "I can barely get up in the morning. I go to bed so afraid of waking up, because I know that when I do, I'm going to have to face everything. Face you, our daughter, my failures. You think I don't care about this family? You think I don't know how torn apart my life has become? I never wanted to move either. I am afraid, Aimee. Look at me; my hands never stop shaking."

She ignored him and looked away.

"You can't even look at me. How can you expect me to go on living as if nothing's changed?"

"People get divorced every day."

"But not us. How many of those people lost their church? How many of them are so consumed with fear that they can't find hope in crawling out of bed in the morning? Tell me how I am supposed to feel, Aimee."

"Numb," she whispered under her breath.

"Emery and I are growing further apart. It kills me inside. I can't take this anymore. I'm not invincible! I screwed up, and I'm willing to spend the rest of my life trying to fix it."

"Joel, you can't fix this. You're a liar and a drunk."

"No, I'm not," he replied weakly. "I'm a minister."

"It's time to wake up. This is reality. You did this, not me. You lost the church; you have the drinking problem."

"I'm not perfect, baby, but neither are you." He handed her the cell phone and walked downstairs to his study.

"I think there's a bottle left in the top drawer," she called down. Aimee dialed a number into the cell phone, put it to her ear, and then closed the bedroom door and locked it.

THIRTY-ONE

"My life is a living hell," Emery groaned, rolling the food cart down the hospice hallway. It felt empty. "I can't take it inside that house anymore. They fight so much. My dad can be so stupid and spineless sometimes. But it's not like my mom's a saint either. I just can't take it anymore!"

Arson didn't feel comfortable being back in the hospital. It was still somewhat awkward spending time with Emery. Part of him was thinking about the little girl. Was she okay? Sure, it wasn't Emery he had run away from seven years ago, but he still had a debt to repay to someone he'd never even met. Emery couldn't forgive him for what plagued him most.

"Are you even listening? Arson?" She stopped the cart and waved her hand in front of him. "Is anyone home?"

He blinked when she snapped her fingers. "What?"

She sighed. "Never mind."

"What?"

"Is that all you can say?" she grunted. "Forget it."

Room 219. There was a stillness unlike anything either of them had ever felt before. It could be sensed the moment they stepped through the doorway. Cold and transparent, like a veil had been split between peace and misery, and this room lay somewhere in between. All they saw was a nurse fixing the bed. She seemed troubled, aware somehow of the questions Emery and Arson longed to ask. But she didn't look prepared to answer anything or maybe didn't know how. She was making the bed with brand new sheets, rearranging the machines in the room, avoiding eye contact with the mask as often as she could.

"We're not lepers, you know," Emery seethed. "You can look at us." It came out harsh, but the emptiness and cold within the room were undeniable.

"I'm so sorry," the nurse said, walking out of the room in a hurry.

"Sorry for what?"

The nurse just kept walking. They knew what sorry meant. They knew that no matter what they said, what they did, that nothing could bring an old, sarcastic man back to life.

"Abe's gone," Emery muttered almost soundlessly.

The light of midsummer reached in from the windowsill over the vacant bed and spread across the room. The truth hit Emery hard. Unable to hold back the tears for long, she threw her arms around Arson's neck.

He wanted to cry too but didn't. Couldn't. He had to be strong. Life was a war and lung cancer a powerful enemy. He had hoped that Grandpa's death might prepare him for a moment like this, but he was dead wrong.

Arson just stared down at an empty bed in an empty room with empty souls. All Emery could do was cry, and all he could do was tell her everything would be all right. A lie. Someday he'd have to deal with Abe's death, the bitter reality of it all. But not today.

"I hate this," Carlos said, closing the blinds of his office. "I hate sneaking around like we're in high school. We're adults, aren't we?"

She wanted him now more than ever. Aimee imagined his lips pressing into her skin. "We're adults with a past. If you keep buying me lunches, the other nurses and secretaries might get jealous."

"I told you not to worry about it. They know enough not to crap where they eat."

"So you're willing to compromise your own position too?"

"I didn't say that. Besides, I'm practically furniture around here. I keep to myself, and I think the rest of the staff knows better than to come between me and my work."

There was a drawn-out pause. Aimee's eyes shifted. "Work? So, this is what, business?"

"That's not what I meant."

"Joel has been checking my phone calls and my e-mails," she said quickly. "I've been able to delete most of the ones you've sent me. I feel like a prisoner in my own house."

"Don't you see, Aimee? He's trying to control every area of your life. Tell me again why you married him."

"He was different back then."

"And what happened to us?" Carlos asked.

"*You* were different back then." Aimee folded her hands and placed them in her lap. She wanted to hold him right then, to feel his fingertips stroke her body the way they used to. Staring into him again, his caramel skin, that black hair combed back in thick, wavy strands, those beady eyes like hunters that always seemed to find their target. She thought about what their life might have been like if she had said yes to his proposal years ago. If she had only been ready for him then.

"What are you thinking about right now?" he asked.

Her eyes came back, and she got up to leave. Something told her to run from the situation before things progressed. "We can't do this, Carlos."

"Why do you always run? You ran from me then, and you're running now. What exactly are you running to? If I could figure out what it is that makes you so repulsed by me, I swear I'd never do it again."

"It's not you. I'm just so confused right now. This is a very difficult time in my life. I love my husband."

"Do you?"

Aimee shrugged. "I'm not who you remember, Carlos. You don't know me. Not anymore."

"Nonsense. We were in love once, weren't we? Things may have changed, but my love for you has remained the same. It has taken me all these years to finally see that letting you go was the biggest mistake of my youth. I kept hoping you'd come back to me, and now you have."

His touch was enough to cripple her. She wet her lips. Slowly, her hands moved upward to his arms. Then his chest. Suddenly, it felt as if she were no longer in control of the moment. She kissed his mouth and held him.

"I've missed you. For so long I've been afraid, Carlos. If I ever even looked at another man, my husband got angry. How am I supposed to live with someone who treats me like that? He's a failure. He loves everything but me."

"I won't let you go this time, Aimee. I'll take care of you. I'll love you more than he ever will, more than he ever could."

She kissed him again, breathing in the same cologne he'd worn the night they made love years ago. He still smelled the same to her.

Aimee drew him closer. "I'm so lonely, Carlos," she whispered.

"Well, you will never be lonely again," he replied, breathing into her.

Aimee could taste the old love of their youth, her fingers running messy through his hair. She breathed deep, wanting breaths. She was alive.

Without warning, the door suddenly whined open. "Mrs. Phoenix, Emery wanted to know—," Arson began, his eyes growing wide. He looked down, almost ashamed, but mostly embarrassed. "I should really learn to knock."

Carlos pushed her away, waiting for the moment of unexpected tension to pass, but it didn't.

"I'm gonna let myself out. You two look... busy. Emery's question can wait." Arson quickly backed out of the office door and slammed it shut.

Carlos fell into Aimee's eyes again, noticing her dismay. "It's okay," he whispered, as if intrusions like that happened regularly.

"What was I thinking? My neighbor just walked in on me making out with my boss."

"He's just a kid. He doesn't know what he saw. Besides, who would believe him?"

She drew back, standing still for a moment, wondering how lost she'd gotten this time. "I'm sorry, Carlos. I have to go."

She fixed her blouse and skirt, rearranged her hair, and made for the door, looking down at the floor as she left.

THIRTY-TWO

Arson's world was changing. What had happened during summer's beginning still left his mind plagued with questions. Before now, he had been sure of three things: that Grandma loved him, that he was going nowhere fast at a job whose sole purpose was torment, and that he was alone. Having Emery around to keep him company helped now and then, but there remained something that separated him from her, if only in his mind.

Prior to stepping into Dr. Pena's office, a stupid endeavor three weeks behind him, Arson had grown callous and familiar with how the world operated. Complications like that were strange and unwelcome. But the world was changing; things were changing.

August approached quicker and softer than other years. With quiet winds, morning fog formed afternoon haze, and the skies began to dim to a powdery gray, inviting gloom. The humidity ended, and warm nights transformed almost immediately to chill. The world was rarely as Arson wished it to be.

Summer remained in the back of his mind, where he kept the image of Emery's mother kissing a stranger. He knew enough to stay quiet, though, refusing to ever bring it up. Mrs. Phoenix was the wife of a minister. They were supposed to be purer, better. They were supposed to carry around Bibles and talk your ear off about something to do with divine providence. Therefore, it was crazy to think that someone like her could be caught locking lips with Dr. Pena. No way she was capable of it.

Let it go, Arson told himself, regardless of how many times his mind wandered. *Just let it go.*

It was becoming more of a challenge, however, to stay away from Emery for more than a day. Each hour apart reminded him of those nights when he couldn't sense Grandma's presence around him or the immeasurable loneliness intensified only by deeper sorrow of his grandfather's death.

Arson enjoyed being with Emery. The time away from the cabin permitted him to dwell on other things beside the clandestine office scene he'd unintentionally interrupted or about Grandma's deteriorating mind. She was getting worse, skulking around the house naked most days with a blank stare on her face, incapable of saying anything other than "Henry's dead," right before falling into a disturbed slumber on the living room couch. She hadn't made scrambled eggs in weeks, hadn't hit him, yelled, showed any emotion at all.

One morning, Arson awoke in a fever as the result of a nightmare. In the dream, he had met his father for the first time but couldn't picture the face. Just another ghost, one who abandoned him before he could even utter the word *Dad*. Arson didn't mention it to Grandma. Maybe, if he tried hard enough, the fire inside might go away, the way pain was supposed to. It seemed like a reality the more he spoke with his new neighbor.

When Emery was near, Arson could glimpse hope for a normal life, free from fire. He wanted to tell her that he was different, how some days he sat behind the cabin and practiced burning up. Tried to turn it on and shut it off. It was hard and painful, but he was sure one day he'd be able to control it purely. On that day, he would tell Emery the truth, when his powers weren't measured by hatred or anger but rather controlled.

He was with Emery when the thought came to him. He began imagining a conversation, how she might react, what he'd say, but her voice shut reason out. "Let's go for a walk," she said.

"Now? Where do you want to go?"

She raised her hands, took a deep breath. "Not sure. Let's just walk. I mean, do we need a destination?"

"No. But how will we know when we've arrived?"

"Why do you always have to ask questions like that? You're so weird. Sometimes it's about enjoying the journey, not always about getting someplace."

Arson nodded as they started out her driveway. He didn't dare reach for her hand. What if she wasn't into the idea? What if she wasn't ready for it? It was a risk he couldn't take.

"The 'rents are killing me," Emery grunted, after moments of silence. "I'm sick of it all. Sick of them both."

"Wh—," he tried.

"And I'm forced to just suck it up. My dad drinks, and it's like my mom's on some other planet."

"Your dad drinks?"

"Where do you think I got the beer for Abraham?"

Arson shrugged. "But he's—"

"A minister, yeah. Was. I've heard it all before. Used to think it wasn't a big deal. But it became a problem. Look, I didn't bring it up, because people usually react strangely when I do, like my family's supposed to be saints or something. My dad's an alcoholic, Arson. It's not something you just go out and blurt out to the world."

The air was bitter. The sound of each footstep, the crunching of the sand and dirt and crushed gravel beneath them, seemed to echo.

Emery continued, "I must sound like a broken record by now. But they're *always* fighting. I try to get between them, try to make it better, but it blows up in my face. My mom has some pent-up aggression toward my dad for making us move and whatever else.

Plus, he's been drinking out in the open to piss her off. Not to mention, he's been lying to me."

"About what?"

"Seems to think my mom's cheating on him. Can you believe that?"

Arson raised his eyebrows, not saying a word.

"I mean, why would he make something like that up? Don't get me wrong; my mom can be a total psycho, but it doesn't mean she's cheating on him with some other guy."

They stopped for a moment. Emery walked off the trail and stared out at the water. Its ripples moved calmly by, lapping up at the stones of the mini beach and rocking a small boat tied to a dock far off. "The water's alive," she said. "Free. I get it now. Why you'd submerge yourself underneath. I get it. If only I could trade places with the lake, just for a moment."

She thought she understood, but Arson knew how different they both were. He commanded fire with pent-up hate and rage; she always tried to put them out. The peace he sought underneath the currents wasn't real; maybe she just wasn't ready to hear that yet.

The wind jostled her hair around the haunting mask. Arson could hear her holding back tears. "Sometimes I wish the water could take me away."

Emery wanted to get a snack at the pharmacy before heading back to her house, or the *dungeon*, as she called it. Arson led her to one of the Main Street plazas, one near Tobey's. It still seemed awkward walking past the building, but he did his best not to let it bother him too much. It wasn't until Mandy showed up out of nowhere that Arson got nervous.

"What are you guys doing here?" she asked, rubbing his shoulder with a smile.

"She wanted a snack from Rite Aid. Apparently they've got some really good chocolates. And this town doesn't really have all that much else."

"Really?" Mandy said. "I'm just finishing up a cone from Tobey's. It's not as good as you used to make it, though." She eyed Arson, ignoring Emery completely. "Heard you got fired."

"Yeah," he answered meekly, crestfallen at the mention of it.

"How do you get fired from working at an ice cream parlor? What could you possibly have done?"

"I think it's for the better." He didn't want to get into it with Mandy, especially with Emery right beside him. He'd messed up once—twice, actually—and was determined not to let it happen a third time.

"Well, whatever. So what's your friend's name? I remember that freaky-looking mask but not the person underneath. I don't think we've officially met. My name is—"

"Mandy," Emery replied. "Heard a lot about you."

"Really good things, I hope," she said with a wide grin.

Arson gnawed at the flesh of his lip. Tension was building as Mandy added, "Let me write down my number for you again. You probably lost it. Boys will be boys." She glanced at Emery, relishing every chance she got to touch Arson in front of her. "I don't think I need to write down my address. You remember where I live, don't you, Arson?"

He nodded, unsure where this was going.

She reached into her purse for a piece of paper and a pen. Using Arson's back as a surface, she wrote seven digits on the wrinkled page, marking it with her name and a heart. Then she handed it to Emery. Before he could ask why, Mandy said, "Me and a few of my friends are getting together this weekend. A little party on the lake. Parents are out of town. Nothing too major. If you're not busy taking care of old people, you should come. It'll be fun. We can all hang out together, and maybe your friend here can tell us some scary stories."

"Sure thing," Emery said, biting back fury.

"Right on. Well, I'm on my way to Shaw's; gotta pick up a few last-minute goodies for the part-ay." Mandy put on her sunglasses and slurped a portion of the cone before walking away. "Ciao."

Emery reached for Arson's hand on the walk back home, and he casually acted like it was okay, at first startled, then willingly accepting. Slight conversations came out roughly every five minutes. Arson acted as if Emery's fidgeting with the paper in her hand didn't bother him.

"Sorry about Mandy," he said. He felt guilty for the unexpected third-party intrusion.

"Hmm," Emery replied, leaning her head up against Arson's shoulder.

"I wish I could know what you're thinking about."

She hugged his arm. "You."

"Really?"

A smile.

Their eyes met.

"It's been a long time since I've had fun."

"I had fun too, Arson. It appears you weren't a failed experiment after all. The other scientists will be thrilled."

"Mission accomplished," he said with a light chuckle.

The night air breathed still, and they continued down the half-lit road. Emery's palm felt different from Mandy's, purer. Passing under a street light, he felt obligated to look at her again, find her eyes deep within the mask. He wanted to kiss her. But when the light was no longer above them, he lost all fortitude and resilience. It seemed like more of an opportunity for disaster and regret than for him to spill his guts.

"Looks like it's going to rain," he said when the dark sky crashed.

She lifted her head upward. "Yeah, I think you're right. I hate the rain."

"Why?"

"It makes me depressed, like something bad's going to happen. Think about it; more car accidents happen on wet roads. Picnics always get ruined. You could leave the car windows down and the interior will get all messed up. Bottom line: rain sucks."

"That all makes perfect sense, but that could happen to anybody. Everybody's had a bad experience with the weather. But it doesn't mean you have to hate it." Arson paused. "Let's say, for instance, it's sunny out, and a guy comes home and his wife is in bed with someone else. Is that guy going to hate every sunny day for the rest of his life?"

She replied coyly, "Possibly."

"What is it, really?"

A moment expired before Emery could force the words out. "I guess it just reminds me of what happened. That night after the bonfire. I don't know. It's stupid."

He stopped. "It's not stupid. You're perfectly normal to have feelings like that. Memories don't die easily."

"Yeah. The 'rents don't seem to think it's perfectly normal, though. 'It's just a phase.' Forget I said anything. I've got to get past this anyway."

Arson was awed.

"You know, you're smarter than you look," she said.

"Is that an insult or a compliment?"

"For now, let's stick with compliment. When we met, I thought there was something different about you." Emery slowly reached her arms around his back to hug him.

Arson hadn't even noticed that they'd already walked all the way from Main Street to her house. He had hoped for more time with her. The last thing he wanted was for the day to end. Not yet.

Maybe this was the beginning. Maybe this was the part of the story where he confessed how he felt to a girl he loved more dearly and innocently than anything. A million different sentences scattered his brain, some creeping up to the tip of his tongue, waiting for release. But how could he confess his secret ability? What would she say? He'd seen people employ this kind of bravery in movies, but this was different. *She* was different.

Arson breathed in the smell of her skin, the natural flavor of her hair and neck, with his eyes closed. It was now or never.

"Emery?"

The mask looked up at him.

"I—"

The door to her house suddenly swung wide open and slammed shut, exiling an unkempt man from within. The man nearly tripped down the porch steps.

"Dad?" Emery asked, running to her father. "What happened?"

Joel sucked down a long drag of beer, then wiped his mouth with the back of his hand. "Arson. It *is* Arson, right?"

He nodded.

"Don't get married."

"Dad, what happened?" Emery asked again, this time louder.

"I'm mar-married to an adulteress," Joel said, burping and slurring his words. "Your mother's cheating on me."

"Oh, not this again. I don't want to hear any more of it. It's a lie."

Joel's breath reeked of alcohol. "Emery, I have proof!"

Arson watched her choke up.

"Your mother thought I didn't know, but I checked her phone calls. And the e-mails."

Wrinkled pages dropped at Emery's feet; some scattered with the wind. "I'm not a liar, and I'm not crazy. I didn't imagine it. It's right there in front of your eyes. She's been lying to us this whole time. Oh God, how could I have been so stupid?"

Emery studied the individual pages. "Maybe you're overreacting," she said. "Who knows? He's her boss. I mean, there must be some kind of mistake or an explanation. Something."

"You are so unbelievably naïve. Like I was. Your mother pulled the wool over both of our eyes."

A scream waited at the back of Arson's throat. He should have said something long before now, said that he'd known all along about the affair, if that's what it was. Regret crept in, building and building. Logic and sense had no place in his mind, not now. Emery would've hated him for it. In past civilizations, Arson was aware that kings and queens killed messengers who dealt out bad news. The news might have destroyed her, the way it was destroying them both now. What a fool he'd been to think a sin like this could be kept hidden.

Joel drained what was left inside the bottle. Reaching inside his back pocket, he grabbed another one and violently broke the glass lip with his palm and cursed as suds foamed out onto the open cut.

"Dad, you should be inside talking to Mom."

"I've tried talking to her. Been trying for months to get close to her, but she's so far away. She ca-can't even look at me anymore, Emery. She doesn't want to talk. Sa-says we should save that for the lawyers."

"Dad, she didn't mean it. Mom's just confused. You'll see."

"This … This has been her plan for a long time. But she never had the guts. Well, now she does. It's my fault … for everything."

"Dad, you can fix this," Emery pleaded. "Be a man. You're both upset. I get it. But you've counseled couples in the past. You can get things back to the way they were, right? You can fix this."

"She doesn't want to fix it!" Joel hung his head low. "I'm not a minister anymore, Emery. I'm nothing."

"I can't believe you're just going to give up." Emery looked at Arson. "So much for sunny days, huh?"

Arson was rigid, practically motionless. What could he do? Say? She was in immeasurable pain. He didn't have to see her face to know the depth of the wound. All he wanted to do was hold her, but she ran inside before he could collect the words.

"What do you want me to do, Emery!" Joel yelled, as she slammed the door. "What do you all want from a failure like me?"

Joel walked up to the house and pressed his face up against the cross hanging on the door. "Why have you for-forsaken me?" he begged in a defeated whisper. "Well, are you just gonna stand there, Arson? Like some stupid animal? You know, ever since I met you, I've been curious. What kind of a name is Arson anyway?"

Arson quickly responded, "Grandma's called me that ever since I was a boy."

Joel belched. "It's a weird, ugly name, you know."

Nod and forget about it, Arson thought. *He's drunk.*

"Say something, kid. Call me a phony, a loser."

Arson's wandering thoughts remained on Emery's well-being, but he couldn't tune her father out. He searched for an answer, but nothing came to mind.

Joel feigned amusement. "Tell me I'm crazy. That this isn't really happening. Do me a favor. I want you to tell that whore in there to wake up. No, I've got a better one. Tell me I'm not a complete failure."

"Emery loves you, I know that much."

"One down," Joel groaned sarcastically. "If this were a test, I'd still be failing."

"Sorry. I'm not an expert."

"What are you doing here? Have you come to collect on my sins and watch me suffer? You're as pathetic as I am."

Arson turned around and, with his head hung low, began walking toward his cabin.

"What's the matter, kid? Can't take a little constr-constr-constructive criticism? That's what my wife used to call it back when she actually gave a d—"

Joel collapsed onto his backside.

Arson turned back around and froze. He listened to Joel drone on and on. As messed up as people were, it was never any one person's fault completely for the end of something beautiful. Blame was easy to shift upon others. All Arson could see was a broken, hopeless man spitting accusations at a woman who was just too flirtatious for her own good. The war could be fixed. Sure, bombs had gone off. But in the aftermath, when the smoke finally cleared, maybe they could build again.

"This doesn't have to be the end, sir," Arson tried in a low voice.

"She told me she doesn't love me anymore, kid. It sure looks like the end to me. You wanna know why I drink? Everybody judges, but no one has a clue what I'm dealing with. This stuff tastes terrible. But I drink it because it makes everything disappear, if only for seconds at a time." He made a *poof* sound like a magician. "Me and Buddy don't need love or a church or a family. We're miserable all on our own. My wife's been a stranger for months, years probably. I just prayed, hoped that my world could change."

Arson grew wary. He noticed Joel staring off into nothingness, a dead glow in his eyes. Lost somewhere. The bottle slipped out of his hand and shattered, beer suds coursing through the rusted nails and wooden splinters of the porch steps. Arson understood what that was like. He'd seen the struggles and pains of normal people—broken, lost souls who'd stumbled around the world in search of something more. But when they got angry, fire didn't breathe out of them; they tried to deal with it the only way they knew how. They lashed out at one another. Cheated on each other. Drank. Or, like Emery, they pretended as long as they could that it wasn't there, believed that it was a lie, when nothing could be further from the truth. When they were hurt, their hands and feet and eyes didn't ache and burn, but their pain was the same.

"I don't love you anymore," Joel reminisced, getting up only to crash down the steps. Arson tried to grab him before his face hit the dirt, but it was too late. "Don't touch me. This is where I belong."

"Fine." Arson shrugged, lying down beside him on the ground.

"What are you doing?"

"Helping you," Arson said, placing his hands behind his head. "The first session's free."

Joel roared with laughter. "You're killing me, kid. But what's the point? I can't even finish a friggin' sermon. Can't raise a daughter right. I have nothing left. Look, you can't make someone love you. You can't fix anything. Believe me, I've tried."

"Have you? You and Mrs. Phoenix are pretty selfish, if you ask me."

"I didn't." Joel took a moment to think. He stopped breathing, blinked, the sweat dripping like mud from his forehead.

"Neither of you can see what you're doing to your daughter. She can't stand being with you both. All you do is fight. Emery can't talk to her mother without lashing out, and she doesn't even recognize you anymore. You're blind if you can't see how amazing she is. She's perfect, but you're too focused on yourselves to see that."

Joel's hands smacked with applause. "Well done. You've cracked the case. Some sophomoric teenager thinks he has all the answers. When you're my age and you've seen the world for what it truly is, seen human beings for what they are, maybe then you'll get it. Life isn't black and white, Arson. It's filled with shades of gray. So don't pretend like you have any idea what it's like, because you don't."

"I don't have to touch fire to know that it burns, Mr. Phoenix. Just because you don't have all the answers in life doesn't mean you should stop looking."

"There are no real answers. The sooner you realize that, the better off you'll be."

"You have a family. You have a wife and a beautiful daughter who are hurting. Why are you out here wallowing in self-pity?"

"I'm not wallowing; I'm self-medicating. I . . . I was asked to leave, Ars . . . Aaron, whatever your name is. Aimee doesn't love me. We pledged our lives to each other, only to have everything crumble." Tears filled his eyes. "God has turned his back on me."

Joel picked himself up off the ground and stumbled his way toward the road. "I get it," he screamed at the black sky. "This is payback, isn't it? I loved my work more than my family. Why not? Hell, I deserve to lose it all. Sooner or later, we all pay for our sins, Arson, all of us." Joel stopped midstride and chucked his beer into the woods.

Soon after, Arson picked himself up and watched hopelessness slip off into the dark.

THIRTY-THREE

Grandma was passed out on the living room couch. Drool dripped off the ends and onto the floor, where a photograph of her and her husband lay. *When will she snap out of it?* Arson wondered, covering her with a blanket to stop the shivers. She hadn't cleaned the cabin, feared the idea of a shower, and refused to change clothes. She smelled. It was as if sorrow were on her bones and on her breath, slipped somewhere under the folds of skin.

Arson had pictured her differently before but never like this. Most days she couldn't recognize him; then others came when she'd call him by his other name. No longer Arson. Never. It still felt strange, but he assumed she couldn't remember his vile ability, how he killed her only daughter by being born.

It had never been a mystery to him why she called him Arson. He had burned her in a way that was beyond healing. He took from her a love so deep, a love he himself could never earn even if he had forever. The frightening divide widening the space between them brought a heavy weight he wasn't ready for. After seeing that she'd become a malnourished recluse, his discontentment turned to pity.

I'm responsible for her condition, Arson mused the following afternoon behind the cabin. He practiced destroying beer bottles and marmalade jars he'd picked up in the trash. Arson enjoyed watching them melt. Seeing the objects liquefy and then burn and become something else seemed to satisfy the darkest part of him, a part he never wished to accept. He had discovered that with enough concentration, even his eyes could create a spark, manipulate a rogue flame, or reduce creation to black mess. His control was growing.

When the bottles were destroyed, their remains dissolved. But there was no peace. He'd imagined the phone ringing dozens of times, even though it was just the sound of the television droning in the background. He'd been sitting in anticipation all morning and had suffered through a restless night. He desperately wanted Emery to call, let him know everything was all right. *She isn't ready,* he thought, staring out at the lake. Maybe she needed more time, like Grandma.

The scratching sound of rocks against his window called Arson out of sleep. With a yawn, he drew himself out of bed and moseyed toward the boarded window. A crack in the wood allowed him to peek down at the masked figure standing with arms crossed. He stared down, confused and excited all at once. Emery was below. The boards Grandma had hammered across the windows made it difficult to focus on her, though. With all his might, Arson dug his fingertips underneath the wood and clenched his teeth. A sliver took some blood, but in an effort to remain quiet while Grandma slept, he managed to create more of an opening. Finally, he broke one of the boards enough to get the window open.

"How romantic of you," he called from above.

She told him to shut up. "Just come down here," her voice demanded.

Arson quickly put on a shirt and a pair of sneakers and raced down.

As soon as the door to the cabin opened, Emery walked toward him and slapped him. "How long have you known?"

"Nice to see you too," he said.

"Don't screw around with me, Arson. This isn't a game."

"No, it's definitely not," he replied, getting back his breath. His right cheek stung. "You were a lot nicer yesterday."

"A lot's changed since then," Emery said. "How long?"

"Do you really want to talk about this right now?"

"The first one was just practice."

"Okay, okay," Arson said. "Emery, I never wanted this. This wasn't supposed to happen. Your mom, she … I didn't think anyone would find out."

"Will you just tell me the truth? Can someone tell me the truth for once? How long have you known about my mother and Dr. Pena?"

"A few weeks, maybe."

Emery threw her hands up indignantly and kicked a hunk of dirt.

"You have to believe I was doing it for you. I didn't want you to get hurt. Your father wasn't supposed to find out. I thought—hoped—no one would find out."

"That scumbag called today looking for my mom. My dad answers the phone. His face says everything. The e-mails, the midnight text messages. My dad was right. Way to go, 007. Secret's out."

Arson drew close; she moved away. "Please, I know how much your family means to you. If I'd said something, you'd hate me, and then you'd hate your mother."

"You're right. I do hate her. And now I'm mad at *you* for lying to me."

"I didn't lie."

Emery's voice got louder. "The sin of omission."

Arson felt like a reluctant psychiatrist. He had never asked to be the dump site for everyone's emotional baggage, but here he was, the only one around when the trucks came rolling in. The rage boiled in his palms, spreading to his chest, the pulsating flame coursing through his veins. *Control it,* he thought. *Control it.*

"How could this have happened?" she cried. "We were supposed to have a new life. Things were supposed to be better. Instead my mom hooks up with some scumbag, and my dad drinks like he's a fraternity loser. Who are they? I feel like I'm the only one acting like an adult. I feel so alone."

"I get it," Arson said. "My grandmother walks around the house naked, crying, staring at herself in the mirror. She just keeps saying the same thing over and over again. To be honest, I don't know what to feel other than rage. Can't help but think that maybe ignorance really is bliss. I mean, if I hadn't reminded her what happened, I don't know, maybe she'd be happier."

His voice grew hoarse, a tear sliding off his eyelid. "She was cruel to me growing up, told me I was a little demon, a mistake. Someone only she could love. She said she loved me, but I never felt it. Now it's like time is repaying her for what she's done to me, and all I can think is that it's my fault. I love her. And I don't even know why."

Emery let out a long-winded sigh.

Arson looked into her eyes. "I'm sorry for bringing my baggage to the table. Just thought I'd remind you that you're not alone. There's a ton of crap in this world and a bunch of people who make it worse. I don't want you to view me as one of them."

She dried her tears and came closer to him. "I'm sorry for freaking out at you. I still can't believe this is happening. I mean, growing up, I saw kids' parents splitting up, saw how it messed with the kids' heads. It's totally different when it's you."

"Yeah," he sighed. "Emery, I swear, hurting you was never part of the plan. I thought if I didn't say anything it would be like it never happened. Thought it would go away, but I was wrong. So wrong."

"Life isn't supposed to be this hard," Emery groaned, cradling her head in her hands. "We're not meant to suffer like this, are we?"

THIRTY-FOUR

Friday arrived, and Arson and Emery agreed to volunteer again. But neither of them was really there. Just two ghosts on autopilot. Arson tried pulling a smile out of Emery a dozen times but failed. She was not the same girl who had moved into the house next door nearly two months earlier. Something inside had changed, switched. A task as simple as riding in the car with her mother was awkward for them both. But as Emery stated to her mother over and over again, they were volunteering for those who needed it, not for her.

Walking the halls of Middlesex Hospital, Arson pictured Abraham in every bed, a wrinkled grin chiseled out of that black, cratered face. Imagined him looking out into a gray world when his eyes failed him for the last time.

The sound of the cart scraping the shine off the hospital floors ripped Arson from his thoughts and drew him back to reality. Emery was methodical as she manipulated every turn with a new attitude he didn't like. *She's just worn down,* he thought. If only her parents could see how much they were hurting her. Arson wanted to flash fire in front of their eyes, make them wake up.

"I haven't seen my father in two days," she said, passing by Abraham's old room. Another weary soul was stuck where he once lay. "Where did he go? I didn't mean to blow up on him like that. I've been so stupid. This isn't happening," she kept telling herself.

"Emery, listen to me. You're not stupid. This is between your parents. *They* have to work it out. It's not your fault that your mom did what she did or that your father took off." He touched her shoulders with his hands.

"It has to be. My parents could never do this to each other," she said, clearing her nose. "Hey, Arson, you're really warm."

"Sorry," he said, removing his hands from her shoulders.

"My dad, the cryptic note leaver, said he had to get away to finish a sermon. But he didn't say where he was going or how long he'd be gone. How can he think about finishing a sermon at a time like this?"

"Sometimes our lives don't make any sense at all."

"They love each other, Arson. I know they do. He'll come back, right?"

He looked away.

Arson and Emery cleaned up when their shift was over. Boredom held them in its grip the remainder of the afternoon, and when Emery wasn't talking about her parents, she was simply silent. There wasn't much he could say to comfort her; words did little against an enemy as lethal and merciless as family dysfunction.

They walked outside. The wind was stirring. A plum sky faded to black as nightfall clothed the world. Emery's mother was inside finishing up. They waited for her to bring them home.

"I was thinking about the party," Emery said, finally breaking the silence. "I want to go tonight."

"What?" Arson replied. "You can't be serious."

"If it will help me forget about everything, forget that my life is messed up, just for one night, I want to go."

He looked at her strangely. "Emery, you *do* remember it was Mandy who invited us, right?" He paced back and forth, white scrubs in his hand, wondering how he'd manage talking her off the insanity ledge. "Do you really think it's a good idea?" he asked with a sigh.

"I think it's the only thing that makes sense right now. I think if you care about me, you'll come with me."

Arson froze.

"But you don't want to come, do you?" Emery said.

"It's not going to end well," he said, reluctantly nodding his head. He held her for a long moment, could tell she wanted to break down. "But I'll go with you if that's what you want."

Arson and Emery stepped out of the car. She ignored her mother's request for a phone call by ten o'clock and slammed the door shut. They spotted a bonfire in the distance, surrounded by a small crowd. Loud music echoed through the night.

Emery placed her hand inside his and started walking toward the party, while her mother sped off. "I'm glad you're here with me," she said.

"Yeah," Arson forced out.

Mandy's backyard was made up of mostly sand, grass scattered about in random spots by the shoreline. A boat sat by her family's dock and rocked to the sway of an angry current. Those by the bonfire pit continued the party, ignoring their arrival, but Mandy greeted them after a few minutes of awkwardly standing by the water. She had on a red bikini. Ripped denim shorts sat high on her curvy hips. Blonde hair dripped off her scalp in golden ringlets. "Welcome to the party!" she hollered. "Hope you guys came to have fun. Either of you want a beer?"

Arson refused, but Emery accepted one.

"Go meet everyone," Mandy suggested to Emery, lighting a cigarette. "They're just dying to hear all about you."

"Um … okay."

Mandy waited for her to leave before she gently brushed up against Arson. Licking her lips she said, "You know, I could see why you like her too. With that mask on, she almost looks like a human being. Don't worry; I won't tell her about us. It'll be our little secret."

"There is no *us,* Mandy," Arson said, walking away. He met up with Emery beside the fire.

He hated the way the group looked at her. Like a freak. They saw her mask as an invitation for sarcastic jokes. He tried to ignore them, but his hands were getting hotter with each passing moment.

Emery lifted the bottom of her mask and pretended to sip the beer.

"Having fun?" she said under her breath.

"Yeah, great party. Are you?"

"You betcha."

Arson spent the next hour getting sicker. Sweat built up in the creases of his forehead, and his white shirt betrayed him, but he blamed it on heat from the bonfire. He listened to the crowd roar with laughter at another perverse rant. He saw now how he'd never fit into a world like theirs, how he was wrong to ever think he could. Those not participating in conversations were scattered across the lawn. Arson noticed a girl completely wasted by the dock. On the other side of the yard, a couple was lying down, making out. Some were taking hits of white powder off knives and picnic plates beside Emery. They offered her a hit, but she refused. Arson could tell she wanted to say something, but she just sat there, almost numb to the chaos.

"So, Arson, how was it?" Josh, one of the track stars from school, said.

"How was *what?*"

Josh looked at his other buddies. "You know. You and Mandy? She's pretty great, huh?"

"Me and Mandy never happened," Arson said harshly, glancing over at his date.

"C'mon, it's okay; don't be bashful. You can tell us," another kid said, spilling some beer. "Blew your mind, huh? Never knew a high school girl like her." Arson had never seen the loser before, and it became clear that he was some college student from out of town.

"I don't know what she told you," Arson began, "or what you heard, but Mandy and I never—"

"She said you were pathetic," Josh said.

Arson wanted to burn his chiseled face off right as he took another swig of the beer, the suds filling his teeth with poison.

"Say, Arson, the freak over there. She's with you, right? Bet that chick needs some serious therapy."

A sharp pain cut through Arson's wrist. Hot breath burned at the back of his throat. He could feel his hands boiling. He wanted to leave. No, he had to get Emery out of there.

Arson glanced at the crowd of girls circling around his date. Mandy glanced back and winked, tossing her cigarette into the sand.

Emery overheard, came up beside Arson, and shoved him. "You never told me anything happened between you two," she said. "I can't believe this."

"Emery, don't listen to them."

"Why? Is there another lie you wanna tell me? I can't believe you actually let her kiss you."

Arson winced.

"Sleep with you?"

"No," Arson said. "We didn't; I swear."

"Oh, perfect. So she kissed you? Was it before we met?"

Arson sighed and eyed the fire pit. The heat tempted the back of his eyes to explode.

"I trusted you. Whatever. I'm going home."

Josh approached them from the side. "You and Frankenstein are perfect for each other."

"Don't call her that," Arson said.

"Or what, freak?" Josh said, spitting in his face. He then poured the rest of the beer into Arson's hair. The brown suds ran sticky through his curly, ash-brown mop and dripped down his shirt. The spectators roared with twisted pleasure as Arson drove a fist into the perpetrator's nose. He swore he heard something crack, but maybe that was just his own knuckles breaking.

Josh coughed out blood with a sick chuckle.

"Arson, what do you think you're doing?" Mandy said in a high voice.

"He's making a big mistake." Josh formed a fist and slugged him twice, once in the gut, the other across Arson's jaw.

Arson could taste the sweat and blood, as the track star breathed out.

"No, wait, you big gorilla. This is my shindig, and it's supposed to be fun. After all, that's what I invited them for. Watching two boys beat the crap out of each other isn't fun. I've got a better idea." Mandy pursed her lips and pushed Emery. "Let's have some real fun," she said, ripping the mask off and tossing it into the fire.

Emery cried out, trying to cover up her face with her hands. "Don't look at me. Please. Why are you doing this?"

"It was fun. Kind of like what me and your boy-friend did. Go on, tell her, Arson. Tell her. I'm sure she's dying to hear all about it."

The crowd sadistically cheered. On each and every one of their faces, Arson could see hatred and malice and cruelty. He could see his father and his grandma, his boss, and everything he hated within himself.

"What's the matter, Arson? You afraid of the truth? The truth shall set you free. Did I get it right, little virgin Mary?" Mandy circled around Emery, taunting her, ordering her friends to grab the frightened, scarred girl.

"Just tell her, Arson. Tell her how we made love. Tell her all the things you did to me when we were intimate," Mandy whispered.

"It's a lie, I swear!" he shouted.

"Have you ever been with a boy, freak? It's invigorating. All that power. Boys are weak, so easy to manipulate, to control."

"Emery, let's go," Arson said, shoving Josh aside. He grabbed Emery by the hand and pulled to release her, but three of Mandy's followers surrounded him. Without remorse, they swung their fists into him, dragging their knuckles through his gut. After he had collapsed on the ground, Josh cracked his ribs with steel-tipped boots.

"She has nothing to do with this. Mandy, leave her alone," Arson begged. "If you want to hurt me, fine. But don't touch her!"

"We just want to have a little fun. Some harmless fun."

"Don't." His eyes turned blood red. "Please! Don't you hurt her!"

"Why do you care so much about her?" Mandy asked, slowly tiptoeing around Emery. "She's boring, pathetic, and ugly."

The group cackled. One of the meatheads lit up a cigarette and flicked some ash into Arson's eyes.

"Oh, look. Baby's crying," the gorilla said.

Mandy grabbed Emery by the hair and brought her nearer to the fire. She struggled but couldn't resist the pull. "What are you going to do?" she said with melted disgrace.

"We're going to fix your face."

Emery's eyes exploded with horror. She turned to Arson. "Help me," she cried, digging her heels into the sand and dirt.

"Let her go!" he said, rising to his feet, his voice ripping through weak lungs.

Out of nowhere, Josh struck him in the head with a bottle. Blood oozed from a gash on the left side of Arson's temple, bleeding into his ear. His body thudded against the ground, and he turned to one side to see Emery fighting to break free. Blinking once, then twice, he tried to get up, to move, but the world was spinning.

"Arson!" she screamed. Mandy put a hand over her mouth and proceeded to drag her toward the fire pit.

He moaned and felt his eyes roll. Suddenly, Arson could feel his entire body ignite with one breath. The burning sensation started in his hands then quickly and violently spread. It crawled out, burning the tips of his stiff fingers.

"What's happening to him?" Josh yelled. "Holy—"

Arson got up from the ground, his bones aching with pain. *Control it,* he told himself. *You can control it.* His muscles and the ligaments attached to them pulsated. Spit dried at the back of his throat, and his heart fought against the bones that imprisoned the torturing flame. His eyes glowed. Burning needles shot out from his skin, sporadically at first, but quickly obedient to his mind. Sweat bled off his body and evaporated before it hit the sandy floor.

The force within him grew fiercer. Lines across his palms commanded the fiery pit and a cigarette to fuse together in one chaotic wind. The fire ripped through him and out of him, seeking each and every tormentor and spectator, apart from Emery.

His bones cracked, the edges of his teeth ground into powder. In his mind, all he could hear was their twisted laughter. The only way to stop them was to silence them. Another burst of red and black flame tore from his hot skin until his body lit up. Arson stepped toward the girls holding Emery once the beginning of his carnage was already complete.

Lifting his hands, he sent wild blasts of fire toward them, ripping the flesh from their once flawless cheekbones. A stir of cries echoed into the dark sky. Tears of anguish burned on the ground. This time it was over. His heart was torn, lost in Emery's eyes and the shallow screams of every burning victim. Their simple tragedy was all he wished to hear tonight.

Josh and his friends tried to escape, but smoke caught them. Their bodies illuminated the sand at their feet. The screams ceased soon after, and they fell into an unconscious spell. Arson stared down at their bodies bubbling with blood and mucus and ash, the fire fusing their necks to their shoulders, arms to their sides, like tormented figurines. Arson then shifted his red gaze to the evening's vile host and released a brutal roar. At once, he sent fire so powerful that it sent her charred body flying into the water, carried in and out by the lake's slow, approving rhythm.

It was with a whisper that the world was hushed, the night cold and still. Arson dropped his head for a moment. He knew that this savagery was a poison, but it was a poison he willingly drank. For Emery. Stopping his rage was impossible until he knew she was safe again. He was Arson, and he'd burn all the cities down if it meant protecting her.

He breathed slow, desperate breaths, his clothes nearly incinerated, his flesh still glowing. The fire was now contained, and that was when the chill came. He looked around, first at the smoke evaporating from his bones and then at the carnage and gasps of the bodies that lay scattered.

He heard Emery's footsteps and turned toward her. "You're safe now," he muttered, collapsing.

THIRTY-FIVE

The trees no longer stirred. The lake's slow and steady moans had died. Wind blew in and drifted by. The sandy dirt beneath Emery's feet felt more like quicksand. She blinked, shuddered, blinked again. Coughs echoed up from the ground, and her tormenters lay motionless.

Emery swallowed hard. With a deep breath, she ran toward Arson. Her hands couldn't stop shaking. Panic had seized her completely. Arson was cold, a blue tint covering his skin. His jaw hung wide while she fidgeted to find a pulse.

"Oh God," she cried. "Oh God, please!"

A million thoughts trampled through her mind, a million days without him. "No, not him," she begged the sky. "Don't take him away."

The boy sat lifeless in her arms, his eyes misty with an ivory frost. She rubbed her face against his.

"Don't do this to me, Arson. Don't give up! Fight!" She felt crazy talking to herself. She held his body closer, grinding her teeth like she'd just been shot, knowing that would have been better than being alone like this.

Anger churned her stomach, eventually pouring out of her with a brutal scream. She couldn't think, couldn't feel. Emery ran her tired hands through Arson's curls, begging for forgiveness. The body didn't look like the boy she knew. His face and skin were so strange without life in them. Tears cascaded down blood-red cheeks, washing the dust and ash from her skin. Emery shut her eyes and kissed his black lips. She stayed, pressing into him, praying for him to return.

"I love you," she whispered, kissing him again.

A split second took her from this place and then brought her back again.

Arson jolted, coming awake. He leaned up, eyes flashing white. "Oh God." He rose with blurred horror in his eyes, staring at the scorched bodies. "What have I done? I—"

"Something I can't explain," she said, panting for breath, weaker than seconds ago. Her mind kept telling her she was asleep. This wasn't real. None of it was real. If she'd pinch herself, maybe she could wake up.

Emery looked down at his arm, the icy veins inside his skin starting to fill with blood, returning to its natural pigment. His body felt warm again.

Arson breathed in. The memory of it all exploded in his mind. He shook with realization. "Are you all right?" he asked Emery.

"I am now."

Kay didn't want to get out of bed. A yawn disturbed her longing mouth, emptying some of the bad flavor from her tongue. With a stretch, she slowly leaned up, the crack of knuckles and age settling in. When she blinked, sometimes she still saw him, shaped out of thinner air, a passing wind, or just pure fantasy. He'd offer to hug her, to kiss her, but as she went to press her mouth into his, he would vanish.

"Oh, my Henry," she said coldly. "Come back, darling."

Lethargic, she stumbled out of bed, thinking of him even more. The late nights he would climb into bed and nestle up beside her, smelling like his work from the lab. The lonely nights in Cambridge during the first half of their marriage were equaled only by these past few weeks. *For so long, you've been able to think he still loves you,* her mind taunted. *But you've been wrong. He's gone, and he's never coming back.*

It was the strangest thing how memories returned, some scattered and too busy to focus, others so succinct. Like her mind was still twenty-something and fully functional, not cut up into meat—the way she felt now.

The late summer breeze chilled her naked flesh. Her body shivered; her chest sank. She dragged sockless feet toward the window and prepared herself to crank it closed. Dawn broke through the night's remaining disorder, and she swore in that moment that Henry was there, kissing her neck softly, his soft breath tickling her still. "Oh, stop it, darling," she said with a smile. Upon her next blink, he was gone again.

Kay turned toward the vanity to fix the white mess atop her scalp and noticed a black car parked outside the cabin. The brown dirt tossed up by the tires was only now just beginning to settle back into the earth. "Who the blazes is that?"

Knock! The door cracked downstairs, startling her. Heart heavy, she felt the jolt of panic spread through her. She scanned the dresser for her glasses. "Where did I put those awful things?" she said, only moments before locating them.

She picked the robe up from the bathroom floor—dust sticking to the threadbare sleeves—and slipped into it. There was another knock at the front door, this time more forceful, and the sound of fists, violent and insistent.

"Who is it?" Kay called down, slowly heading out into the hallway. She tied her robe loosely on her walk down the stairs. The knock persisted a last time before ending completely. She pressed her eyes against what she referred to as the spyglass located in the center of the door and saw a man wearing a black coat and sunglasses. He appeared to be stretched far too thin, brown hair with spikes of gray blended in. He had a long face, jagged features, and sharp ears. She couldn't clearly make out the person within the face, though.

"What do you want?" she asked, remaining completely still. "Who are you?"

Slowly, she went to remove the lock bolting the door and wrapped her misshapen knuckles around the brass handle, bit by bit drawing the door backward toward herself. "I said who—"

The door broke open with enough force to knock Kay backward onto the floor. She dropped hard, her spine sinking with a crunch. The coated figure stepped out of the blinding light and removed his sunglasses, slowly revealing glad eyes.

"You!" she said, forming spit with her tongue.

"Hi, Kay. Did you miss me?" the figure replied, grabbing her jaw with a gloved hand, threatening to break it if she spit at him.

Their eyes met. "I let the devil in my house," she weakly said, washing his face with her spit. She swung her ankle into his crotch.

A grin parted his younger mouth as he bent over in pain. He cursed at her several times, wiping the saliva from his cheek. He then grabbed her head and aimed to break the stairway's unpainted wooden spirals with it. A beam cracked, the top of her forehead spilling red.

"Get outta my house," she seethed, crawling up the foot of the stairs. Kay pulled her body up and labored to gather what strength still lingered in her weak veins. Her mind raced—frantic, panicked, and tired with fear. In a staggering pant, she tried to get to the upper level, but the invader grabbed her robe and yanked her back down.

Without much thought, she struck her left elbow into the side of his head and watched the man spin back into the front door, veins bursting at the sides of each temple. His face was thick with frustration.

Gasping for breath, she finally reached the next floor. If she could make it into the bedroom, maybe she could—but there was her attacker, right at her back, a grin stitched into his face like fabric. His shadow slowly moved closer. She could smell his vile breath, began shaking when he put the black glove on her skin.

My God, where's Stephen? she thought. The man eyed her, staring down. She must have seemed so weak and frail to him. "What do you want, you no-good filth?"

"Shhh." With an index finger pressed to his mouth, he raised his eyebrows, clutching her throat with a grip that started loose but became choking. "He's not here, is he?" the man said.

Circling around her, he noticed a square mirror affixed to the wall. His eyes told her that what came next would be painful.

Spinning her around, his grip got tighter still, and he watched her face change color inside the glass. His teeth flashed white, a sick smile stacked behind thinly painted lips. With a grunt, he pulled her neck back and bashed her head into the mirror. Glass showered onto their feet, blood dripping from Kay's scalp and mixing into her white-gray hair. With great force, he swung her body around and threw her down the stairs. The crash of broken bones and pounding flesh against each stiff step chilled him as he watched. There was pain in her eyes, her cheeks flushed and cracking.

Kay spent a few seconds trembling once her body hit the bottom. Through narrow slits, she watched the figure's footsteps draw nearer, as he scaled the stairs down to where she had landed. All she could hear was the sound of her wrist bending backward with a sudden snap, before she stopped moving altogether.

THIRTY-SIX

Arson's eyes peeled back. He awoke to bright lights and a cold room. He'd been sleeping for several hours, and a task as simple as squinting became a challenge. After seconds of fighting it, he managed to look down at himself, disgusted by patches with cords attached and needles feeding life into his blood—or taking life out; he wasn't sure. There was a lukewarm towel across his forehead. He felt displaced, removed somehow, somewhere else. With each new breath, the stench of hospital sheets dissipated, and the sight of his weak, pale reflection brought on new paranoia.

Loneliness.

Fear.

Panic.

Get me outta here, he thought. *I'm not Abraham Finch. I'm not Grandma Kay. I'm Stephen Gable, Arson G—.* The nature of his identity was a mystery to him now. Who was he? What was he? He didn't know.

A cold draft blew in suddenly from the hallway. It was Emery. She reminded his heart of what beauty meant. Reaching for his hand, she sat beside the hospital bed.

"You're awake. Thank God."

It was strange seeing her without the mask on. "Yeah, looks like someone was looking out for me after all," he said weakly.

"I'm just glad you're still breathing." She turned on the television, as if it could help distract her from the questions begging to be answered; nothing was on but infomercials and sitcom reruns.

"Emery, you look pretty shaken up."

"Oh, I'm fine," she lied.

Arson brushed his hand against her back softly.

"Do you remember anything?" she asked, obviously distressed.

In the back of his head, he could hear the screams of people burning. All he said was, "Are they dead?"

Emery answered slowly. "I think they're all breathing. But their faces are burnt off. You went to town on them. No one's woken up yet; the doctors don't know if they ever will. Some kind of coma. Arson, what did you do?"

Arson turned away and shut his eyes. The time had finally come. "No more secrets," he said. "I'm not like other kids. I was born with a curse." He chuckled to himself, knowing how stupid the next part would sound. "Sometimes, I get a little ... hot."

"Hot?"

"Hotter than normal. Look, I can't exactly explain it. But think of it like a match. All it takes is a little spark. The right amount of pressure, and then—"

His hands made an invisible ball, and then he illustrated it blowing up.

"Wait. So you can, like, explode?"

"Sorta. I don't know what to call it. My body creates too much energy, heat energy. Maybe it's hormones or something else inside me, I don't know. But I"—he looked at her for a long moment—"can start fires with my mind."

Emery sat down. To Arson, it seemed like she was experiencing a system overload.

"Do you have any idea how crazy this sounds?" she said, raking her fingers through her hair.

He nodded. "But it's the truth. I was born with it."

"How is somebody *born* with it?"

"I don't know."

"Is there anything you *do* know?"

Arson sighed. "Whatever it is inside me killed my mother."

"Whoa," she said, sinking back into herself. "Heavy."

"Look, I didn't want this curse, this ability, whatever you wanna call it. I've tried my whole life to blend in, to try and control it, so no one would ever find out. But it isn't as easy as it sounds."

"Oh, right, you mean the part about you going nuclear!"

"Please keep your voice down. If somebody hears you—"

"Yeah, right. Sorry. This is all just a little too freakin' weird. I mean, this isn't a comic book. This doesn't even make any sense. Are you hearing yourself right now? You can create enough energy to burn crap just by thinking it."

"Yeah. Are you...afraid of me?" Arson said weakly.

Emery glanced down at the floor, head hung low. She allowed the entire scene at Mandy's house to replay in her mind. How in one second he was just this normal kid and the next, he was going nuclear, burning people one by one. "No," she said. "It's actually...kinda cool. I'm just trying to wrap my head around it all."

Arson's eyes changed. "Emery, I'm not your normal teenager. I get it. I'm not even special or anything stupid like that. I'm actually pretty messed up. Something's wrong with me."

A tear slid down her face. She wiped it away quickly. "Maybe not. You saved me, Arson."

"I couldn't let them hurt you like that," he said, flustered. "I didn't have a choice."

Emery took a deep breath. "I know. It's okay."

"It all just happened so fast."

"So how does it work?" she asked, trying to distract his guilt.

He was surprised by her intrigue. In all his life, he had never had anyone to share it with—his horrible ability—if that's even what he could call it. He was always ashamed, afraid of it. But Emery was so different.

"It happens whenever I get emotional. Pissed off or scared or whatever. I *am* still trying to control it." He stared up into her tearing eyes. "I've never been so afraid in my entire life as I was with you last night."

"What did it feel like?"

Arson paused momentarily and then resumed. "Like a tornado rushing through my entire body, ripping and tearing me apart. It's never been that strong before. I mean, I thought my skin would peel off. Everything burned and ached. Then I lost myself in it. Didn't care who got hurt, even if it was me, as long as you were safe." He bit his lip. "I blacked out. Next thing I see is you standing over me, telling me you love me."

"Oh. You heard that?"

"It was the only thing I *could* hear while I was asleep."

Emery looked away and collected her thoughts and the words to say. With a sigh, she broke the silence. "You weren't sleeping, Arson. You were dead. Man, it's like looking at a ghost. After it happened, you collapsed. I checked for a pulse a dozen times, but there was nothing. Your whole body was like ice, and your skin turned blue. You were gone for an hour."

"Whoa," he gasped.

"That's not the weirdest part. Try not to freak out, okay?"

He nodded.

"The strangest thing happened. I kissed you; then I held you for a while. Something felt different. Felt cold, and the back of my eyes and head ached. I know it sounds insane, and maybe I'm just really tired, but I saw you, Arson. You were gone."

Arson didn't move. He couldn't.

"Please say something. Tell me there's an explanation for why you can do whatever it is you do. Things like this don't just happen. I mean, teenage boys don't spontaneously combust, die, and then magically come back to life."

Arson stared blankly at her for a while.

Emery rubbed her face. "I sound mental."

"You're not mental. This is all a little strange, I know. It's not easy. But thanks for not freaking out."

She held up her index finger and thumb and pressed them within centimeters of one another. "I'm this close, trust me."

Arson lay with a look of bewilderment in his eyes, thinking about the violent events of the previous night. He couldn't believe what he was hearing.

"Please talk. I don't like this uncomfortable silence," she said, biting her fingernails.

"Was I a good kisser?" Arson asked, trying to sound both charming and serious.

Emery shoved him in the chest.

"Look, I should be dead, and I'm not. I don't really need an explanation. Maybe, in time, we'll figure all this mess out. But for now, stay calm. I'm alive, and you're safe."

"This isn't normal, Arson," she answered behind clenched teeth.

"I've never been the expert on what's normal."

There was a light tapping on the door. Emery jumped. "Oh, right. There's a guy out in the hall. Agent Lamont. He already questioned me, but I didn't give him anything. Not sure why the local cops are sitting this one out, but this loser seems like a total nut-job. He's going to ask you about what happened. Be careful, Arson. The guy creeps me out." She leaned in. "Look, for the record, our lives might suck and be full of mistakes. But meeting you wasn't one of them. And neither was what you did last night. Thank you. They could've hurt me, but they didn't because you were there to protect me. You're my hero. My own personal guardian angel."

Arson felt oddly all right.

"I'll know why you did it. No matter what happens, I'll always know."

"Has anyone told my grandmother where I am?" he asked.

"Oh, I called her from the ambulance, but she didn't pick up."

Odd.

"Could you let her know I'm all right when you get back to your house? She was probably just sleeping. Hasn't exactly been herself lately." Arson fought the panic creeping through him, but he faked certainty pretty well.

"Of course. Well, the 'rents are probably outside having conniptions. They didn't want me talking to you. I guess they're still trying to figure this whole thing out. Don't worry, I didn't tell them about you, not the truth anyway," Emery said. "Man, the way they're acting, you'd think it was the end of the world. Do you think things will ever go back to the way they were?"

"Maybe."

She shrugged. "Just promise me you won't ever scare me like that again."

"Cross my heart," he whispered. "No more bonfire parties."

She wore a slight smile. "Anyway, I should go."

"You don't ever have to be afraid of me," Arson said.

Emery hugged him. "I just want to stay here with you."

Another knock at the door disturbed them, followed by two piercing eyes. Emery quickly wiped away her tears. She looked heavily into Arson's eyes and kissed him.

"I love you."

"I love you too," he said. "More than anything."

Once she exited the room, Lamont shuffled in. He was a stiff, awkward-looking man with no hair and a creepy-looking black beard. His eyes were bullets and his teeth gatekeepers of hot, stale breath. His shadow met Arson first.

"My name is Agent Lamont, FBI," he said. "I know you've been through a very traumatic experience, but..." He waited for the door to close behind him. "Look, kid, I don't know what happened, but you better have some good answers."

Arson tightened up and swallowed hard as Lamont pulled out a notepad.

"As it appears, your girlfriend's the only one without a mark on her. Except for that pretty little face of hers. So, Mr. Gable, what do you want to tell me?"

Every word came out like packaged poison. His teeth looked rotten in certain parts. In fact, the more he played with them, Arson realized some of his teeth weren't real. He popped them in and out of place with his tongue. The strange image was enough to make anyone queasy.

"I went to the Kimballs' home to party, all right? I wanted a good time."

"Does a good time involve leaving eleven kids in a coma and one dead?"

Arson's neck jerked.

"Oh, that's right. One of them didn't make it. That's murder. Eyewitnesses said they saw you *light* up." His voice cracked with disgust. "Care to elaborate?"

"That's crazy," Arson replied.

"As crazy as someone coming back from the dead?"

An eerie silence plagued the room.

"Now don't screw with me, kid. I'm gonna ask you one last time, what happened last night?"

Arson felt his nose twitch as he snarled and moved within the hospital bed. How had anyone seen? The roads were quiet, not a soul around. No lights in any of the houses.

Nothing was adding up. Who was this man? What did he want? Arson slowly turned to face him. "I burn things," he said in a low voice.

The grim-faced agent drew closer and was now peering out of two narrow slits. "Well, you cocky little punk, do you want to tell me what these kids did to deserve it?"

Lamont was recording their conversation, making a checklist that would undoubtedly be used later. Arson didn't care. Suddenly, everything replayed over again in his brain, as if his entire life had been recorded, not just this moment.

He pictured his mother screaming in pain, imagined what it might have looked like as the doctors pulled him from inside of her, soaked in blood and ash. He could see Danny taunting him to throw the firecracker that cold night in Cambridge. In an instant, there was Mandy, along with all her sick friends, burning and agonizing.

"I'm the one you came here for, Agent Lamont," Arson confessed, the words spilling out of him. "I'm the one you want. Whatever you want, I'll do it. Leave Emery out of your investigation."

"Emery, that's right. Emery Phoenix. That's her name, daughter of Joel and Aimee Phoenix. Age seventeen, like you."

"You don't need to ask any more questions. I did it. I burned those people."

"Why?"

"They were going to hurt her."

"The beauty queen that just left? Seems to me like somebody beat 'em to it."

Arson wanted to shut him up. Kill his awful laughter. The sick cackle echoing from this scumbag's wet throat sped up his heart rate. He locked gazes with the man and held it there.

Lamont got closer. "Am I getting you upset? Did mocking your little girlfriend hit a nerve? What do you really want to do to me?"

Arson held out his hands and unfolded each fist. With gritted teeth, he pictured Lamont's face melted off, quiet. *Time to end this,* he thought.

He cracked his fingers and commanded his hands to burn. He'd felt the rage, let the fury bubble inside with his blood. He blinked and took a deep breath. Counting his heartbeats, he began picturing Emery as a little girl without her mask, without the fears or the confusion of the world. Arson could see her as she was, as she had always been, a beautiful face, lit like the eyes of God.

Arson blinked again. Nothing. Where was it? That dormant flame. Arson bit down hard and fought to call it out again. He stared down at his palms, but they were still cold.

"You didn't burn them with matches, did you?"

Arson panted, afraid once more for what might happen. He avoided the agent's eyes and stale breath and focused on the window. Down below, Emery was walking toward a black car.

Lamont's lapel radio suddenly chirped. "The girl's in sight," he heard it buzz.

Arson's head jerked frantically, his eyes flashing. "Wh...What's going on?" He continued staring out the window, but in seconds Emery was out of sight.

The static from Lamont's radio chirped again. "We've got her."

The agent walked toward the window and twisted the blinds shut. "Good," he responded, careful to drag out the word.

"Where are you taking her? Help!" Arson yelled toward the room's camera. "Help! Nurse! Someone's taking—"

"Shhh. Keep your voice down. Wouldn't want to hurt her...more than we need to."

Arson lunged out and grabbed Lamont's tie, trying to choke the life from his heartless veins. "Where are you taking her!" he spat.

"Do you really want to be responsible for her death? Let go of me, or we will give this story a very unhappy ending."

With an angry grunt, Arson obeyed.

Lamont loomed over the boy. A broken smile split his jaw. Two glass eyes shot into him.

Arson struggled to create fire, his face dripping with cold sweat and fear. He bent his fingers, spread his palm, and chewed the lower half of his lip. All the concentration in the world wouldn't bring it back.

Lamont noticed what he was trying to do. "The fire's gone, hmm? Don't worry, we'll get it back. You know, you've been somewhat of a mystery to us for some time now," Lamont said with a creepy slur.

"If this is about an accident seven years ago, I'm sorry. It was a mistake. Emery had nothing to do with it, with anything."

The man clapped, and his face read a sick kind of delight. "I like you, kid. You're so unbelievably predictable, weak. I guess there's a part of you that's still human."

Lamont reached for two pairs of handcuffs and attached one to Arson's wrist and to the hospital bed's metal frame and the other pair of handcuffs to the opposite end. With wide eyes, the agent gripped around his skull. Arson tried to resist but couldn't. He wasn't strong enough. A sharp prick pierced the back of his neck.

"Now that I know we're playing fair, we can figure out what makes you what you are and what exactly you're capable of."

Arson was powerless. He couldn't move, couldn't speak. The left side of his face became paralyzed. *Get her back,* he heard his conscience scream. *Whatever you have to do, get her back!*

Lamont breathed out through crunched nostrils, spreading his tongue across scabbing lips. He slipped a stick of gum into his mouth and began to chew it methodically, angrily.

Arson forced one word out as he stared, defenseless, through the window. "Emery."

Lamont shut his notepad and smacked his jaw. "You're no savior, kid. You're just a freak."

The room began to spin, his world warping and distorting with each blink.

Agent Lamont was grinning. He picked up the boy's head and toyed with it, breathing his hot breath onto him. His fingers slid across Arson's face. "It's over."

Arson felt his eyes grow heavy, the white room dizzy and fading fast. A thudded heartbeat became a slow, dull hum. "It's over." The words kept replaying in the back of his mind. This filthy FBI agent in front of him—if that was even what he really was—was right. It was over. He couldn't be Stephen Gable anymore, not ever again. That boy was too weak, powerless. That boy had died on the beach hours ago.

He was Arson now; he'd have to be. But where was the fire when he needed it? What was happening to his body? A tear streamed down his cheek. He felt like he was hanging on a cross, the handcuffs clenching down upon his wrists like nails and this hospital bed his wooden spine.

One last time, he tried to start a fire, a spark, something. The drug Lamont stuck him with was working, faster than he might have guessed. How much longer could he stay awake? With each groan and movement, there was Emery's face, and Grandma's, slipping farther and farther away.

Blink.

"Sooner or later…"

A deep breath. Panic spilling over his bones. The fire had forsaken him. All he had to do was…

Blink.

Quickly, he began to fade.

"We all pay."

A hollow gasp drew itself out from Arson's throat. From above him, he heard the faint vibrations of dark laughter slithering down the dents in his spine. The black was closing in.

It was cold.

It was quiet.

Can't get enough? Check out The Borrower,
a chilling short story from the mind of Estevan Vega.

THE BORROWER

Rain and sleet soaked the black world, and a stray wind howled in the dark, disturbing the short stubble on the Borrower's face. He was wearing a cloak and little else, but the colorless garment hugged his strong frame tightly, keeping his body warm despite the winter chill. Gasping, he fought to keep a steady pace, taking shorter breaths and longer steps. He would be there soon.

With every footstep, he was taken back to the memories he'd longed to wish away. Dwelling on them—on her—was enough to tear down the walls of Jericho. But he couldn't help it, tonight of all nights. The memories were like living, moving flesh, flashing pictures unable to be turned off. They were burdens fortified by timeless tragedy and loneliness.

His mind drifted to the battles and histories he'd reluctantly called his own, yet both memory and history seemed like foreigners now on the shores of his weathered soul. He gritted his teeth, finding some kind of sick enjoyment in turning the edges of each jagged tooth into a white powder, only to feel them resurface moments later. So he clenched his fists, tucked in his head, and ran faster.

The hum of the dark city drowned out all the sounds except the lonely melody of his heartbeat. Only moments ago, it seemed, he was riding along the Mediterranean, hunting a faceless man—if the being could even be called that—in Barcelona. One who might have gotten away or perished, he couldn't remember.

Or could he? Yes, that was the most troubling of all. He *could* remember. That was his burden, wasn't it? He could remember everything, with detail—the un-quiet morning, the blood and rage. The way the dew stuck to his lips or how the sand felt beneath his boots.

The cries of the ocean returned tonight, as if they were a soft lullaby, soon to be swallowed.

The Borrower closed his eyes, wiping filthy drops of rain from his brow. "Not tonight," he whispered. "Just forget. That's what you must do."

He knew it better than anyone. Though he couldn't understand it, he knew the riddle of how a moment might turn into forever, leaving all of life as nothing more than a map of uncharted islands in a sea of wanderers. A snap of the fingers. A tide rolling in and rushing out. But not for him. For him, life was not just a moment, nor a sum of increments, but a line without a start. God was the blink contained in everything and every human soul. What power and privilege. How he longed for it, how he needed and pleaded for it. God, a microorganism and a drop of water. A skyscraper and a breath of wind.

He was taken back again. He couldn't even have a moment to himself, a moment to remember the good things in life, how it all felt ... at first. Instead he was alone, trapped on that damned beach, listening. The crows were above him now and all around him, unkindly rushing through the past and present, where he was lingering. Dark shapes glided and unfolded the air behind and in front of him, their caws repeating.

"Soon. Very soon," he said.

With one blink the world looked sound and flawless, but inside it was filled with robbery and murder and unclean men, unclean streets. It was nothing new to see or to experience. The taste of reality had already begun to spoil.

To his right, he passed a nursing mother whose stare was polluted by the city smog and haze of underground subways. The car crash six blocks ago and the bodies burning like lost embers or a smoke signal that no one would ever see flashed before him. A groaning heartbeat, and then, nothing at all. Life was not the only gift God could give. He knew that now, he was sure.

Another blink brought him to the beach once more. Stuck. "I don't want to think about it anymore!" he cursed into the night. "Be gone." But it remained, crawling into his mind and resting there. The pictures flashed.

A bloodstained dagger wetting his gritty palm. It seeped into every line and curve. As he looked up into the hungry eyes of the one he pursued so valiantly and shamelessly, those cheeks of his stretched back into a moonlit grin, and his eyes started to spin. "I don't want to die!" he remembered himself crying. "I'm not ready to die."

As his feet hammered against the split asphalt, he felt as though quicksand were dragging him under. It was a pile of angry mud, greedy and wanting and never satisfied with the dirt or ruin, always longing for more, filthy and without gratitude for the futile life it was created to be.

The Borrower swallowed and kept moving, ever watchful of his surroundings, the night spies. He could hear their feathers unraveling a new language as they cut through the dark air. His feet were never heavy, but tonight, it was like dragging lead.

But at last, he reached the end. He came to a halt in front of a lonely group of buildings. A cramp suddenly twisted his ribcage, and for a second he wondered how Grace had felt gasping for her last breath. Didn't know why of all nights, that stuck out to him the most. But it did. There was no shaking it. She had seemed so delicate in his hands. It was strange how different someone could look without life in them, without something to fill those shallow pools we call eyes; without some word or smile to disturb our frosted lips.

Grace was gone.

His gaze moved along the brick face of the building—the vines and shingles and flickering lights. Just one of many other connecting frames, contingent upon that which came before it. Weak and powerless on its own.

Lightning angrily split the heavens.

A roll of thunder grumbled in the distance. He wiped his face and opened the small gate. With careful, calculated steps, he walked toward two angelic pillars on either side of the entrance to apartment 316. The white paint covering the door was faded and came off like clay. A flimsy banister hung down from above the door and shadowed the entryway, which had dead flowers collected in pots of stiff dirt.

He knocked, only seconds before realizing the door was already open. "Come in, Christopher," a voice invited from within. The voice was thick and coated, somewhat raspy. "I've been waiting for you."

The Borrower shut the door behind him as each crippled flower inside the pots began to climb and spread up out of the rough dirt, coming alive with petals, stems, and vibrant colors.

He followed the cough and the near-choking old voice from the other room. The house was dark, lit only by the moonlight. It took him back to the beach, where he refused to linger. Back to the grin on the man overshadowing him, the man he wrestled for hours, fought, and cut.

"Why don't you take off your cloak and come into the light?" the old man said, putting on a breathing mask and sitting up in his big chair.

"Hello, John," the Borrower whispered, revealing his face in the moonlight.

"It's been a long time, Christopher. But you've come back to me at last," the old man replied, lifting up his breathing mask with a whine. His eyes glanced out the big, open window to his right, and he focused on the flapping black shapes stirring along the rooftops. "So, you've brought company."

"I realize that perhaps they may be unwelcome, but wherever I go, they must follow."

"Even into hell?"

"Everywhere."

The old man leaned up against his knees, and the Borrower could hear the crack his bones made with each shift. How he winced and bit his tongue with the slightest amount of pressure. "You kept your word, Christopher. But why? Why did you come back here?"

"You are the last."

The old man keeled over in a coughing fit, blood curdling in his lungs before spilling out that wrinkly throat.

"You are stronger than I imagined you might be, John," the Borrower said softly.

"Well, I've had a lifetime to practice. My God, when did I get so old? Do you remember what eighty-seven feels like?"

"No."

"Don't you remember anything before it happened?"

"It's not good to dwell on the memories for long," the Borrower said, picturing how the breeze felt against his cheek that day on the beach.

"To hell with it. I don't want them anyway. They're nothin' but excess baggage. It'll be better just to forget everything. That way it won't hurt, right?"

The Borrower nodded slowly, slipping back into the darkness.

"What does it feel like?" the old man asked, leaning in his chair. "Does it hurt?"

"For a moment," the Borrower said, shedding his cloak. "When it's over, it will feel like a very long dream."

"Those creatures are still waiting outside. Good grief, look at them. Skulking little vermin, aren't they?"

"They like to watch."

The Borrower took a step toward the old man. He noticed him recoil, feeble and full of fear, even spilling his coffee on the Persian rug.

"Do not be afraid, John."

"Wait, Christopher. Please, just wait."

The old man reached for his cane and stood up. "Do you ever wish you could see Grace again? That was her name, wasn't it?"

"I don't have time for this."

The old man exploded with laughter. "That's just it; you have all the time in the world." He reached into a nearby hutch for a bottle of champagne. "It's been many years since I decided to break this old friend out. Oh, how I've missed the taste."

The Borrower watched his eyes glow.

"Now, where did I put that da—?"

"John, I didn't come here to celebrate and inebriate with you. Your vices are your own. We have business."

"We have *business*," the old man mocked. "Is that all you think about, son? Business. Be mindful of your humanity, Christopher. You mustn't forget you *are* still flesh and blood."

The Borrower held out his hands and stared down at them, a look of disgust bleaching his face.

The old man fidgeted with the bottle's cork, slowly unscrewing it until it popped, champagne sparkling over the glass lip and spilling onto the floor. "Indulge me."

Another roll of thunder crashed above the city, lightning sailing through the mist and the clouds. The Borrower's eyes flashed white. "One drink."

"Thata boy." The old man poured two glasses and handed one over. "Cheers. To a long life."

Silently, they clinked glasses and took a long sip.

"What's on your mind?"

The Borrower tilted his head, unsure of what to say. He stood there for a moment, quiet as the dead.

"Well?"

Finally, he broke his silence. "I've been living on borrowed time, John. My soul is fatigued, but my body does not feel worn. My heart feels fear, but there is nothing in this world to fill me with horror. Can you imagine being thirsty but never finding water that can truly quench your dried mouth?" He paused to finish the glass of champagne. "I can only grant you this one wish. You are certain that this is what you want?"

The old man put down his glass. "I have never been more sure of anything in my entire life, son. Forgive me for calling you that. I must seem like a small child to you." A smile split his wrinkled lips. "Won't you tell me about Grace first?"

The Borrower paused and studied the old man. Frail, hunched over, and pale. His frosted lips reminded him of Grace's. Hesitant, he shifted his shoulders and stared out the window. At long length, he parted his lips and spoke. "She was . . . all I could ever ask for. Grace was perfect. Every line of her face. Every smile. Innocent and full of life. Even her anger was flawless."

"Nothing is flawless. I should expect you to know that after all these years. Everything dies, Christopher. Everything 'cept you."

A sigh.

"What would you say to her if she were here?"

"Sorry."

A long moment drifted by them both.

"Listen to me, John. When it happens, things will be different. *You* will be different. There is no way to undo it. Your life will change forever."

"I expect it shall. Don't tell me you're getting cold feet now, Chris—" The old man began to cough and reached for a hand mirror. "Christopher, I've been living this way for far too long. Weak and fragile. I've missed who I used to be. I miss my youth."

The Borrower drew the blinds. "Looks like it stopped raining. The sun should be coming out shortly. Are you ready?"

The old man set his cane against the oak coffee table beside him. He stared at the picture frame holding a much younger face beside that of an elegant bride. "I'm not afraid anymore. I made a wish when she died. That's when you came to me. Do you remember?"

The Borrower dipped his head and held the old man.

"Me too. Now stop stalling. Do what you came here to do."

The Borrower looked straight into his eyes. "Years ago, I wrestled with God on a beach. One of us died that day." He drew closer, the darkness surrounding both their faces. "I wasn't totally honest with you, John." The Borrower grabbed the old man's cheek tightly, and his palm shook the pale, wrinkled flesh beneath it.

"Oh, it's cold," he heard him shudder.

"I know," the Borrower said, growing weaker. He struggled to keep his hand up. "Close your eyes. It will be over soon. I will grant you this wish, but one thing must stay with you."

"Oh God," the old man gasped, looking straight into the eyes of someone longing to be dead.

Gravity dragged the Borrower's face toward hell, his flesh and skin like loose clothes on a weathered body. He caught a glimpse of his reflection and quickly looked away. A piece of skin slipped from his jaw, exposing the gray skeleton beneath it. The flesh became ash on the rug.

Meanwhile, the old man's skin reshaped itself, turning softer, more youthful. Kinder eyes replaced cold, calloused mirrors. Ears shrank behind a well-manicured scalp. Teeth now reformed from decayed gums. He screamed and cried and changed.

"I got to live forever, but I was left my memories," the Borrower whispered, barely audible with the sound of wind and chaos whirring in their midst. He tried to cradle the youth in his hands with an arthritic grip but couldn't hold it up any longer. His power was now reversed, his energy depleted. His chest was caving in, broken. "Everlasting life."

The old man's body dropped with a loud thud, as the Borrower lay on tired knees. A ray of sunlight reached through the darkness and scratched his old, worn-out face. Another flake of skin peeled off onto the stained rug.

"Christopher? Are you all right?"

"You are changed now," Christopher said with weighted breath. "It's your burden now, my friend." His eyes were lost and wandering.

"What do you see?"

Christopher answered slowly, "I see an end."

John's shoulders sank, and he used his palms to lift a rejuvenated body. "Can you see her? Do you see Grace?"

"No. I see light. I see the end of all things. Finally, I have rest." Christopher's head rotated slowly toward the young man standing in front of him. "They are coming, John," he said, falling over and collapsing into black dust.

Suddenly, all of the windows in the room shattered, and violent caws echoed through the open space. The sound stung at first, causing John's ears to bleed and buzz. But the crows did not attack him. Their black feathers and eyes and wings took shape around him. "You are the Borrower, John Chambers."

"What are you?" he asked, his heart beating more slowly despite this new fear.

"We are the guardian watchers. We dwell with you always, even until the end. Now take up your cane and walk. There are many to encounter."

"Many?"

They unfurled their spiny wings and stared with lidless lenses, remaining silent.

"Where must I go?"

"Wherever time takes us," they stirred.

"But Christopher. What happened to him?"

"You set him free."

John remained still, counting his heartbeats and waiting for them to disperse. "How old was he?"

"He was the second," the murder answered, as the violent spread of their wings folded and unfolded air and wind and light. "Four centuries old. Now, be still. Time is ever against us, and we have much to accomplish."

John nodded, trying to walk. Pain writhed through his waist and right leg. "One thing must stay with you," he muttered to himself. Slowly, John reached for his cane and shook to keep his balance. He bent over and reached for Christopher's black cloak. It fit him loosely at first, but then it adjusted to his thin frame. With a deep breath, the Borrower limped his way outside, wincing at the pain.

He closed the apartment door behind him and glanced down at the flowers that had come to life since Christopher's arrival during the night. He watched the murder of crows unhinge in flight and suddenly vanish within the gloves of the city.

With a slow blink and a churn in his gut, the Borrower covered his young face, hiding it within the cloak. He moved toward the concrete pathway and hesitated at the gate, staring at an old life, a once-life he knew was now at an end.

listen|imagine|view|experience

AUDIO BOOK DOWNLOAD INCLUDED WITH THIS BOOK!

In your hands you hold a complete digital entertainment package. In addition to the paper version, you receive a free download of the audio version of this book. Simply use the code listed below when visiting our website. Once downloaded to your computer, you can listen to the book through your computer's speakers, burn it to an audio CD or save the file to your portable music device (such as Apple's popular iPod) and listen on the go!

How to get your free audio book digital download:

1. Visit www.tatepublishing.com and click on the e|LIVE logo on the home page.
2. Enter the following coupon code:
   d9cd-e1c2-d61b-0679-175f-bdee-f437-b43a
3. Download the audio book from your e|LIVE digital locker and begin enjoying your new digital entertainment package today!